The New Heir

I0562033

Nadia Marsoli

The New Heir

Nadia Marsoli

Prologue

Samuel
Twenty-two years ago, Edinburgh

I enter the bedroom on the lower floor. It's warm and dark, and his leather and mint scent welcomes me, something his illness hasn't taken away from him.

Rosita called the boarding school I've been attending for the past five years.

Her message was urgent, and they couldn't wait for my graduation in a couple of weeks. Grandpa needs to talk to me.

"My-boy," he calls, in a tired and raspy voice.

I step closer and take a seat on the old leather armchair by his side. As I do, he tries to sit straight. I jump on my feet and hold his shoulders, pushing him back to a lay position.

Whatever got him like this, has taken his strength away too.

"I need to talk to you," he murmurs.

What could be so important? Why now?

"Grandpa, whatever it is, please just rest," my voice breaks.

"My boy–this is important–this will be the last time we talk–"

"Grandpa, please, don't say that," I beg, aware that his words are the truth.

He is nothing compared to the powerful man I last saw five years ago. That man is now transformed into a pale, skinny, empty shell, with a soul fighting to remain here, unwilling to lose this battle.

I need him. We have been apart for far too long, but I can't imagine a life without him.

"You listen, my boy," he orders, in between teeth.

I push the armchair closer, holding his hand in mine and locking my gaze with his.

Even there I can't find him. They aren't bright, light green. They are dark, empty, out of life.

"Do you remember my night walks?" He asks, giving himself a break after every word.

I remember seeing him a few times, walking around the house, and moving things around, but I never understood what was happening. Many times it's like he disappeared into thin air.

"You know the small corridor heading to the kitchen?" He asks. I just nod again. "There's a..."

He stops the story when someone opens the door—I turn to find my father standing there.

"Father, you must rest," he orders as usual. "Samuel,

please leave your grandfather. You will have time to talk later."

Grandpa tightens the hold of my hand, shaking his head and pleading with his eyes.

But father's rough cough is a simple order for me to leave the room.

Once the door closes behind me, I can hear his monitor screaming like a siren, and he is gone.

There is no point in me going back in. I can feel it. I just lost him, the only person I could talk to, I could trust—he is gone, and I am left here surrounded by ghosts, traitors, and strangers.

I walk back to the front of the house, crossing paths with Stella, who rushes inside the bedroom, crying and yelling, pushing Father out, but it's useless. It's too late.

I enter my bedroom, take a well-needed shower, put on my black full suit, and head downstairs, find our favourite spot in the garden, and sit there, letting the summer wind surround me, the sound of the birds, the soft branches moving.

I closed my eyes, and I let my head travel back in time, when I was a little boy, before they took me away from his side.

It's the day of the funeral. We've just returned from the graveyard when Father calls me to his office.

We won't talk about Grandpa—nobody talks about him—it's like he never existed.

All his belongings have disappeared. I asked Rosita, but silence was her most frequent answer.

Stella is gone, in silence, hidden somewhere.

That is not an option for me.

"Collect your belongings. We will travel to London immediately," he orders.

Standing straight, rolling my shoulders back and slightly raising my chin I confront him.

"Father, I am not coming," I answer firmly, my fist tight on each side, anger fills my veins.

He doesn't say a word. We have never found the correct communication system that a father and son relationship should have.

The silence has been his treatment, deciding behind my back, and making me face the consequences.

Stepping aside and letting my life be taken away from me.

That will not happen again. If I let him take me to London, I will be lost. I will kill what is left of me.

I couldn't defend myself when he sent me to boarding school at thirteen. I am eighteen now. I won't bend that easily.

That hideous military prison, hidden behind a large building, and a well-known name didn't break me as he thought it would, not completely, and that is killing him on the inside.

I hold his gaze for a moment longer before I turn ready to leave the office.

I hear him approaching me and his hand holds my

biceps. "Son!"

I pull to free myself, but his hold tightens, and before I know my fist hits the wood wall panel by the side of his head.

I missed on purpose. He didn't blink or move. He expected me to do so, he would have taken it, and even when I hate him with all my soul. When I want to hurt him as deeply as he hurt me. I am aware I will hurt myself too, or worse my mom.

She matters to me. She has nothing to do with all of this. She is just one more victim in the ruling world of this man.

I break the distance between us. His turquoise empty gaze studies my face as I speak low and clear. "You have no power over me."

A deep frown grows in between his brows, his eyes turn dark, and his lips part without words coming out. He should be wise in the next words that he intends to exchange with me. I have no mercy for him–I want him to suffer, to emotionally and physically pay for what he took from me, what he did to my life, and he disrespected me as a human being and as his son.

He deserves to suffer the loneliness and hatred of us all. He will be the one paying for the consequences of his actions for the rest of his life.

I will make sure of that.

His hand releases me. I pull the office door open, shaking my burning knuckles, and I head to the dining room.

Fucking old thick wood panels.

My beautiful mom is sitting there, staring at thin air, a food plate rests in front of her, silence is her companion and she doesn't move as I bend, and whisper in her ear, "I love you, Mom," dropping a kiss on her soft cheek, and I walk out of the room.

I stand in the hallway, looking around me, at the many rooms that hide many secrets and memories. This was my home, my safe place, my fortress to save me from the world out there.

Now, after that night that changed it all, I am a stranger inside these walls. I don't belong here. I must leave.

My black leather suitcase rests by the side of the front door, one last look around me, up the stairs where I left Stella minutes ago, aware it might be the last time I see her, to the dining room where mom sits, and to the office where he hides.

I take a deep breath, walk to the front door, hold my belongings on the way and jump into the back seat of the family car that Jeremiah holds open for me.

I let him drive away to an unknown destination. Away from this dark castle, never looking back.

Chapter One

Samuel
Present day, London.

The sun fights to get through the heavy curtains while my upper arm covers my swollen eyes.

I roll over and sit up at the edge of the mattress. My vision is blurry and my head is heavy.

This constant hangover that happens every day. Even now, when I haven't touched alcohol in far too long, the sensation remains in me, as a reminder of who I used to be.

The clock on the nightstand reads 5 a.m.

Time doesn't matter. One day ends, and another starts, a tortuous continuation, a blend of days and nights that have suddenly turned into years.

Today is different. I know on which day of the week we are, what month and what year. I can remember where I was on this day, what I was doing and how I was feeling for the past twenty-two years.

Another reminder that I am not eighteen anymore. A

whole life has run through me and I haven't paid attention to anything that passed in front of my eyes.

I can't remember what happened yesterday, either a week, a month, or a year ago. Just this day, the day my entire life changed.

My palm rubs my face, I shake my head, and stand, grabbing some shorts on my way out of the bedroom and I head to the gym downstairs.

There aren't any shades here, so the early morning end-of-June sun hits me through the glass walls facing the rear garden, while I follow my daily routine.

I stop when my muscles ache, unable to hold me up any longer. That's the way to know I am alive. That I am not trapped in my dark nightmares. This is the real world.

One where I spend far too long analysing the simplest things. This morning is how symmetric and green the grass looks, or how the blue sky seems transparent, if it wasn't for a couple of clouds floating around.

Peace doesn't last long. My mind won't tolerate it, not when my life's punishment is to remember all that I did, the actions I took, and the consequences they gave me.

I was a child.

That is what young people do, think they are the leaders of the world, make stupid decisions, and–

My hands rest on the window, my head falls and I press my eyes shut when the memories, the disturbing thoughts, and the consequences from the past travel across my body.

I used to blame my grandfather for leaving me, my father for taking me away, my parents for disappearing, and my sister for moving along like nothing mattered. I am the only one to blame. *I left.*

And for that, I received this life, a world of darkness where anything that I lay my eyes on gets damaged, destroyed, and broken. Loneliness is my life partner, and even when Grandpa believed there was something good inside me, I couldn't find it.

I was a crap son to my sweet mom, a terrible brother to my sister, and now, many years later, I am the worst person anyone could wish to have by their side.

Shaking my thoughts away, I head to the shower, letting the cold water clear up my mind and let myself focus on the day ahead of me.

My dear grandfather, Scott Smith senior was a unique man, someone that under that sweet smile and light green gaze hid way too many secrets.

He died today, early afternoon, in his castle in Edinburgh.

Leaving me with an emptiness that I doubt will ever fill up. Instead he did something to be present for the rest of my life, this year after my fortieth birthday, he gave me the highest position in SaStel, our empire, one that by birthright I should have lead after my parents' disappearance, but I didn't, I was far too busy destroying my life.

There is no way to let this pass, not when Stella has stepped aside for good, taking her mom's duties as her full-time priority.

The heaviness on my chest grows as I move ahead with

the morning, stepping out of the bathroom and into the closet.

Standing in front of the dark line of suits–my armours.

They make a sense of value grow around me. They hide me away in the inside, and just give the world around me what they crave, a replica of my father, the incredible, kind and successful Sebastian Smith.

I hate him with my entire being. He messed up my life as a teenager and destroy me as a young adult.

He took away my chance of be who I really wanted to be, he crashed my dreams and goals with the intention of made out of me a little minion he could controlled and walked around as he did with the pretty doll he created out of Stella.

I growl in between teeth when I see some crease on the suit I wanted to wear for today.

It's not just Monday's meeting, is as well the first one I will do on my own, as head of the company, I need it to be spotless, perfection, but that can't be with this one, neither with the other three I checked.

"This must be a fucking joke," I growl, fisting my waves.

Rosita can't be doing this to me, she knows how important it is, I turn to go and find her, when I see a suit bag hanging on the side of the full body mirror, I walk to it, run the zipper down and tilt my head to a fresh, spotless, three-piece, black shirt and narrow matching tie, there are shiny ebony shoes resting below.

There's a card hanging out of the breast pocket:

They would be proud,

R x.

The suit fits my six feet four like a glove, after I redo the tie over five times, I nod at my reflection, brushing my fingers to fix what I messed up, I shake my head and shoulders, lock my gaze with the motherfucking good-looking man in front of me.

He looks undefeatable, spotless. He is the shell I travel around the world in. He intimidates, amuses, and pleases people. The real Samuel is far too damaged.

I turn to the dresser, to complete the full outfit and mark a point on the day, maybe to fill the strength cup too. I collect a gift that Rosita kept for many years. It was meant to be my twenty-fifth birthday gift, a token that has been passed down for three generations, and I didn't deserve back then. Perhaps I do now.

My great-grandfather's 1815 'Homage to Walter Lange' special edition watch.

A piece he wore, but couldn't give to grandpa, it was part of his inheritance, it didn't have a meaning at the time, he passed it to father when the time was right, but neither of them got the opportunity to give it to me.

Push everything away!

I stretch my neck and roll my shoulders, heading to the desk in the corner and packing the documents on the briefcase.

Brought back to reality by Rosita with a soft knock.

"Your ride is here," she says.

I nod, collecting my mobile on the way out, kissing her cheek and walking out.

That is not the way I should be with Rosita, she has took care of me since I was a baby, she was there when I return to found out I had only Stella left, she was by my side on my darkest, holding me up scared that I will drown, and the one who helped me to step away of the blind path I was stuck in.

That doesn't take away the resentment I can feel from here, the disappointment she has felt for years, the concern that I will fail this one too.

I have invited her to leave, but she won't. She needs to know I am ready to be on my own before she does.

What the fuck is that supposed to mean?

My *fratello*, my chosen family and best friend–Matteo, is waiting by my Black Badge, as I walk out.

"I am walking to the office."

"You want company?"

"I need fresh air," I assure, tapping his shoulder, offering the briefcase and walking away.

Heading towards Knightsbridge, where SaStel offices are. I pull out my mobile. There are no notifications that I should care for, and there is just one call that can confirm everything is going as schedule.

"Morning Samuel. I was in the conference room," she says, out of breath, her heels click on the background letting me to know she is running around, "everything is on the screen. The folders are on each seat. Catering is in place.

And you should be here on time, do you–"

Helena is the golden assistant any business man will dream of, she is professional, keep everyone in line and have the work done before you think about the deadline, to that add she is gorgeous, but to me she is a pain in my ass.

The amusement in her voice and face when is obvious I am out of my comfort zone, tempts me to fire her, but we both know SaStel will not survive without her.

Helena keeps running the schedule for the day, when my eyes fall into something far more interesting.

She is not interesting. My eyes, mind and body are reacting and the young lady across the road.

To her hazelnut hair pulled back in a low bun, the contrast it has with her pale skin, the little nose and full rosy lips.

I can see her profile in between the cars, how she kneels to comfort a little girl, similar hair and darker skin.

I observe the full scene as I cross to their side of the road, leaning against the wall under five feet away from them.

A pushchair with a small version of the little girl stands, calling the stunning young lady 'mama'. Three of them hug, sharing a few words that make everyone giggle, and she stands.

Her gaze travels in circles around them, a deep frown grows in between her brows and her shaky hands brush her hair back.

Are they alright?

My legs are in full motion to approach her, when the

brightest blue eyes I have ever seen, matching the clear sky lock with mine.

Time pause, my mind is engraving every inch of her being in my brain, studying her body when the little girl ask to be carried—slim body, covered in a short sleeve long floral dress, and by the distance between us, I am at least a head taller than her.

Now with her daughter in the arms, she turns the pushchair towards me, and after giving me one last straight forwards sight she walks my way.

My body is tense, my throat is blocked, and my head is empty. I step forward, ready to approach her, with no reason or plan, when a couple of tourists block my way.

"Palace?" the woman asks in a hard Eastern European accent. The stunning angel walks past while a giant map is placed under my nose. I spot Buckingham Palace.

Every second that I don't make a decision, she walks further away from me. "Straight to the end of the road, turn right, when you–" I explain, the anxiety doesn't hide away.

She is going. I won't be able to find her if she reaches the end of the road. I am talking to people, something I don't do on a desperate attempt to free myself and run after her.

What is wrong with me?

I can't let her go. The foreign couple has made me turn to them. I frown at the confusion in their faces, and back to the top of the road when the sweetest giggle rings around me––it was hers.

"No, English," the couple answers.

A part of me wants to shout at them to fuck off and learn how to read a map, the other wants to laugh at how absurd and hard is to communicate with certain people.

My brain chooses the second. I laugh.

I look around, concerned about who might have seen that.

Blowing my head off when she looks over her shoulder and smirks at the situation she has put me into.

I shake my head, bite my bottom lip and take a deep breath.

This absolute stranger is doing something to me, and I am not willing to let go of it, not just yet.

"Follow me," I gesture to the couple, marching towards her.

A few steps later I am on a safe distance from her, tense as I hear the couple chatting on my side.

We reach the traffic light. She is standing in front of me, confirming her height and grinning when her long fingers brush the skin at the back of her neck.

I feel it too. Her presence is playing games inside me, awakening a curiosity I thought was dead long ago.

"Tour guide?" asks the gentleman. I close my eyes, loudly exhaling. She looks over her shoulder and we both laugh.

The road fills up, people push and stand far too close to each other, I step forward, the warmth of her body turns my torso into flames, her sweet scent become the air I inhale, I am fully influence and intoxicated by this angel.

The lights change, trapping us in a chaos I am not used

to. I am the shield that protects her back, but people are dangerously pushing her by the side and worst the pushchair.

She slightly steps back, our bodies meet and I jump out of my skin when my entire being receives an electroshock.

What the fuck was that?

Her body tense, and something awakens inside me, my hand lands on the centre of her back, and the other arm extends forward to keep anyone from stepping closer.

Her shoulder presses into my chest and our gaze meets. I fall down into her deep blue eyes. I can't breathe. I am drowning, but she needs me. That is my priority and focus. I guide them forward, holding her closer as the crowd narrows the path.

The heaviness that builds inside my chest minutes ago explodes and an excruciating pain takes the little air I have left away from me.

I know about pain, emptiness, but this is something far too deep, uncontrollable, and unknown.

We step onto the other side of the road. My arm holds her, her head remains on my chest and time pauses just then.

It doesn't last long when the couple step close with the hideous map once again.

My arm drops and she take the queue to walk away, I turn my head both ways, to the couple that I now feel I have to help once more and the angel that has messed up my entire existence by simply standing far too close to me.

"That street, Constitution Hill, Palace," I point down the

road in front of us.

"Palace!" The woman cheers and laughs as she searches in her purse.

"That is unnecessary," I clarify and turn to find her, but she is not here anymore.

She is across the road, her daughter now stands by her side and they chat, pointing at the gates of Hyde Park Corner.

My mind won't focus, my body shakes anxiously and my chest contracts at the thought of never seen her again.

I pull my mobile out of my pocket, stepping closer to the crossroad, "have a wonderful day!" I exclaim. She turns and I film and photograph every move her body does, and every gesture her angelical face gives me.

I turn it off, hiding the device away, observing as she walks inside the park, considering the possibility of skipping work and following her.

Helena must sense something is happening when she calls me once more.

"Matteo is here, and you are not, I swear Samuel—"

"I am here, take a fucking deep breath," I hung up, turning to the office, rewatching the pictures and video.

Walking inside the building, up to my floor and into my office with my full attention fixed on her.

"What is that?" Matteo startles me, seated on the couch across the office with the newspaper resting on his lap and a coffee.

"Comfortable?"

"Avoiding her," he points out to Helena.

"I can't blame you," I assure, sitting on my desk chair and turning to the view, Hyde Park lays under my office window, my eyes travel around on the desperate hope that I might be able to see her, from this distance and height.

Helena's clicking heels quick me off my nonsense and I turn. "Samuel, they are here."

I nod, observing my assistant-secretary-friend.

She is a fake blonde beauty, almost as tall as me, skinny as a post, and dusky eyes. Nothing to do with the angel I just meet.

"Can we go?" she asks as my gaze travels across her figure.

"I was just thinking that outfit is perfect."

"For what Samuel?" she asks, rolling her eyes on the way to the conference room.

"To keep the male board members distracted."

"You are disgusting."

"The fact that you don't like men, make them salivate for you."

"Because of men like you, is that I prefer women."

"Can't blame you, Natasha is a sweet candy."

"Get in there before," she pushes me to the door.

"Ladies first," I gesture, letting her break the ice of the meeting.

"Good morning," I greet, taking my seat at the head of the table. All heads turn to me, studying every inch of my frame.

I keep my guard up. My body doesn't move and my expression is cold.

Mr Rolland, father's right hand, gives a nod, so I move on to break the silence.

"Welcome to the century publication session, please open the folders."

I wait as they have a look at Helena's elaborate presentation.

My body trembles over the leather chair, the silence grows thicker and I decide to break it as I did when I practice this speech with Helena many times.

"For decades SaStel has followed a traditional approach to develop stories, interviews, and promote businesses."

Helena's speech runs smoothly over my mind. I walk around them and robotically said what I should until a flower based similar to the little angel, brings her to my mind. I pause, shake my head, and clear my throat.

I move along, talking about the boring past of the company, what the past generations have done, complimenting the ones who's father's have been with us for a lifetime, pointing out some of the most successful publications we had to the day and slowly returning to the summer publication that will be launch on the annual gala.

An event that grandpa started in memory of his parents after they tragically passed on a road trip back to Edinburgh.

"We will settle on the future of this country, the current styles, products, gastronomy, travel destinations, but especially on the entrepreneurs. We have selected the best of the best in every department. Giving one the opportunity to be our cover," I inform them.

A low murmur starts. My gaze burns Mr Rolland's, to what he clears his throat as a sign that they should return to the silence I need, so they can listen.

"The other five businesses will receive an interview and the opportunity to share their services during the annual gala," I continue. "The magazine will be available online and printed, and publish it during the gala, not after as it's tradition."

"What are you trying here, boy?" Mr Rolland asks in a low voice.

"Members of this board," I say, walking in a circle around them. Everyone becomes uncomfortable in my presence. "Some of you have been here for decades. All of my teams are ready to create what the new readers crave. It will only be possible if we join the current trends and adjust our focus." I explain, opening the door and giving way to the illustration, press, and editorial teams to join us. "Everyone must put aside what our traditional readers needed. They will not be here forever." I say, resting my hands on my chair. "Thank you for joining me today. In a week's time, we will meet again for touch-ups. Please get back to me with the new drafts," I say to Isaiah, head of the illustration team, walking out of the room as they continue the meeting I won't be present for, so they can't tear me apart.

I don't return to the office. That meeting was the only thing on my schedule, and suddenly the building becomes too small for the clear air and space I need.

Matteo is waiting outside, ready by the car. I shake my

head and walk to the crowd of people that fill up the popular roads of Knightsbridge.

I have no destination, only the need to walk away from who everyone needs me to be.

By Friday, the meeting should have been settled, approved and everyone working their best on it.

That is not the case. It has been a week filled with endless phone calls, unreadable emails, and a constant knock on the door.

But I have something that has kept me centred, that calms me when I feel the pressure on my chest overpowering me, something I now doubt I could live without– my angel.

She is the first and last one I see every day, the one that keeps me company on my sleepless nights, that makes me want to move along with the day, with the hope that she will walk down my road once more, that she will storm inside my darkness and kick me out of my skin once more.

"We have to talk," Helena says, startling me out of my daydream. "That woman again?" she asks pointing that my mobile.

"None of your business," I say, putting the device away and listening to what could be happening now.

"Samuel, we can't early published this edition."

"You too?"

"Can you be logic?"

"I thought you were by my side," she agreed to all the decisions I made until today.

"Samuel, we don't have a cover. Without that, there is no way we can finish the edition on time."

"You have a list longer than your legs, find one, and stop worrying too much," I say, turning away from her and deleting some more unnecessary board members' messages in my inbox.

"There is not one worth of the cover, we need the best, they are goof don't get me wrong–"

"Can you take care of this or not?"

"Are you questioning my job?"

"Why are you complaining so much?"

"Get into the conference room, talk to the editorial team yourself and then you come back to criticise my work."

"What do I have you for?"

"To serve you coffees and answer your calls," she says, turning and walking away.

I walk to the meeting they have booked without my knowledge and regret it as I open the door.

The room feels heavy, everyone is talking over each other, and an epic headache builds from the back of my head straight to the centre of my brows.

I sit there, listening to everyone discussing the possibilities and consequences of a poor decision, one I am not ready to make without Helena.

Many hours later, a cloudy mind, and exhausted physically and mentally, I walk out of the room with a bigger issue.

We won't be able to publish in advance, but neither on

time if I don't find a business in the next few days.

And the warning from Helena, that I either find it myself, or we won't have it at all. She is testing me. She better have an alternative plan, or we are screwed.

Matteo is waiting out as I leave the building.

"Is everything okay?" He asks.

"I need fresh air," I explain, hiding my hands in my pocket and looking away. "I will see you on Monday."

"What about Blue Valley?"

"I will go to Stella's and to see the new place. You can take the weekend."

"As you wish, *fratello*," he says, resting his hand on my shoulder. I look back at him. We nod and he jumps into the car, driving away.

I walk around for hours, lost, confused, aware that this week something has changed inside me, something I feel I am losing control over.

What is happening to me?

It has to be that woman.

Something has awakened in me, something unknown, something addictive.

Two dangerous things for me.

Curiosity has taken me to the limits of my existence.

Addiction made me lose who I thought I was, bringing a new man that I couldn't control.

The sun is lower when I head back to the apartment. It's empty. Rosita must have left hours ago.

I head to my room, pack a weekend suitcase, head to the back garage, jump on the McLaren Speedtail and ride as fast as I can away from the city.

It's 5:30 p.m. when I park on Stella's drive way, perfect time for dinner.

She offered a dinner on Grandpa's honour, a way to celebrate his memory and share him with Scott, who doesn't just share the name with him.

I take a moment to study Stella's new hidden place, one of the smallest properties we own. A cottage in the countryside, in a village that barely anyone has heard of, surrounded by families, elder people and green fields.

She wanted to move here after she found out Scott was on the way, but I wasn't prepared for her to step aside just yet, and neither I was on the years that came after that.

All changed after Donnie, her husband passed away, the city, the lifestyle, the rumours, everything became unsuitable for the mom's life she chose to start.

After all, here Scott can have the opportunity of enjoying many outdoor activities once school is over, and their Old English Mastiff, Mr Wrinkles has plenty of space to run.

Before I can knock, Scott opens the door and jumps over to me.

"Uncle Samuel, you are here!"

I smile when his handsome face comes to view—he looks nothing like us, and for that I am grateful. It gives me peace to know—he has the chance to differ from us.

I put him down and head to the kitchen, following an unfamiliar smell.

"What is that little monkey?" I ask, bending down and

twisting my nose as an unpleasant scent hits me.

"She was cooking all afternoon," he whispers in my ear, using his hands to avoid Stella hearing him.

"Hi stranger," she sings.

She looks like a complete disaster. Her fake blonde waves are in an ugly nest, resting on the top of her head. Her cheeks and arms are dusted with a white powder. And every surface around her is cluttered.

I help myself to the cupboard, taking some wine glasses and a cup, pouring some red for us and juice for Scott.

"I think we all need a drink," I murmur, gulping a full glass at once and pouring another.

I can have some wine, is not like I will drink my weight in alcohol as I used to do with the whiskey.

I rest hers next to where she is murdering some vegetables. I have no clue about cooking, but that is not the normal sound knives do as they meet the board.

"Dinner should be ready in ten."

I kiss her dirty cheek as an attempt to act casual, leaving a taste of flour and cornflour on my lips. And I walk to the family room where Scott is waiting for me. I rest my wine and his juice on the tea table in front of the couch and I join him.

"I have a little surprise, boy," I say, taking out of my jacket the new game Rosita bought for him. She knows dinosaurs are his favourite.

We are half way through the game. There is no more clutter coming from the kitchen, and I look at my watch.

We are moving closer to bedtime. It's Friday and there

is no school tomorrow, but I can't be the only one starving in the house.

I let him move forward on the game, vaguely surviving so he won't snap out and come to the same conclusion that I am–dinner is not ready yet.

"Dinner is ready!" she calls a few minutes later.

"You owe me another round," Scott complains as I make him lose his last life in the world of dinosaurs.

"Later," I assure him, holding my hand out so he can give me the remote, and walking behind me to wash our hands at the toilet near the kitchen.

I halt as we enter the dining room. The table is full. There are more dishes than during Christmas lunch. Scott's face looks alarmed, but I just squeeze his shoulder and we both sneer at the scenario.

She has cleaned up, changed clothes, and come back to be the normal Stella perfection. She is relaxed and smiley, letting me catch a new spark in her eyes.

The glass of wine and the bottle are as I left them. I frown and choose to let go. I won't ask in front of Scott.

We talk more than usual during dinner. SaStel is the topic. After all, that is what we have in common, and Stella is curious about my first week on my own.

"Our great-grandfather built an empire, grandpa brought it to the world, father kept it alive, and I'm just trying to adjust it to the new, young people," I assure.

"Where will you find excellent businesses worthy of SaStel?" She asks.

"There's an incredible market out there."

"Have you met them?"

"I trust Helena with the ones she has found already, and soon we will find the perfect one for the cover." I answer and she rolls her turquoise eyes on me.

"Ambition is wonderful, but you need to be cautious. This is an old empire to come and fu–damage it now," she sends me a wink, knowing she was about to use her forbidden language. "Besides, if this edition is so special to you, why do you need to put Helena into it?"

"Because that is why I pay her," I say sharply, standing and placing Scott and my plate on the counter.

I send Scott to brush his teeth so we can talk. There is something going on. This has nothing to do with Grandpa or SaStel. She can't hide it from me.

"What's wrong?" I can't help but sound irritated.

"This isn't what I was expecting," she says.

Ungrateful, as usual.

"You choose this place, this house, this fucking hidden life, grow the fuck up, Stella."

"I am trying to live a simple life. Take Scott for activities after school, parents meetings, anything that other moms do," she says with a miserable sight. "Kids don't want to play with him. Moms share a 'hi', smile and turn away–"

"Have you considered the fact that they know who you are?"

Nobody wants to be around us, not after everything that the press, gossiping, and ill-willing resources were shared.

We passed from the spoiled orphan siblings to the public enemies 2.0.

"I just want to be a mom that can invite her friends for coffee, playdates and birthday parties."

Now everything makes sense. Scott's birthday is a few weeks away, and she knows he has nobody to invite, just her fake friend's children.

She never had real friends, just annoying people looking for fame and gossiping.

"I can take Scott with me this weekend."

"He can't be in the city."

"I have the new place, maybe some time in the park. He is good with people. I just need to supervise."

"Few hours at the park won't fix this," she points around, the mess that surrounds her, a chaos she can't control.

"Nothing can be worse than last year."

"That is not funny," she sighs.

For Scott's seventh birthday, she followed one of that bitch woman ideas on hiring a large venue, filled up with far too much shit for the children, private chef, endless drinks, entertainment, and a little extra gift for the guests–food poison.

"I can't find a skilled caterer."

"It's a child party. Get regular food."

"You are kidding, right?"

"Stella stop trying to live in a world you don't fit on, that party didn't suck because of the food quality, it was the fact that you tried so hard to hit them in the face with our wealth that it turn into your event, not his."

"Do you think you can do any better?" she asks, teasing

me.

Tired of her pathetic attitude, I grab her laptop from the counter and take a seat by the island.

As usual, Samuel to the fucking rescue!

"Baker, party organiser," I mumble, searching online. It can't be so hard.

Over a million searches show up in front of me, but as I change it to closer locations, I have around twenty. My eyes spot one in particular.

"How does Ruby Sweet Dreams sound?"

She turns, with an awkward smile. Why is she smiling that way?

"She is a local baker. Her calendar says she will be available for the party," I continue, pushing the laptop aside.

Her expression changes and I rise, eager to run away. What is going on with this woman?

"I will take Scott with me, contact her, book her and stop whatever is going on there," I say, pointing at her face.

"Yes, boss," she says, cleaning away her tears, walking to the laptop and having a peek at the screen. "Maybe she could be your front page." She mocks.

I ignore her sarcastic comment and the tingles on the back of my neck.

This is a serious matter.

I head to Scott's bedroom. He is reading one of his new books, all about wizards and potions. I sit on the floor with him, resting my back on the pillows that surround his little bookshelf, in the reading corner.

"What if you pack a small bag and take Mr Wrinkles to *Little Castle*?"

He slowly places the bookmark on the page he was reading and puts it back on the self.

Sprinting to the closet and bathroom, collecting his things in his dinosaur sleepover bag. I stand by the door, observing my special nephew.

There is something special about him. He has Donnie looks, light brown hair, green eyes, and a charming smile.

Inside his little body there is something I haven't seen before, a kindness, a light, something that is easy to feel and hard to name.

Donnie wasn't around enough to enjoy him, to know what an incredible son he had. He was a good guy, easygoing, very similar to me in many things.

But never a husband material.

Clearly Stella and Donnie were into the looks, because they couldn't have been more opposites. She tried to make it work. She took care of him, that I have to give it to her.

She didn't deserve what they put her through.

Stella and I might not have the regular siblings' relationship, but I care for her, and for Scott. And just that will make me fight anyone that tries to harm them again.

"I am ready," he says, pulling me away from my thoughts.

I follow him downstairs, wave our goodbyes and head to my new house.

The biggest property in the neighbourhood. It is across from the main park entrance, except for a cottage on the side, it has no other neighbours by the side in at least twenty feet, giving privacy and space for the back garage, where mostly my biggest cars and bikes are parked, and has an extensive front gravel space.

It was a little countryside castle from over a hundred years ago, and I didn't want to change a bit of the outside when I found it.

The walls are made of dark brown rocks with creepers growing in and out of them. Thousands of flowers have blossomed in the past few weeks, giving some brightens to the dark castle it was when I came here first.

Before I put the key in the lock, Rosita opens the front door.

"Mi niño!" She cheers, opening her arms for Scott to run to cuddle her, and Mr Wrinkles to circle around, guiding them to Scott's bedroom.

Stella and he have been working on renovating this room. It's a significant improvement. The walls are like a jungle, so real it makes the room endless. There are dinosaurs drawn everywhere. The carpet is brown to match the walls, and Mr Winkle's house is a small wood cabin that matches the room.

Scott is in bed quicker than I realise and Rosita is nowhere to be seen. "Good night, my boy," I say, dropping a soft kiss on his forehead, making sure the blanket is in place before I leave the bedroom and walk back to my gloomy reality

Chapter Two

Ruby

Naima and Aidan are having a bath while I clear up after dinner.

It's all giggles and screams when my mobile rings and I pick it up from the island as I see Louise's—my social worker's name on the screen. "Hi, Louise." I say, cleaning the counters.

She was at the court office with us on Monday, guiding me through the entire trial and staying slightly longer, trying to find more information.

"Ruby, there's something you need to know," she says.

"What happened?" I ask. My voice trembles, and panic grows in my core.

"Advik's lawyer has pleaded for a reduction in his sentence," she says.

"What do you mean?" I ask, in shock.

"After your testimony, his lawyer gave a speech to the

judge. The lawyer and governor fear for Advik's life."

"That's impossible," I say in a panic. "The judge can't do that."

What type of judicial system do we live in?

"Ruby, the governors protect and prioritize inmates who are suicidal or in danger from other inmates." Suicidal? For what I care, he can hang himself. "The lawyer proposed he could finish the rest of the sentence in a community center, doing some services and therapy. Under control that he doesn't break the restraining order..." is that all?

"He can't be free!" I exclaim.

"I understand your frustration," she says, in her usual calm voice and measured speech, making me anxious.

"You don't understand," I say.

I run my fingers through my hair, rubbing a thumb on the scar that fades away over my eyebrow. Every muscle in my body aches at the thought that he will get out of that place.

"Have you agreed with it?" I ask, she didn't reply so I move along. "He almost killed me! Try to kill my daughter! He doesn't deserve freedom!" I say, growling through my teeth.

"On those matters, there's nothing we can do. It's all under the judge's decision," her professional, cold tone replies.

I hung up, dropping my head as my hands hold me in the counter. My mind was working faster than I can control it.

Planning on what the next move will be, I blindly

trusted the system, this protection center, followed their advice and guidance as if I couldn't make my own decisions.

That will change today, I can't just seat here and wait for him, accept what people that don't take his actions as serious as they are.

We are talking about a dangerous man, with a simple motive in life, end me.

I shake away those emotions, returning to the orders I need to finish and the bedtime routine, that I push forward as I don't have to spend the next two hours pretending and lying to Naima.

She is six, far too smart for her age. Life hasn't been gentle with her, taking away a big part of her childhood, one that I work hard every day to recover.

They are exhausted after our shopping trip in the afternoon and asleep before I finish the second paragraph of the bedtime story.

I return to the kitchen, packing the two boxes of eight cupcakes each, princesses and superhero themed, for the twin's birthday party tomorrow, together with twenty-four shortbread biscuits for the moms and fifteen mini sandwiches.

Next is a five-inch chocolate cake with strawberry filling, covered with a green fondant turtle, for little Malcom's birthday.

The trickiest part of my job is packing. One wrong move and everything will be destroyed for what I like to deliver them personally. This time both have insisted, as my apartment is on their way home from the station.

A soft knock announces Susie, the twin's mom, a kind a funny lady that found me through the local library publicity I hanged around couple of weeks ago.

Something I doubt will work, but has my schedule for the next couple of months nearly filled up.

"Good evening, Susie," I say, opening the door.

She is shorter than me, has black hair and dark eyes. In her mid thirties, kind and funny.

"My beautiful Ruby," she calls, stepping in and giving me one of her awkward hugs.

She is shorter than me, what forces me to bend down, and even I can't say it out loud. I don't like physical contact with anyone that is not my children.

"I will get your order." I say, stepping back.

Once Susie left, I have enough time to pack the cake before Daniel, Malcom's dad, knock on the door.

"Hi Daniel."

"Hi Ruby, you alright?" He sounds tired.

I nod and rush to pick up the cake.

"There you are," I say, opening the lid. "Enjoy your party tomorrow and send me pictures of Malcom and the cake."

"Take care Ruby, we will see you soon," he says.

I lock the front door, make sure the garden door is secure too, and head to the shower, washing the day away.

Walking back to the kitchen, uploading the new images in social media, interacting with some people interested in my work and deleting some junk mail.

I've been told by customers that I should share my

image, that will help with bookings and growing my platforms.

But I have no intention of selling my image. I want to sell my art, and most importantly, avoid to be easily found by the psychopath that apparently will be released unfairly for his own safety.

I prepare a chamomile tea, collect my mobile from the kitchen charger, and walk out to the garden.

Is a small space, enough for a craft picnic table, a grass section for Aidan's expeditions, a sandpit and some herbs I have planted in the back.

I loved cooking since I have memory, always dreamed of serving new meals to my family every day while we share how our day went. But that was not the type of situation I lived.

The children and I were given the scraps of what he didn't want, the fridge was empty for as far as I can remember, and the pantry had some cans that I wasn't allowed to open, unless I was warming it up for him.

My stomach twist at the condition of how we lived for many years. Naima didn't know what a healthy, or at least proper meal was until a few months ago.

Aidan survived of my breastfeeding, taking away the little nutrients that I could have left inside me, as anything he gave went straight for Naima.

Now, I spend hours exploring in flavors, making them taste different meals to see what our favorites are, there are savory and sweet treats on daily basis, and they love when I get orders, as they know I will need their opinion before I can give it to a customer.

It was hard, but I haven't done too bad. I won this battle, and I will fight with all I have to win the war against this monster.

The ringtone of an upcoming email pulls me out of my dark thoughts.

A birthday party coming in a few weeks. They need a full catering service, as well as party organization.

I am good on the cooking world, not that much on decorations, invitations, goody bags and that short of things, but I could try. After all, she is giving me plenty of time. This will be a big deal order, and we needed more than ever.

***

Good evening, Stella.

Thank you for choosing us for your son's birthday party.
We are available on the date you have inquired, and the services can be provide it.
I would like to invite you for a first meeting, when we will discuss the details and you will have the opportunity to share any specifics.
Please find attached the link to my website, where all the designs I have worked on recently are available.

www.rubysweetdreams/birthdayandweedingsalbum/2341z

Sweet Dreams, Ruby. 😊

* * *

You are a lifesaver, Ruby.
I can give you some specifics now. He loves dinosaurs. I need a party with that theme.

He is obsessed with lemon, flavor and color, so you can incorporate in anything, and there must be menus for everyone, properly labeled and organised.
It will be in the afternoon and move along to the early evening.
Please send me your availability for the first meeting.
Thanks so so so much, Stella. Xxx.

* * *

Dear Stella,

I could book you in for tomorrow morning and go through all the details.
Lemon and dinosaurs sound good to me.
Would 10 a.m. work for you?

Sweet Dreams, Ruby. 😌

* * *

10 a.m. will be perfect.
Thanks again, looking forward to meeting you.
Stella. Xxx

* * *

Dear Stella,

That is all booked for tomorrow Saturday June 25th at 10 a.m.
My address is Apartment 3, Daisy Road.
Sweet Dreams, Ruby. 😌
* * *

Locking the garden door, closing the curtains, and moving the wheeled little pantry cupboard to block the full door. I collecting my event folder and a fresh tea on the way to the couch, where I do all the needed research for the morning.

It's late when I send Miguel an email with all the ideas that I prefer to present printed at the meeting.

Before I let go of the day, I prepare a bowl of pancake mixture for breakfast, and our clothes. That will save time in the morning.

I double check the front door, pushing the dresser that holds the house key and shoes towards the door to make sure it's blocked, too.

The kids are peacefully sleeping when I secure the bedroom window, and I lay exhausted by Aidan's side, extending my arm to cover both of them, and letting go of everything, at least for a few hours.

I can smell the wood that burns on the fireplace back inside the house. I can hear the crack of my boots on the dry fields. I can feel the sun warming my pale skin.

But I pause at the hair on the back of my neck stands on end, I can feel it without seeing it.

Mom's gorgeous sunflowers surround me, taller than me, hiding away what now twists my core nervously. I tense my muscle in anticipation.

I can feel his presence, his proximity, by the side of my eyes I see the movement on the wheat, and how he walks my way, a bouquet of sunflowers wrapped on a pink paper on his grip, a mischievous grin growing by the side of his lips. Those that long ago I badly adore.

His pace is slow, cautious, as if I could be fooled that he is testing my reaction when I should be the one with the guard up ready for anything.

His brown gaze fixed on mine, those fake apologetic eyes that long ago I let them fool me.

My wrist get twisted so he can place the bouquet, I let it rest on my palm, tensing as the back of his other hand brush my cheek, through my jaw, until it is resting on my neck, my breath stops, ready for what is coming, moving to my nape, and brushing his fingertips around, almost tickling my skin, but his hold become harder, almost painful, pulling me closer to his face, one that long ago I couldn't take my eyes away from.

Resting his forehead on mine, I can smell the liquor, making my stomach twist, pulling me even closer until his lips touch mine.

"I missed you, my sweet girl," he murmurs to my lips.

I jump out of my skin, returning to the apartment, to the bedroom, and to the bed where the kids sleep peacefully.

Drange in sweat, my muscles ache from the tension and anxiety.

In silence, I walk to the bathroom, stand under the water, and let the temperature regulate, letting it wash away everything, making me aware I am awake.

I collect a comfy maxi t-shirt on the way to the kitchen, the wall clock marks 3 a.m., I prepare some coffee, collecting and mixing all the ingredients for the cupcakes I want Stella to taste, the mini pizzas, and sandwiches for the picnic I had planned and squeezing some lemons for the fresh lemonade.

Letting everything rest, I walk out into the garden with my first cup of coffee.

The fresh air clear the cloud over my head and I smile,

ready for what I know will be a big day.

That phone call won't determine our future. I have worked extremely hard to let all of this go–not again.

With my second coffee, I work on the kids pancakes, the whipping cream for the cupcakes, placing the tray in the oven and working on the dough for the mini pizzas.

Before I wake up the kids, I place the cupcakes in the resting tray and head to the bedroom. Turning off the alarm, laughing at my two babies jumping on the mattress—who is screaming for help.

"Little monsters, stop for a second," I say, holding Aidan in my arms, and guiding Naima with the other hand.

I seat them by the island, giving each their plate with pancakes, and a cup of fresh orange juice.

"Eat babies," I talk as I move around. "I will get your clothes. We need to visit Miguel's."

I change into short and oversize shirt, fresh clothes for the kids, as after the appointment I will take them on a picnic at the park and with the heat wave we are having this week, I want to make sure they don't feel uncomfortable.

I walk back to them, pushing the empty plates away, and changing them as I make them aware of Stella's visit.

They aren't comfortable with strangers inside the house. I usually have a chat with the customer, mostly by the phone, or they will stay with Miguel while I meet face to face.

"I want to stay with him," Naima protest.

"She wants a big party. I can't meet her anywhere else," I explain.

"We can be with him while she visits."

"Baby, you can play in the garden while I work. Please understand that we can't always ask Miguel for help."

"Wasn't he happy with us the other day?"

"Naima, you are a fantastic child. He never said anything like that, but he has a shop to take care of."

"Can we go there for Sunday dinner?"

"I will ask him later."

Since we arrive in Blue Valley, Miguel has helped with the business, the children, and our process to adjust to a neighbourhood like this one.

It's a quiet village, filled with families, elder people, and nothing interesting happening, unless is a gossip scandal.

There were too many questions when we move here, ones that Miguel quiet down in no time, and never heard of ever since.

After a quick visit to the bathroom, I pack some cupcakes for Miguel to taste and we head to his printing shop round the corner, holding hands, and mumbling a new song Naima has made up.

Their joyful and innocent spirits are what keep me going every day, one step at the time, replacing our past.

Naime runs to hug Miguel as he finishes placing the board outside, and I hold Aidan up to join them.

"*Buenos días señor* Miguel." I greet.

He is Cuban, and I am half Mexican. No excuses for me not to practice a language my mother taught me since I was younger than Aidan.

The same one that Advik forbade me to speak, or teach

the children, all because he didn't understand it.

Nowadays, I practice it with Miguel, and we both teach the kids, helping them connect with my native routes, to a past life.

"*Buen día,* Ruby," Miguel says.

He is a short gentleman, with black hair, tan skin, a thick mustache, and a big round nose that holds his reading glasses.

"*Hola* Miguel! Can you please help mama to get ready for an important meeting?" Naima asks, placing the cupcakes box on the counter.

"Does mama have an important order coming up?" he asks, replacing the sweets with a pile of documents.

"She is organizing her son's birthday, and wants me to cover the entire menu," I say, letting my fears take the joy away.

Opening the little box, he takes out one of the lemon cupcakes, "*Mi hija,* you cook like an angel, and anyone who tasted your food can fell the love you put in it."

"I am good at sweets."

"I have tasted both, and with no doubt, you can nail this. She will love it and so will her guests. This is your opportunity to become the best caterer and baker in the neighbourhood."

"I'll need a bigger kitchen," I argue back.

"Keep working hard and you'll own that little cottage," he says, pointing to the other side of the park, to the house Naima calls *one step closer to heaven.* "Take this," he says, handing me the pile of documents, "show that lady who

Ruby Rao is."

The apartment is spotless, the pictures displayed, the fresh coffee and cupcakes scent the room, and the kids are all set up with toys, drinks and food in the garden, when a soft knock announces my customer at the door.

I shake away the nerves, plaster my business mask on, and open the door.

"Good morning, Ruby?" Stella asks. I nod and welcome her in.

Stella is gorgeous, taller than me, slim figure, long wavy blonde hair, skinny olive skin, a perfect white smile and the deepest turquoise eyes I've ever seen.

"Please this way," I point into the open space, shaking my head to stop studying her.

I am used to dealing with female customers, but there is something in her that makes nearly impossible to stop looking at her.

"May I offer some coffee?"

"Black, please," she says, taking a seat at the dining table, where all the images are ready for her to have a look. "You have children," she says, pointing at them in the garden.

"Apologies. It was a short notice to get a babysitter."

"Nothing to apologies for, is mom life," she says, giving me a sweet smile, "where are you from Ruby?"

I stop serving the coffees at the personal question, fear running through my veins.

"You have a lovely accent," she keeps talking unaware of how awkward the situation has become. "I'm Scottish, but I lived here far too long to keep the accent," she says, separating the images from two piles.

"I am from Texas, but move away many years ago."

"This is fantastic," she moves away from us, and back to the party conversation.

Offering the cupcakes and the coffee, I take a seat next to her.

"This is far too much. The venue I have in mind is too small for this," she points out, putting aside the large party images. That is better for me, otherwise I will need to hire some help.

Opening my notebook, I make notes of the images she has chosen.

"When is the party?"

"Saturday, the 16th of July."

I nod, glad of the over two weeks time frame that gives me. I am not the type of person to judge the book by the cover, but a quick look on Stella tells me we are talking about high standards. This is not a simple garden party at home.

"How many people are attending?" I ask.

"We're new to the neighbourhood, you know, new school," she explains, laughing nervously, I nod and write more notes down, "at least fifty, those are the friends coming from the city and family," she says, moving more images away.

"I will need you to confirm at least a week in advance."

Stella nods and places more images in between us. All are elaborate designs, nothing I haven't tried already.

"You mentioned a dinosaur theme. I was thinking of a small two-layer cake. The bottom can be brown and the top green—representing the jungle," I explain, finding some images that represent that I mean, "for details, you can choose in between flat figures or 3D," I say, showing her other samples.

"I like those to fill up the cake," she points out. "We need a big T-Rex."

"That can be the topper," I murmur to myself, making small drawings in the notebook as reference.

Two cups of coffee, a couple of cupcakes are biscuits, multiple notes, and an easy flowing conversation after Stella and I agree on the last touch ups for the party.

She wants a full catering service, decoration, invitations, goody bags, activities for the children, drinks for the adults.

I am unsure if anyone out there offers all of these services at once. She certainly knows better than me.

And by the disastrous party they experience last year, I can't blame her for not be happy to hire multiple people.

"I need your full dedication," she says, filling up a check. "this should be enough to cover the party cost and your exclusivity," she says, pulling the little paper away.

My hands shake as I hold it. The air rushes out of my lungs and my head spins at the amount written down.

"Everything alright?" she asks, closing her check wallet and putting it back in her handbag.

"The total is—"

"I am hiring you full time. For the next couple of weeks, I expect constant updates, the best quality and excellent presentation. The total is correct."

I clear my throat, trying to regain the composure. She is paying me far too much of what I would have asked.

"Am I doing some kind of celebrity party?" I ask.

I can prepare a regular party, but if we are talking high standards, the quality and type of food will have to be different. That would explain the thousands of pounds for food and decoration; high quality comes with a high price.

"He is a member of the third richest family in the world," she says, standing and arranging her blouse as if wasn't in the place she wants it.

"I will start working on this immediately, and keep you updated," I assure, shaking her hand.

"Any other meetings will have to be booked during school hours," she points out.

"Of course. Have a lovely day, Stella."

"You too, Ruby," she says, walking away, leaving me standing glued to the spot.

The moment the door closes behind her, I rush to the garden, holding the kids up, spinning them around and laughing as tears roll down my cheeks.

"Mama!" they exclaim.

I place them down, kneeling in front of them and holding their hands, letting their innocence increase the joy in my heart.

"Give me two seconds baby," I say, rushing back inside the house, holding the mobile, running through my contacts and dialing a person only in my dreams I ever thought I will.

"Good morning, Grace Thompson. How can I help you?" She greets.

"Hello, it's Ruby. We meet–"

"Ruby, how are you? I've been waiting for your call."

Have she?

When they assigned me this apartment, Grace was someone Louise introduce me to for future opportunities.

I was grateful they gave us a place to stay, but as well of the possibility of finding something better in the near future, another apartment where the words *Women Aid Center* weren't written on the wall next to my door.

I am not ashamed of the reason we are here, but I know who I deserve to be, and what the kids and I should have, and I won't stop until that happens.

"I have a lovely apartment next to yours–"

"Grace, I am calling about the cottage."

"The cottage," she says surprised, "I wasn't expecting it this soon."

A few months ago, she showed us some properties, all good for a fresh start, a big step ahead of where we were at that time.

But she did shows us too a new property that came out in the market, a little cottage with a large garden in the front, a rustic touch that stands out of any other property around it, specially the mansion that stands steps away from it.

The massive place will be like reaching heaven to us, but as I remind the kids when we saw it, we need to keep our feet on earth. That is the reason Naima named the cottage *one step closer to heaven*. And it will certainly be, as it has all what we could dream of, the space, the location, everything a person like me should hope for on her own.

"Well, I just finished a meeting with a new customer," I explain, bitting my nails. "I've got the money you asked for."

Not even in my best dreams will I ever imagine that in such a short time I will have been able to collect what I needed for the first payment, and now with Stella's payment, I will cover a few of the mortgage installments.

"Ruby that is impressive."

"Is it still available?"

A sense of worry grows in me, thinking someone might have got it during these months.

"It's available. I had a few people interested, but nobody deserves it more than you do. The person managing the property wasn't happy with the choices I have made it easier to hold it for you," she confirms.

"Thanks, Grace, for your patience and support."

"I have some paperwork to work on, a few phone calls, but they are desperate to sell now that the mansion has sold. I will get back to you on Monday," I thank her for her support and hung up.

Laughing that the kids jump over me, after waiting patiently for the call to end.

"Do you understand what I just talked about?" I ask. Naima nods and Aidan looks confused. "Mama just called Grace, making an offer on the cottage we loved so much a few months ago. Do you remember?"

"The one next door to our dream house?" Naima asks with a bright smile.

"That one baby!" I exclaim.

"Can we visit it again?" Naima asks.

"I can ride by it on the way to the afternoon surprise," I offer to their gorgeous smily faces.

They both nod, walking back to put all their toys in place, I take the time to pack all the food and drinks, filling the carriage of the bike and once I secure them, riding around the neighbourhood letting the wind blow my hair back, the sun warm my skin, and a bright smile light up my spirit.

Our destiny stands in front of us, a perfect future open ups for us, and I am ready to ride straight into it.

I depart home many years ago, lost and unsure of who I was or where I was heading.

Today, that changes for good.

Chapter Three

Ruby

6 months ago, London

The lack of air awakens me. I can't breathe. My head is drowsy after I fall into a deep sleep for the first time in a long time.

Kicked into reality by pain, when my body turned and my back falls on the mattress, forced to face my death sentence.

The liquor odor makes me sick. I can't see him, but I am aware of who is straddling me.

I cover my face after his fist opens the fresh wound on my cheek. My other hand searches for my old phone under the pillow, pressing the side button multiple times, hiding it under my head as the emergency services get alerted.

I am not sure they will arrive on time. My body is too weak after what I went through protecting Naima.

Fearing for my life and the safety of the kids, when he

hits me harder, I cover my head as he pulls my panties down, and forces himself inside me.

I can't move, but I can shout, and I do until I hear footsteps approaching, trembling at the thought that he has brought someone, that this is the end of me, that I won't be able to protect them anymore.

Everything stops. He isn't on the bed anymore. The kids are screaming at the top of their lungs, their voices are getting closer, until they jump on my side.

I hold them tight, hiding them in the gap between my legs and my chest, making a shield that won't break that easily.

"Everything is going to be okay," I whisper to their trembling heads.

I can hear the footsteps approaching me and I can feel someone standing at the foot of the bed.

"Ma'am, I'm Officer Clark and I'm here with my partner Officer Lewis," a gentle male voice explains. "There's an ambulance downstairs," he says, giving me all the information he considers I need. "We will escort you and help with the children."

"They are okay with me. I will hold them." I assure.

"I have something to cover yourself," he says, dropping something on my side.

I pull up the trousers the best I can, tightening my hold on the kids as I turn on the mattress, touching the carpet and pushing myself to standing. Pain is excruciating, but my determination, the sense of freedom is stronger.

With every step that I take away of a house that has kept

us prisoners for over five years, I remind myself that nothing matter most that me walking out of here with my children in my arms.

I pause by the door, right beside one of the man that has come to my rescue.

This is not the first time I have to walk around the house blinded. He enjoys taking senses away from me, like the time he punched my ear so hard against the wall that all I could hear for days was a buzzing noise. Or the time he kicked my face and I couldn't breathe or talk properly for weeks.

But nobody knew about that. I doubt neighbors knew of our existence. As for the fear of punishments, the kids barely made any noises.

"Ma'am, my partner and I will guide you downstairs."

"I can do it on my own."

"I am sure of that. We just want to feel helpful," he confesses.

If I didn't know better, I will say he is offended that a woman on my condition is not crying and begging for their help.

I never had it, so I would find it hard to know how to do so.

There is someone tall and strong standing in front of me. I step closer, and even when I can feel his hand suspended in the air, somehow holding me, he doesn't touch me.

The other officer is one step behind us, letting me take my time, reaching the lower floor, shivering as the cold air of the night hits my expose body, that soon gets cover with a thick blanket, I wince as the fabric touches my wounded skin, but I embrace the warmth it gives us.

"Ma'am, I am the paramedic," a male says, approaching us. "I'm going to help you up to the gurney. Just stay still," he informs, lifting us up effortlessly, resting another blanket over us and taking us away.

I can hear people murmuring, gasping and sobbing, my neighbors I supposed, the ones that lived steps away from us for over four years and never knew or care of our existence.

My head rest back, somehow finding a peace in me that makes little sense, but I know is the relief of stepping into an uncertain and unknown future, where he doesn't exist anymore.

We reach the hospital faster than I realized, and my determination and strength deflates as multiple voices surround us. I cover the kids and tremble when I feel someone standing on my side.

"Ma'am, I am head nurse Wan," she says in a calm, low voice, "I will accompany you inside where my team and Dr. Lopez would take care of your examination," she continues and I nod.

The gurney moves forward, a set of automatic doors open and the cold air swaps for a heavy warm one.

I inform the kids of where we are and that there is nothing to fear for when nurse Wan walks away, assuring to return in a moment.

All my guards jump up to place when a set of clicking heels approaches us unannounced, pulling a side of the blanket aside, exposing the kids and trying to take them as she speaks up.

My hold tightens and I growl. She is stronger than me, but so are the boots that march on our way and the familiar voice that now orders her to stop.

"Please, don't do that!" says Officer Clark. He must have followed the ambulance. "They will remain with her at all times."

"Officer, there are rules and policies to follow," the rough woman says, with a voice that matches her attitude.

"I'm well aware, but my colleague and I will be around and help with them as much as possible," he says, in his previous determine tone, mixed with what feels like insecurity.

"Thanks ma'am, but Social Services won't be need it here." Nurse Wan says, followed by multiple footsteps and murmurs.

Why would Social Services be here?

They want to take my kids away from me, the victim in all of this, but they didn't care about their existence all these years.

I exhale in relief as we move forward, to a warmer and quieter room.

I can't see them, but I can feel each and everyone in the room. Their thoughts are louder than any words they could say.

Plastic packages are being open, rubber shoes move

around the room, metal utensils are being placed over another metal surface, their breath is heavy, but their heartbeats are stronger.

I can't see what they see, but I can feel it. I know is ugly and makes them uncomfortable.

Is it not part of their job to see this constantly?

Someone enters the room, the determine footsteps stop by the end of the gurney.

"Evening Ma'am, I am Dr. Lopez," the voice of an elder man says. There is knowledge, calmness and control of every word and move that he takes to stand closer to us.

"Ruby,... I am Ruby," I whisper.

"Ruby, it's nurse Wan," she says next to the doctor. "I know you are worry, but my nurse team has brought two beds and we will need you to let us take the children," just by hearing that, our hold tightens, "that way we can examine you better, they won't leave the room, I can promise that, we have some food, books, and toys." She says, trying to convince the three of us is not a separation situation.

Naima's head shakes. Aidan rests his little head closer to her and they whisper something to each other.

"Mama is here babies," I whisper to them, kissing their heads, "the doctor needs to clean mama up," I said.

Naima pulls away from my chest, her soft palm rests over my jaw, her little thumb caress a clear area, my head tilts and I feel how she holds Aidan up.

Someone approaches them. I can feel how they take them away, emptiness hits me, but hearing the way how they interact with the nurses, the noise of paper bags, and Naima explaining images of a book to Aidan calms me. She is a little girl, someone that in a short life has faced the ugliest side of life, building a fire and strength inside her that makes me know, no matter what happens to me, she will protect Aidan.

"Let's get you in a clean gown," a woman's voice informs on the other side, gently taking the blanket and t-shirt off me.

Dr. Lopez and nurse Wan talk me through every move that happens before it does.

"Ruby, I need you to rest sideways, in the opposite direction of my voice. We will start with those wounds," she explains.

"Please, raise your hand if you need me to stop at any time, Dr. Lopez requests.

I turn as they ask, exposing the consequences of protecting the kids last night after Naima didn't look at him as he was delivering his usual threats before he walked out to drink.

The sound of the belt tearing my flesh echoes in my mind as a cold liquid falls over the wounds.

They cover the back of my head, my arms, back, bottom side, and part of my legs.

"Everything is going to be okey," nurse Wan whispers, holding my hand. When a cold cloth rests over my flesh, the pain makes me dizzy.

I take a deep breath and let go, give them the time to clean all my wounds, and cover myself.

Chapter Four

Samuel

Thomas' name pops up on my screen as I walk out of the closet, pulling down my t-shirt. "My man! How are you?" he says.

He is the contractor that has helped us on multiple of our properties and SaStel before I took over.

I didn't want to step into an office that would just give me old memories of Grandpa or father, and he was the one helping with Scott's bedroom.

"Saw your email, man! That house is a dream come true."

"I need you to start today," I order.

"How about twenty minutes? A couple of my boys are in the area. We will come, take pictures, and measurements. I can bring you some materials. How does that sound?"

"Not a minute later. My nephew is with me."

I hang up, and walk downstairs when Stella's name bright on my screen.

"Stella," I greet sharply.

"Oh my God, Samuel, you won't believe it!"

I pull the mobile away from my ear to don't end up deaf.

What is wrong with this woman?

I enter the kitchen. Scott and Rosita are finishing the picnic bag for the park as I mouth her name.

"Hi mom!" Scott exclaims as walk pass, collecting some water from the fridge and sitting on the dining table.

"Do you mean it went well?" I ask.

"I found an angel, Samuel. She is perfect, professional, beautiful, and kind. She needs help, and she's helping me." Stella explains.

"How so?" I ask, rolling my eyes at her comment.

Something is being planned in her mind and it's irritating me. Stella never compliments or speaks nicely about people, especially beautiful women.

Thomas arrives before I can find out what she has done.

"This kitchen is amazing, man!" Thomas exclaims, followed by six employees and too much stuff. I knew every single inch of this house would surprise him.

Thomas takes possession of the dining table with all that I sent last night while I roll my eyes and mouth–*Stella*, making him shake his head.

My sister looks adorable, but it can be a big pain.

"I will help," Rosita murmurs.

I just gesture for the boys to go on with her so I can finish with the call.

"Continue," I order, stepping out into the rear garden.

Let's hear the brilliant plan.

"I paid her twelve thousand pounds for exclusive service." I choke on the water.

"What?" I ask.

I knew giving her freedom in finances wasn't a great idea, and here is why.

She is a bored fucking stay-at-home mum with too much money available.

What type of party is she organising?

"You should see her ideas, her passion. She would do an incredible job." She can't stop talking.

Pulling the mobile away, I take a breath and try to listen to her again.

"Oh Samuel! That will send her business to another level, don't you agree?" She asks, while my mind is processing the fortune this lunatic just spent on a eight birthday for Scott. "When you meet her, you will love her, Samuel, I promise," she keeps talking when I put the mobile back on my ear.

"Very well," I mumble. "Its great news."

"Fantastic..." I hung up ignoring anymore nonsense.

I finish my water, run my hands over my waves, and take a few deep breaths.

Stella is the queen of building headaches, and I thought she was better.

Fucking lunatic.

Twelve grand for a birthday party, fuck me.

This makes me wonder how much she wasted last year. I wasn't around–she didn't want me there, for sure another fortune.

I need to contact Nathaniel. He is our lawyer. I fucking hate him after what he did to Stella, but I need to make sure there is a clause that can keep my little sister under control.

I am the head of the family now. It's my duty to make everyone safe, and stable.

Rosita, Scott, Thomas and his employees are walking out of what will be the new theatre room on the lower floor as I walk out of the kitchen.

"I can get that finished by Monday," he says, pointing to the close door behind him.

I take them to my bedroom. "I want new carpets and the colour of the walls."

"This is as old as my grandma," he mutters, walking inside, "take measurements, we are taking this off now."

"I need it done before the evening," he nods, flicking his fingers to his employees who start working before we leave the room.

"Bathroom and closet?" he asks.

"You can have a look, but everything looks good for now."

I walk out, heading to the opposite side of the corridor, where Rosita', Scott' and two guests' rooms are. One could have been Stella's, but she rejected the idea of family under one roof.

"Scott needs a bigger and more secure window. He likes to spend a lot of time in there. There is not enough light for him."

"You want one of those that take the full wall?"

"Is that safe?"

"Some of them only have opening areas on the top part. He won't reach it unless he climbs."

"Scott is not that type of boy. That is clear. Follow me."

I take him to the oval extension. It's the biggest room in the house, the walls are made of glass, so it has the perfect light all day.

"Man! This room is another world. What are we doing here?" he asks, checking the sketches I sent, "the office, that might take as a while longer than you expect. Windows have to be secured, carpet,--"

"I want wood floor."

"Yeah, that is my point. We need to replace that, too."

"Let's make this sweet and sound. My carpet today, paint Monday when I am back in the city, theatre room ready for next weekend, and this," I say pointing around us, "I need it for the end of July, I won't be working in the city while Scott is on holidays."

"Kitchen?"

"That is Rosita's."

"I will talk to her."

I tap his shoulder, find Scott reading in his bedroom with Mr Wrinkles head resting on his lap.

"Did you see the park in front of us?"

"Yes, mom took me there twice."

"What about we let this man's work, and we take Mr Wrinkles to run around the park? I don't know you, but we need the fresh air."

"Rosita said we will have a picnic in the garden."

"No, in the park," *gosh nobody listens.*

"Let's go then."

I follow them downstairs, collect the bag, dog leach, and we head to the park.

The park is across the road, with the main gate a few steps to the side. *Little Castle* is a great location, and I know Scott and the dog appreciate it.

I listen to all his stories about Stella trying to do activities that mysteriously get cancelled at the last minute.

I know the truth. She knows is better for him to don't be around kids that won't be kind to him. I won't be the one telling my nephew that.

The moment we cross the gates, the warmth of the sun, the scent of fresh grass and the lake in the distance, my body turns cold, all my hair stands on end.

What was that?

A tickle runs from my feet to my face, and there's a buzzing in my ears, but the worst is the pressure on my chest.

What is happening to me?

I shake my head, to put away this weird sensation and focus on reality.

Mr Wrinkles pulls the leash and I hold him tight, looking down to where Scott was standing minutes ago, and now is empty. He is gone.

What the fuck have I done?

"Scott!!" I release the leash, turning in circles looking for him.

Panic is blurring my vision. It's impossible for him to

have gone far. My heart is in my throat, I'm out of breath, I'm having a panic attack, and I need to focus.

Turning on the spot, I see Mr Wrinkles running towards the lake and then I see Scott. He is feeding the ducks.

He is feeding the fucking ducks?!

I run like my life depends on it, kneeling when I get closer, "are you–" I say, making sure he is fine.

My head tilts and I frown when I meet the confusion in his round face.

Why is he confused?

He is the one who disappeared.

His little chin push forwards and I follow the direction.

There is a girl and a boy, younger than him, standing behind me, holding a bag of bird food. Two sets of wide blue eyes observe me and I draw an awkward smile on my stupid face.

Scott was trying to make friends, and my controlling side was here, ruining it all out.

I look in between them, focusing on his new little friends, my head tilt and something tries to clicks in my head.

I've seen these kids before.

I give Scott an apologetic smile, stand, stepping back so they can feed the ducks again.

A soft hum makes me turn. I freeze when I see her, her snow skin, messy bun, and angelic face.

She's here, in front of me—it feels unreal.

My chest contracts, my throat closes, and I lose the little air I was holding with all the running and panic.

She is kneeling, a paper bag full of bird food resting on her lap.

"Is this your son?" she asks, pointing at Scott.

I bite my lip to hold a stupid smile as I hear her cute Western accent.

She doesn't focus on me. Her gaze moves around, never stopping.

Is she looking for someone?

I can't take my eyes away from her.

Of her gorgeous face that I missed very much for the past five days, the picture was not enough or did any justice to her beauty.

Or the white fabric that covers her top part of her body, falling forward as she stands, giving me a glimpse of her white bra underneath. Her legs are exposed, they are long, slim. I lick my bottom lip just with the desire of running my fingers over them before I wrapped them around my waist.

I'm suffocate on my skin. The t-shirt and shorts I am wearing feel like a neoprene attached to my body. I move on the spot in need of some air, but we are under the sun and far too close to her.

"He is not my dad, he is Samuel, my Uncle," Scott says.

Bringing me back to reality, I look away, clear my throat and with a loud exhalation I build some words in my lips.

"Nice to meet you. I am–" her gaze moves around my face and I can't breathe, kicked miles away when she smile, I look away and find the words, "Samuel, Samuel Smith," I burst out, dying on the spot when her deep, bright blue oceans meet my mine, I can't tell where or who I am anymore, not while *she sees me.*

Doesn't she recognise me?

My mind, body and broken soul are travelling on different journeys.

I wonder why she is acting like if we are total strangers. My hand is in between us waiting for her to shake it and my soul comes back to life with an electroshock the moment her soft skin comes in contact with mine.

Our skin melts, we tighten the hold, and my chest expands when I see the same confusion I have on the inside, plastered on her angelic face.

"Uncle Samuel, these are Ruby, Naima and Aidan," Scott introduces them.

Ruby breaks our hold, pulling me back to the present moment—at the park, by the lake, with the children.

"We are out of food kids," she says, shaking her head, avoiding me. "Let's clean our hands and eat something."

When she turns, Mr Wrinkles follows her. This dog will follow anyone at the mention of food.

"Would you like to join us?" she asks Scott, from a nearby picnic matt, kneeled to scrub the dog behind the ears and letting him leak her cheek. "Well, if your uncle is okay with it," she looks at me again.

"Are you sure?" I ask, but she doesn't answer.

She just guides all the kids to take a seat, cleaning each of their little hands and faces, opening a large basket, to prepare the endless amount of food that it's inside there.

I smile on the inside as she places a plate away for the dog.

Attentive and gorgeous, can she get any better?

"Come on, Uncle Samuel." Scott gestures for me to join them.

I sit on the grass, resting my basket and the leash on my side, rubbing the dog ears after he finished all his food, appreciating the fresh air under the tree shade and fixing my gaze on her every move.

She is too fucking perfect to be real, the simplest most natural beauty I've ever seen, her moves are special, the way she takes care of the kids.

I don't miss the way her gaze travels around the park.

Are we waiting for someone else?

There is no ring on her long, delicate hands, and I will bet something that there is no man in her life, she wouldn't be looking at me this way if there was one.

"Samuel?" My eyes drop to her fleshy lips, dark pink, almost red, a small heart shape on the top.

I lick my dry lips, and my chest contracts at the thought of brushing hers.

My entire body shakes, my arm turns into flames and I jump out of my skin when her soft hand rests on my forearm, *I never felt more alive.*

"Samuel," she whispers, a cute frown grows in between her brows and I bite my lip to avoid touching her, her lips move, I can't hear her, but I can feel how her hold tightens and I am brought back to reality as she pulls it away.

"Yes?" I ask in shock.

Why she stopped touching me?

I need her to touch me.

67

"Water or lemonade?" she asks, as I catch the way she analysed her palm.

She felt it too.

"Lemonade, please."

I observe the way she pours it, how she holds it with two hands, letting go of the own I could have touch to avoid me.

She felt it too!

"Food?"

She offers a platter with mini pizzas and mini pies.

I nod, take a mini pizza that blows me away—I'm floating on the clouds. Heaven is in front of me and an angel is serving me.

"You love mama's food, right?" Naima asks.

She is a small version of Ruby, a different skin tone but the same incredible blue eyes.

I just nod and smile around the next bite, "this is Spectacular."

Fuck she knows how to cook!

Yes, she can get better.

"Do you live around here?" Naima asks.

I nod again, washing the food and dryness of my throat with lemonade, aware that is the effect they are having over me, is not just Ruby, is them, this place, this food, the way they are looking at me, I feel exposed and unguarded.

"Naima," Ruby calls, "focus on your food."

"Do you work around here?"

She keeps going, I finish my drink, clearing my throat and ready to act as I should.

"Uncle Samuel works in the city," Scott answers for me.

"London?" Naima asks him, her eyes travelling from Scott to me.

"He works in a magazine," Scott says proudly.

"What type of magazine?" Naima asks.

I can't take my eyes away from Ruby reaction to the children conversation, to her blushed cheeks, her slight move on the spot, how her fingers play with a loose lock of hair, dying on the spot when she finds me.

"Not sure," Scott continues, "there are lots of clothes, jewellery, food, parties, that type of." He has described it perfectly.

"Are you a writer?" Naima asks me.

"No, I am..." I start.

"Mama ball please," Aidan stops the conversation and all eyes move away from me.

I take a deep breath, in need of shake away this cocktail of emotions.

Ruby takes all the food away, running behind the kids and I turn facing where they stand now, playing all together.

Could life get any fucking better?

Yes, it could, if Ruby could be mine.

That is something that could never happen, for her good she should run the opposite direction that I am heading.

I belong to a world someone like her should never enter.

"Uncle Samuel! Come on!" Scott calls.

I jump up, not thinking this through as I join the game, Mr Winkles runs around us helping Scott and I against them, the game become even.

Scott and Naima are the goalkeepers. Aidan has his own game going on with Mr Wrinkles, leaving it to Ruby against me. She is better than I expected, running around me kicking the ball without mercy, giggling as I miss catching it and slowing down as she reaches Scott.

"Can we join?" A group of six boys approach us.

"Absolutely!" Ruby exclaims.

Now this turns into a fair game, I clearly suck at it, my high and speed helps my clumsy feet though.

Scott has never been a sport lover, and I haven't play in decades.

Ruby determination to kick my ass turns this into a more personal matter, and I get ready to give her a fair play, or not, we will see how she reacts.

She is like a magnet that pull me closer and closer; I believe if I try to run I wouldn't be able, and as much as it hurts, for the first time I want the pain, the agony, the discomfort, I want it all; *I need more.*

Naima and Scott get replaced by the other children's parents and the teams become bigger and bigger.

Ruby is on full mindset, determination builds on her blue oceans fixed on me, running around, laughing when I miss taking the ball away from her, and she face the real challenge, the new kids and parents.

I growl a laugh as she rush by my side victorious, she is playing dirty games with my mind and body, but I know how to play too.

Let's test your limits angel.

I observe as she kicks the wall my way, my arm extends on her direction, catching her small waist, pulling her away from the ground and letting Scott take control of the ball.

The entire world pauses, her laugh is all I can hear, her scent all I can smell, her heart all I can feel.

Nothing else exists with her on my arms, the only thing that matters is the way her eyes study me and they rest over my lips, as mine travel across her angelical face.

I tremble, afraid the moment I let go of her everything I will fall.

Not in the ground, but into a darker hole that the one I dig for myself long ago.

A boy from her team passes by, I let go of Ruby's waist, keeping her on arm distance to catch the ball and I rush to the opposite team goal post, ready to play somehow.

Naima is my opponent now, laughing as she runs my way, determine to take the ball from me, I move aside, slightly brushing her shoulder and halting when she freeze, her tan skin turning pale and something unknown growing on her small face.

I let go of the ball, approaching her, observing how she jumps out of her skin as I nearly touch her shoulder.

Ruby rush to her, holding her tight, "Mama is here," she whisper.

"He... he touched me," Naima says.

My palm aches and I understand the mistake I have made.

Why have I touched them?

Suddenly I want to run away, I want to go as far as

possible from them, people getting affected by my darkness wasn't something I concerned myself about it.

In this precise instant I will put my hand off if that will take away the expression that Naima little face holds, or the pain in Ruby's eyes.

I created that, and for that I should run away.

Scott runs around us, unaware of what is happening, I can't take this moment away from him.

I walk back to the mat, facing the game with Mr Wrinkles by my side.

My eyes travel across the imaginary field where Scott is having a great time, while my thoughts torture me.

Ruby jumped away the first time I touched her back in London.

What a fucking stupid arsehole I am, thinking that meant something, it did for me, for her was a reaction to someone's touch.

It didn't mean anything.

I can't hide how much that realisation hurts me, but there is something that hurts even more, deeper, my blood boils and my muscles tighten in rage.

What happened to them?

I observe how Ruby and Naime return to the game, holding hands and smiling as they were before I step into their lives.

I never have to push people away, they make their way out on their own, Ruby has me standing in between her world and mine, both ends far too dark, wondering what matters the most.

Bring lightness to them or try fixing myself.
Who would ever care if I do or die?

Chapter Five

Ruby

Who is this man?

I run around the kids, focusing away from him, observing him from the distance.

Analyzing discretely a man that stormed inside our afternoon picnic, our peaceful time feeding the ducks like a summer storm over a clear sky.

I wouldn't feel this way if he picked Scott and walked away.

The fact that he couldn't take those deep turquoise eyes away from me, the way he studies me unapologetically, the inappropriate proximity or physical contact, the familiarity with whom he moves around us.

All of that bothers me.

Is that how men behave around strange women?

How would I know?

The only man I've been in contact with showed me how evil, manipulative and controlling they can be, and how vulnerable and useless they can make us feel.

Samuel's looks can't soften that thought.

Not even when a side of me appreciates the way he is behaving, talking, and even slightly breaking any strangers' proximity safety codes.

"Mama, tired," Aidan says, asking to be held up, bringing me back to reality.

I walk back to the matt where Samuel and the dog observe my every move. I place Aidan on the grass, looking at the ducks as I kneel to clear up the picnic.

Looking over my shoulders to Naima who keeps playing with the others, bringing warmness to my heart, knowing she belongs here, around kids, under the sun, inside the innocent bubble of youth.

My mind is everywhere, Louise's call last night, Stella's meeting, Grace's conversation, and now, Samuel.

I pack as my eyes travel between Aidan and Naima, jumping out of my skin when I hold the lemonade bottle and my palm turns into flames.

My head turns in that direction, finding my hand rests over his, the contraste of my pale skin over his toasted one.

The softness and warmth of his skin, over the cold drink dripping in between his masculine, long and strong fingers.

My eyes travel across his muscular forearm, dusted with dark hair, up to his define biceps, that tense as I look across the dark material that covers his torso, I can see his chest raise rapidly, matching the beats of his pulse over his neck.

My free hand fist the matt, eager to draw the line of his

jaw covered with a dark stubble, across his full lips, over the straight line that defines his nose, through his thick eyebrows to soften up the frown that grows deeper as I study him.

Or over his thick, charcoal waves that frame his gorgeous face, brushing his ears and resting over his nape.

Confirming how much I am losing control when I look into those two hypnotic oceans, the air blows his scent my way and, a mix of eucalyptus and mint intoxicates me, the world around us disappears, my body burn under his gaze and I come back to live when his fingertip brushes my jaw.

I move away, standing, collecting what I can and loading the bike carrier.

This is madness.

Panic grows in my chest. I am doing it again. I am letting a man control my mind and body. Samuel is far more dangerous than Advik could ever be. That hideous bastard uses physical strength to keep me docile. This irresistible man could make me bend to my knees with a simple smile or a deep stare. Who knows what a word coming out of whose lips could do to me.

I need to go.

Turning desperate to leave quickly and hide away, has me hitting my face with his muscular chest, my hand land on his torso, and before I can think they are exploring his define body over the thin material, his heart beats travel across my arms and my wounded heart and soul bring me back to reality.

My hands drop to my side. I step back to turn and lose

balance when his hands now holding my hips spin me around. The back of his arms becomes my balance point and my head falls back to meet his.

A sweet touch of cinnamon scent reaches me at this height and distance. When he faces move closer, his fingertips brush some loose hair behind my ears, drawing a burning line down my nape collarbone, up my throat and across my bottom lip.

I lose all the air that was held inside my lungs on a soft moan and I melt as the corner of his lips raises.

He is well aware of what he is doing, and I will be a stupid naive woman if I deny it, too.

"Mama," Aidan's voice throws me off Samuel's dimension and back to reality.

I step back, making sure my hair and clothes are where they should, shaking my head and rolling my shoulders, desperate to run away.

"Can we walk you home?" He asks.

My mouth is working the way to decline something a part of me wants more than anything.

"That won't–"

"Mama," Naima calls, "can Scott and Mr. Wrinkles walks us home?" she asks.

Trapping me in between what I know is the correct choice, walking away from this man for good, and what I really want to do, spend every second I can in his presence.

A soft nod confirms that they all win, and my poor rational consciousness kick me in the butt, reminding me of the consequences of letting him give a step far too close.

But haven't I let him in already?

I haven't. The power of stepping away, putting distance and forget about his existence is on my side. Once I reach my apartment and I close my door on his face, Samuel will exit my life, and land on my mind forever.

Everyone helps with the remaining things, Aidan seats on the carrier, and Naima walks side by side with Scott and the dog, while I accept Samuel's offer of pushing the bike up the little hill side that ends across the road of our apartment.

"How long have you been living here?" He asks.

"Six months," I say.

"Liking the neighbourhood?" he asks.

"It's a quiet area, and people are nice."

"Seems a good family neighbourhood," he agrees.

"It's safe, with excellent schools and nice green areas," I say.

"It's looks better than the city, that's for sure," he says.

He lives in the city?

A million question overload my mind. The most alarming one is what a city man will be doing in the countryside.

I stop, letting something that has been bothering me all afternoon in the back of my thought travel forward and making me seen what that little voice was warning me about.

Samuel doesn't feel familiar with inexplicable, unnatural, unknown reasons.

He does, because I have seen him before, his casual

clothes, his charming and friendly behavior, his hypnotizing aura has blinded me all day.

I can see it and remember it now, he is the mysterious man that cross my path on Monday, I was confused and lost in that moment after the failure appointment at the courtroom, and the fact that I've never walked London roads on my own before.

The overwhelm sensation of that many people surrounding us, and the way he steps up, cared for three strangers and pushed the crowd away so I could cross the road.

That small gesture brought out of pure kindness.

"Mama?" Naima calls from the top of the hill, next to the gate, bringing me back to reality.

"Sorry, you were saying?" I ask Samuel, pretending I didn't just remember who he is, playing his game to test his limits.

"That Blue Valley is better than the city."

"Maybe, but the city, the buildings, the vibe, being able to find anything—that is incredible," I say. "One day I want to hire a tour guide and do a proper visit," I let the comment sink in. His eyes narrow and his head turns away. Now we both know. "Do you know any?"

"I know what you mean, I spent my childhood in between the countryside and the city, honestly nothing beats the green fields and the fresh air, so when my sister found this location, I didn't think twice and found a place around here too."

"Are you planning to stay?" I ask.

Aware that he is hiding something, turning the conversation around to make sure he is not caught in his own lies.

I can't be around a liar, and neither do the kids.

"My place here is under renovation, and my job is back in the city."

"Oh yeah, your magazine job in Hyde Park area, right?"

My accusation comes out before I can think it through, and it hits him hard, understanding I am not playing his game of lies any longer.

"Ruby, I can explain–"

"There is nothing to explain. You knew us all this time and kept it for yourself."

"So did you?"

"No, I didn't," I say, facing him when we reach Scott and Naima, holding her hand, claiming my bike back, and crossing the road.

"Ruby," he calls, "is not what you think."

"Thank you for the help, Samuel, bye Scott," I say, helping down Aidan, and parking the bike on the side of our door.

"Are we going to see you again?" Scott asks.

"Maybe at the park another time," I say, avoiding Samuel's gaze that burns my skin.

"Uncle Samuel will take me to the park at the same time tomorrow," Scott says.

Is he trying to set up us to meet again?

"Am I?" Asks Samuel. Scott punches his leg, and I can't help but smile. "I am!" he exclaims.

"I have some work to take care of, but if I finish on time, we might pop in for a bit."

"Mum has to buy ingredients for her orders. We ride to the store after the bridge every day. The bike doesn't have much space." I clear my throat in the hope that Naima will stop, but she doesn't get it. "It will take us all day, maybe next week," she continues, making me feel guilty.

"You go grocery shopping on the bike with the kids?" Samuel asks. My gaze lands on his and I frown at his alarmed expression.

"Well, I don't have another choice," I say.

There are no buses services, and a taxi will cost a fortune.

"He will drive you!" Scott says, "that will take you less time, and you can meet me after that," he continues.

Taking away the possibility of Samuel to make a decision.

My head tilts, begging him to stop this madness. We are complete strangers, we come from different worlds where my daily routine is based on bike rides, cooking and playing board games, and his is work on big posh offices and wear expensive suits.

"I could take you," he says, blowing my mind on how reckless he can be.

"Baby, can you help with the carrier?" I ask Naima, handing the apartment keys and signaling to Scott, so Samuel will send him away too.

"Scott, help Naima please," he says, without breaking the eyes contact with me.

Taking a step closer, looking over my shoulder to make sure the kids are distracted, I face this dangerously gorgeous stranger.

"What are you doing?"

"I was just trying to be kind."

"Samuel, you lied to me. I know who you are, and you think you can storm inside our lives and behave as complete strangers one minute and old friends the next?"

"You don't take help as graceful as I thought."

"I am not the damsel in distress–"

"Does that make me Prince Charming?"

"More like the Evil King. I will take care of my things and you will walk away from our lives. Are we clear?"

"Why are you so stubborn?"

"Because a man that mysteriously helped us in the city a few days ago, has popped in my afternoon picnic miles away from where he belongs, pretend to not know who we were all day, broke all the boundaries in the world and now wants me to get into his car and let him play shopping day with me and my kids for a day?"

"You walked by my apartment in London, that's why we cross paths on Monday, my sister and Scott live here, that is why I am in the neighbourhood, and I was offering a friendly ride to the store, not a full day."

"We will be fine, thank you," I assure, turning away.

"Why can't you take the help? don't do it for me or for you, but for Naima and Aidan."

"Do not put my children in the middle."

"The middle of what, Ruby? I am just trying to help. Yes,

I am a complete stranger, if makes you feel any better I do not like new people's company. I don't know. This feels different, like something I have to do."

"Samuel–"

"Take me as you will with a taxi driver. I will take you where you need. Help you unload it to your door step and be out of your way before lunch time."

"Scott wats–"

"I will take care of that. Please don't make me feel guilty knowing I let you do your regular ride around."

Scott runs to Samuel before I can decline once more.

I can't deny that it's a tempting offer. I know we are all tired of the daily rides. Stella's order is far more extensive that other customers, and if I organize it well, I could be done in one day.

"I don't have car seats," I say.

"I will figure that out," he assures.

My head turns, my chest contracts at Naima's expression, my strong little girl puppy eyes are breaking all my guards.

"Unbelievable, at 8 a.m. here." I say, pointing to the little path in front of our door.

"Done!" he exclaims, grinning at his victory.

I shake my head and bite my lip to hide away my own smile.

"Until tomorrow, kids," he says, waving his hand, "Ruby," he murmurs in a raspy voice, making my entire body shake.

Melting in the spot when his eyes brighten up, his white

killing smile comes on display and he winks at me.

I rush inside the apartment as they walk away, opening the garden doors to let fresh air clean the heavy air inside the apartment, clearing away the picnic basket with shaky hands and jumping out of my skin as Naima calls me.

"Are you okay, mama?"

"Why don't you wash your hands? Dinner will be ready in a few minutes," I say, walking around and warming up the oven for a last touch up on the vegetable pie I have prepared this morning.

"Samuel and Scott are nice," Naima comments, washing her hands at the kitchen sink.

I nod, preparing the dining table, cleaning Aidan hands, and serving the plates, while Naima keeps brining them up, sharing all what Scott has talked to her about.

And even when I dislike the idea of how attached she feels to a little boy she just met, my heart expands at the thought that one day, in the near future she will open to others, and childhood will take away her social struggles.

Dinner becomes eternal with *irresistible* Samuel as the main topic. I chose to grab a pen and paper and work on the shopping list, nodding at Naima's conversation and helping Aidan with dinner.

Pushing bath and bed time forward, and spending a few extra minutes under the shower washing away the afternoon, the steam of my body, and the inappropriate thoughts out of my head.

I can't take away his scent, the warmth of his body, the

sensation that his presence and his touch had awakened in me.

My hands rub the soap in small circles, tinkling my skin, my eyes close and I travel away, to a moment where Samuel, soft and masculine hands are the once cleaning my body, brushing my breast, rolling down my tummy and landing in between my thighs, caressing the ache that screams in deep in my core for release.

My forehead rests on the cold tiles, my hand holds me in place while the other, the one my wildest thoughts is imagine as if it was Samuel take me to a place where I am touched in unexplored places, where my head spins in pleasure, and my body shake in need for more.

I turn the cold water on, letting the sensation bring me back to reality, shaking him and this desire away.

What is wrong with me?

I spend the next few hours trying to finish the list, while my mind let curiosity wonder how spend a morning with Samuel will be, seat on a car next to him, have a conversation, the questions I would like him to answer.

Dropping the list aside, I walk to bed, forcing my mind to stop, we both know what happened the last time I let curiosity take control over my rationality.

He has a past too, I can see the darkness behind those hypnotic eyes, the pain and burden of caring a heavy weight over your shoulders, what makes it clear I should walk the opposite direction than his, after all, an afternoon at the park and a morning shopping can't change my properties, and they do now include a tall, gorgeous man.

At 4 a.m. I roll out of bed, after a night filled with chaos and uncertainty.

Walking to the kitchen, I take my time preparing some croissants for breakfast and fresh orange juice.

With the dough resting, a filled mug of warm coffee I walk out to the garden at the best time of the day–dawn.

The sunlight fights between the houses until the town come back to life, reminding me of the time back home, where I used to see sunrise and sunset from the safety of our little farm.

The outside world didn't matter, I had it all what anyone will dream of, but I was too young to appreciate it.

And now, fifteen years later, I will give anything to spend one more day there.

Tears roll down my cheeks at the thought of my parents, the farm, the animals, the innocent Ruby that had big dreams.

I walk back inside, finish breakfast, prepare a lasagna for either lunch or dinner and shower before I hear the kids jumping in bed, singing and laughing.

It took time to adjust to the sound of their laughs, their joy, their innocence, and now is the one thing I can't live without, the one I miss the instant they close their eyes.

"Good morning," I say from the door, unable to hide my own silly smile.

"Zoppppiiinnnggg!" Aidan says, making me laugh this time at the horrible trouble he is having with S and Z.

Miguel says it's a transition, one that I want to enjoy

every second and cherish every day, my baby boy, and his special, wonderful soul.

I take them for breakfast after I change them, so I can have my own time getting ready and making sure the list is completed before Samuel arrives.

Taking longer than usual choosing my clothes, I take a last look in the mirror, admiring one of the outfits Sarah, my neighbor encourage me to choose a few weeks ago.

I look over my shoulder in the mirror to make sure all the marks are covered under the little top and I exhale in relieve knowing he won't see them if he steps too close.

Months and care have fade nearly every scar *he* draw over my exposed skin, the internal ones will need a lifetime to heal, but those I know how to cover them with a sweet smile and kindness.

"Mama, you look pretty today," Naima says as I walk back into the kitchen.

Turning the oven off and cleaning Aidan messy cheeks.

"Thanks baby," I say, readjusting my top.

"I don't mean the clothes," she says.

I look up at her, tilting my head, reading her mind and blushing at the thoughts traveling across her little mind.

She asked me to wear these clothes many times, always receiving the same answer *'on a special day'* apparently something in me has chosen that day is today.

A Sunday morning, for an adventurous trip around different stores, and markets. With a dangerously handsome looking stranger.

I can't deny it. The man I accidentally cross paths with

a week ago, carries this magnetic aura around him, that I have no doubt attracts the attention of anyone that dares to pass next to him.

Letting my curious mind and my rational thought fight against each other. Reminding myself that this is just a favor he is doing to us. A little help he offered and I should take it with cautious steps.

There is a thick line I draw months ago in between the rest of the world and us. And today, I have no intention on trespassing it.

Chapter Six

Ruby
Fifteen years ago, Shepperton, TX

The phone rings while I'm on the porch cleaning my muddy riding boots after I finished my farm chores.

Mom is by my side stitching up my trousers for the third time this week.

The result of my clumsiness, she have to forgive me for life.

Dad let us know is Lisa, our neighbor from the farm next door, someone I wasn't aware of until few months ago when dad asked me to join him at the supplies store, and there she was.

We are the same age, and lifestyle.

Both home schooled, mostly farm duties and house chores.

I have seen other teenagers once when we ride by the main town a few miles away from home, but she is the only one I have ever spoke with or be allowed to spend time with.

The existence of a life outside of these fields is based in old books that mom and I read.

The same that makes me dream of a future where I could travel around the most popular cities, wear fancy clothes and taste new food.

Until then, I will have to follow my parents desire of keeping me hidden.

"Hey Lisa," I say, cleaning the mud away of my hands on a dry cloth.

"Ruby!!" she exclaims, making me pull the telephone away. "There's a party tonight," she whispers.

Pulling the cord, I step out of the kitchen and dad eavesdrop at the dining table reading his newspaper and having some coffee.

"You know I can't," I whisper.

Dad has let me visit her farm on my own a handful of times, there is no way he will agree for me to go at the local bar.

"You will never leave if you never ask."

She is correct, but my fear of his rejection is bigger than my desire of exploring a Friday night out.

"I will call you back."

I hang up and walk back inside the kitchen, leaning on the edge of the doorframe, hiding my shaky hands behind me and taking a deep breath before I say a word.

"Dad, can I talk to you?"

His eye look up to me, I chew my bottom lip and he drops the newspaper on the table, giving me his full attention.

"Everything okay Ruby?" He asks.

"Was Lisa, the neighbor."

I say nervously, forgetting he was the one picking up and calling me out.

"Joseph's daughter, yes, very polite girl," he nods like he's agreeing with himself.

"She was calling to let me know there is an event happening at the local bar–"

"You want to go out?"

Is he asking or affirming?

"I've never been out, and since you know her, I thought you'll agree."

"I don't think you'd be interested in that type of thing."

Is he serious?

The furthest I've been is Mrs. and Mr. Johnson store with him waiting in the car while I got some girl supplies.

"I think it will be a good way for me to socialize.," I say, lowering my head, begging for a five minutes of freedom when I could be a simple fifteen years old, and be around people.

"You will be restless, I need you, especially now that we have a new calf." He is right, but I'd rather tired tomorrow than lose this opportunity.

"You are right," I say. He nods and smiles. He loves when I tell him that. "But I promise I will catch up on work. You won't feel any difference."

"Trust me daughter, you will feel it," he says.

He's not threating me, just warning me I am not yet

aware of what is coming my way.

"Let me try once, and for ne—"

"No Ruby, there is no next time. Tonight will be enough for you to know that you aren't ready."

And that is a firm statement. I better prove him wrong, enjoy the night and work hard tomorrow.

He nods and I rush to the telephone. "Thank you, dad," I say, dialing my friend.

At 7 p.m., I'm walking in circles in my room, brushing my long waves with my fingers, pulling down the old flower dress Mom let me borrow so it will reach the knees, and my new boots make the old wood floor crack underneath.

I am excited and nervous, Lisa should be here any minute, and I can't believe we will drive away, enter a bar, hear a band, drink and eat new things, speak with others, maybe even dance.

Wait, I don't know how to dance!

Lisa's truck horn echoes in the silence of the evening, I walk to the kitchen, hugging and kissing mom.

"Te quiero mama."

Dad is by the porch as I walk out, returning from the barn making sure everyone is safe and warm.

"Have fun," he says, I rise on my tiptoes and kiss his cheek.

"I love you, dad," I say, jumping down the steps and into the truck.

"Are you ready for the best night of your life?" Lisa asks, with her mischievous laugh. She is such a naughty girl compared to me.

We drive for over twenty minutes before we reach a building on the side of the road, it has so many lights, anyone can see it from miles away, if wasn't for the corn plantations at the other side of the road.

As we enter the parking space, the music become louder, specially when someone walks in or out.

Echoing in the silence of the dark night, I step down and look around. There is nothing but us visible in miles, and that awakens a sense of insecurity in me.

The music makes the ground vibrate, shaking my entire being, I feel more nervous than I should at something that awakens in me, making me feel different—alive.

I grin at the similarity of this place with the western movies, the wood floor, the neon signs hanging on the walls, the couple dancing country next to the stage, the barrel tables with unmatching stools, the wall decorated with country singers posters, the scent of fresh soap and beer.

I observe the spotless boots, clean denim, platted shirts and cowboy hats in men, the decorated boots, flowy dresses, and loose hair in the women.

Farm life is hard, is not just for men, and the fact that women are pulling their feminine side just for a night out, and that men has kept their messy, greasy looks at home to present their finest for one night too, makes me smile.

Reminding me to the old pictures hanging at my house, where a cowboy fall for a foreign Mexican city young lady, and from there was history.

Lisa walk us to a reserved table in front of the stage, a

lady introduce the new band, and I don't miss the moment my friend blushes and giggles to the singer who is testing the microphone and the guitar.

"Do you know him?" I ask her.

I know she has been here multiple times, since she had an older cousin over for the entire summer, it wouldn't surprise me to know she well know the entire bar, after all she is the extrovert between the two of us, with her around, silence never exists.

"I meet him a few weeks ago," she says. "He walked me to the truck and kissed me."

She already kissed a boy?

My head turns to the singer, under the cowboy hat there is no boy, there is a man that at least is twenty. She is out of her mind and her dad will kill her if he finds out.

"He has a cute friend we want you to meet," she sighs.

A cold sweat rolls down my spine at the idea of talking to another person, a young man, a band member, at least five years older than me, with nothing in common.

"We came to hear the band, right?" I ask nervous, Lisa giggles and clap her hands when the singer does so.

"Hello Shepperton!" The singer greets the bar, nodding at the rest of the band and they all start playing.

The bar vibe changes as he starts singing, some follow the lyrics, others dance, and some like me clap and enjoy it.

After a few songs that everyone seem to knew by heart, he pause, explaining they are about to sing something original, "this one is for you," he ends pointing at Lisa, winking as she blow a kiss.

The small interaction makes me blush too and realize what is happening here.

Her father wouldn't allow her to come on her own, she needed a chaperon, an excuse to see him.

She didn't want to go out with me, and the idea of her tossing me aside to go and have sometime with him after this song, where they announce a break will happen, has me on full alert.

Would she leave me alone for him?

I miss the entire song, gazing in between them both, building a plan on my mind at what could I do if she leaves me.

Do I remember the way back home?

There is no way I could call dad and make him come until here, he trusted me to be responsible, and he believes Lisa it's too, now I can see she is not, and that scares me.

The band joins us and I tense, keeping my head low and nodding when one of them talk, playing the part of paying attention to someone I don't know, or care of what he has to say.

The waitresses filled the table with a variety of dishes and we all get a drink called milkshake.

I have only seen it in movies, and I have to admit it is delicious.

As much as I will love to taste the food I can't my stomach is a knot of nerves as I observe Lisa melt on the singers lap while he whispers things to her.

One of the member chats about a tour they are preparing for the next few months—they will cover the entire southeast coast.

They speak of places I've only read about in my books—my dreamy head can't help but wonder how magnificent would feel to travel, pack a bag, and leave for months—to see other people, other towns.

"Girls, join us!" the singer says, "we have space for two more."

I laugh so hard everyone turns their heads to me, and Lisa disapproval gaze makes me rose, excusing myself and walking away on search of the toilets.

They are out of their mind, and so it's Lisa. If asking dad for a night out was hard, I can't imagine how will be explaining I will leave the town with a group of grown men, and ride around the country while they cheer cities in different's states.

The line to the toilet's is long for both, I rest my back on the wall and watch the bar, observing how the ambience has changed since we have arrived.

The lights are low, people more cheerful, that must be the alcohol, there is less food and more drinks coming out of the bar, and the dance floor is full of couple dancing any song that they play.

After at least five songs I reach the door, I should be next, if the lady in front of me, who looked highly intoxicated and in need of some fresh air, makes it out of the cubicle.

"Seems like someone drank the entire bar, right?" a young man asks me from the men line across the corridor.

I turn to face him, unsure if he was talking to me.

Under the dusky corridor light I can see he is not from around here.

From his toasted skin, charcoal hair, long face, and charming smile, to his LA hoodie, loose denims, to his trainers.

I tilt my head, studying him, thinking where he can be from without the intention on asking.

"I was saying, they are taking too long," he says, a eastern accent drops at the end of every word.

"They are," I confirm, crossing the arms at my center.

"Are you from around here?" he asks.

I look at my boots, making sure the clothes I thought I was wearing, matching the vibe of every women in the room are still on, where he is the one wearing a complete foreign outfit.

"You aren't, right?" I ask, turning the conversation around.

"I come from India," he confirms my suspicion of eastern accent.

"Wow, that's far," I exclaim, looking at the toilet door and drilling a hole in that woman head from the distance.

What is taking so long?

"I'm in America as a backpacker."

"Sorry, as what?" I ask.

"I left my country, came to America, and move around the entire country with my backpack," he explains with a wide smile, "I sometimes sleep in my tent, other times in road motels. It's the best way to know a country and culture."

"That sounds incredible, I never, you know—farm life."

"You are a cowgirl!" He sounds delighted at that. "I guess you love the animals and quiet life."

"I've never known better," I answer, raising my shoulders.

"What do you mean?" he asks, drawing a cute frown in between his thick brows. "You've never left Shepperton?"

"My farm, not until today."

I shake my stupid thoughts, unsure why I am sharing far too much with a complete stranger, a young man, a foreign, multiple reason to stop talking to him.

The toilet opens up, the woman can barely stand, and even when I will love to help her, I need to hide and end the conversation I shouldn't have started.

After taking five extra minutes inside the toilet to make sure any male would have walk away by now, they always say ladies take longer, I wash my hands, make sure my dress is in place and walk out.

The young man I talked to is gone, and so are Lisa and the singer, the rest of the band is by the bar having a chat with the bartenders who giggle at whatever one of them is saying.

Panic makes me run outside, just to realize her truck is also gone.

She left me.

My suspicions where correct, she used me, she needed someone to be allow out of the house so she could disappear with a singer.

I look around me, we are miles away from home, in the darkness in the middle of nowhere. There is only one way to make it back, walk.

Crossing to the corn plantation I replay the journey here on my head, reaching the end of the road where I know we turn.

I cautiously walk in a straight line in between the pavement and gravel, all lighten by the moon that now rests high in the sky.

Anger and frighten has me walking on a fast pace, I can see my farm at the end of the road, my mother's sunflower plantation stands opposite to Lisa's farm, on my left.

I know this grounds, but I am unaware of what hides in between the flowers. The movement paralyze me and I sprint to our fence, jumping to the other side as I feel someone following me.

"Wait!" I hear the person rushing out of the plantation. "Please stop!"

I step back from the fence, my eyes fixed on the fence where I know someone stands, looking at me.

"Hello?! Toilet girl?"

Did that man follow me? I need to run back home and hide, this is not safe.

I jump out of my skin when I feel Dalia standing next to me, this cow is the nosiest and most protective animal we have.

"I'm good, girl," I assure rubbing her face and kissing her.

"I need your help," he says.

"You need to leave. This is a private property!"

"Someone stole my backpack!" he exclaims.

It might be the truth, he might need help truly, but he has followed me for miles when he could have asked help by the bar.

"What do you want?"

"Can I borrow your mobile?" he asks, "I will try to get a lift somewhere."

"I don't have one!"

"Someone you can ask for one?"

"Sorry, but you have to leave."

"Can I get something to eat? They took all my money, too."

Gosh, he is making it harder to not help him, but something tells me I shouldn't.

"Wait away from the fence!" I warn.

Dalia and I walk away towards the barn, I grab some milk and bread, collecting a fabric bag and a pocket knife dad like to have handy and I head back to the fence.

"Step away, I will leave a bag there for you," I order.

I hear his steps backing up on the gravel, I take mine slowly, resting the robe of the bag on his side of the fence and walking back to Dalia.

"You can take it now and leave my property." I say, heading to the barn to put Dalia back where she belongs and me to the house, I don't have much time to sleep.

After a good few hours' sleep, I shower, change, prepare some coffee and head to start my chores before anyone else.

I'm done in the barn, feeding, cleaning, and letting everyone out when dad walks in with fresh coffee on each hand.

The goat soaps that the Johnsons' let me sell of their stores need to be delivered today, so I take everything out under his close look.

He is enjoying seen me taking care of the farm, I've seen him doing this all my life, always better at it than at mom's housewife duties.

I was born to be around animals and nature, not inside a house cleaning and knitting.

But I won't deny I love cooking, that is the one thing I love to spend time with mom, and dad body shape can easily say how much he enjoys it too.

The day pass by faster than I thought, every animal has been taken care of, I spent hours caressing the new calf, the barn and stables are ready for the end of the day, and I have given dad a day off that I know he needed.

As the sun drops in the horizon, I head to the stables, making sure everyone is locked, comfy and warm. Arranging all the tools I used during the day and refilling food an water when a noise startle me from an empty stall at the back.

Tiptoeing, I grab the shovel and open the stall door, I can see a body resting on top of straw. The clothes are covered in it, and a pair of familiar dirty boots are the closest thing I have.

I kick them, waking up the intruder as I raise the shovel. Shocked when I found toilet boy rubbing his eyes and looking at me confused.

"What are you doing here?" I ask, holding the shovel up to his face, he is not smiling anymore.

"I found this place," he says drowsy.

Chapter Seven

Samuel

The cold water runs down my back, my forearms and forehead rest on the wall tiles, trying to clear away my heavy thoughts and sweat after a longer than usual gym session. The pressure on my chest won't let me breathe.

I walk out, rest my hands on the sink and lower my head, I shake it, roll my head, curl my shoulders blades.

It won't go away.

I raise my head, to check me in the mirror, I recognise who I see, someone I haven't seen in far too long.

Someone I try to bury on the deepest of my darkness so I will never have to face him again.

Is that young Samuel, the lost boy that fall into intrusive thoughts that took him to make mistakes, to push away anything that could help him afraid that facing his demons will be more painful that hide them away.

If someone told me back then how much they will grow

and swallow me, I would have reach any hand that was offered to save me.

Ruby, her presence, her life, her past, her pain, her fears, her entire world has brought way too much to the surface.

Some will say I found a purpose to move along in life, but how safe it will be move away of my darkness and enter hers?

It doesn't matter, I am unashamed of how nervous, scared, and excited I am.

Could I save them without shuttering them in the process?

I don't know how to be gentle, thoughtful, kind.

I am used to taking what I want, use it as I please and toss it aside.

That is not an option with them, I need to run away from them, step away before is too late.

I will take them shopping, I gave my word. After that I will disappear, no matter that I know how close she lives, where I can find her, or that I could have one of my men following her every move, just for their safety and my sick curiosity.

I will ignore the way she looked at me, the way her body's response to me, the way she touched me, the way she called my name.

"Enough!" I growl, hitting the marble countertop.

My waves, my face and my closet pay the consequences of my rage, pulling, slapping and throwing things that stand on my way, even if it's the wrong shocks, or the shirt that I have in mind and now is not good enough for the day.

It's just one fucking day. Tomorrow I will be back in the city. Seven days to forget her, to hide away, and avoid any accidental encounter.

This town is too small for both of us to share it. I will crawl to her doorstep if I don't walk away while I have time.

I pull a shirt off a hanger, storming out of the room as I head downstairs, finishing my buttons before I reach the lower floor. Rosita is there, a small smile on her lips, opening her arms as I approach her.

She can't be content with this? There is nothing good coming out of this.

"Show that lady who Samuel Smith is. Open your heart, *mi hijito*. It's time," she whispers in my ear, brushing her palm over my broken heart.

I pull at Ruby's earlier than we discuss, giving myself sometimes to calm down, and control my thoughts and body.

I step out, having one more try at the car seats that the delivery man secure for me last night. I walk in circles, back and forth on her pathway, unsure what to do next.

Coming face to face with something that I didn't see yesterday, a plate on the side of the apartment building with the words 'Woman's aid centre,' engraved into it.

I knew something happen to them, I just couldn't put my finger into it.

Here it is, right in front of me. They are hiding. They are being protected.

From what are you hiding, Ruby?

Resting back on the car, I realise there are no windows at the front of her flat.

Should I knock?

I push myself forward, walking slowly, raising my hand to knock when the door flies open. Ruby stands on the other side, breaking eyes contact and blushing as I grin, hiding my hands inside my jeans.

She gestures for me to come in, walking away.

I reconsider how far in the wrong direction I will step the moment I close the door behind me. The moment the warmth of her house welcomes me, her fresh scent of wildflowers and a bakery surrounds me, I lost control of who I am and what my pervious intentions or thoughts were.

I am walking into her darkness, following her through the apartment, ready to get lost in her world.

We walk into an open space with a little dark green couch in the corner. She has covered it with a colourful blanket that makes it cosier, and a dining table sits in the opposite corner with three matching chairs.

At the end, there is a small open kitchen, herbs, colourful bowls of fruit, and jars of every size and shape filled up the space.

And in the furthest corner, a glass door leads to the rear garden.

"Good morning, Samuel," Naima and Aidan welcome me in unison.

I smile at them. "Morning."

"Breakfast?" Ruby asks.

Holding a large plate full of croissants, while her gaze is over a long list, she is holding in the other hand.

I take that opportunity to observe how stunning she looks today. Her hair is loose. Long, dark waves that end at the curve of her spine, an off the shoulders floral top and a green wrap skirt.

The material of both is far too thin, acting as a second skin, one that brightens up the one underneath and gives me a full view of her curves.

Fuck me, she is gorgeous.

If perfection needs a human shape, it will be this woman.

My chest aches on a deeper level when my broken soul attaches the pieces of who I could have been long ago. What a sweet torture.

A soft cough brings me back to reality, to Ruby's kitchen, with the kids having breakfast behind me and this angel standing a few steps away.

"Drink, Samuel."

I bite my bottom lips, drinking her, devouring every inch of body and grinning when her brow raises.

"Won't say no to an espresso." I say, grabbing a croissant.

The rooms spin as the pastry touches my lips, "this is *Spectacular,*" I murmur in between bites.

"There you go," Ruby offer me the little cup of coffee.

I take a sip, is delicious too, this woman doesn't stop surprising me, and killing me when she whispers the list bitting the pen, moving her hair forward and plait it. Woman you better stop the torture!

Naima and Aidan have finished their breakfast, clearing up what they can, Ruby talks and it takes me a long minute to hear her.

Her cheeks turn pink, her bottom lip hides behind her teeth and her head shakes slightly when I clear my voice.

"We are ready," she says, finishing her braid and cleaning the kids mouths and hands.

"Just Tesco's?" I ask, finishing my coffee and leaving the little mug on the sink.

Ruby turns and her cheeks blush with my question. *Fuck me, she looks even more beautiful with that natural pink shade on her cheeks.*

"More than one store," I say, nodding while I finish my croissant.

We head out of the apartment, Aidan rushes to hold my hand, I observe how good does it feel that this little boy trust me to get close to me.

Not doing too bad after all.

There is something making him nervous, the closer we get to the car the tighter he holds me, it becomes clearer that he is either scared of them or not used to.

I turn to face him and go to my haunches—I learned with Scott that visual contact, and to explain things step by step is important.

"Do you see this car big boy?" I point at it, and he nods. "It's mine. Inside there are two car seats. One is blue, and the other is pink with flowers."

His head tilts, a small smile grows in his cute face and I want to smile myself.

"We will help you up and drive to the store," my hand moves closer to him on an attempt to caressing his little arm and calm him, Aidan raise his arms, protecting himself and I want to punch my own face. "I'm sorry," I whisper, afraid I scared him more than helped and that all I am doing is push them away.

My gaze falls to the floor, my hand hides on my side and I am blown away when Aidan jumps on me and gives me the tightest hug I've ever experienced in my life.

I look at Ruby, her eyes are filled with tears as she holds Naima on her hip, I can see the sadness and pain in their faces, someone hurt them way too deep, they are not used to new people, and here I am storming inside their lives.

I don't say a word, there is nothing that I could say to help them, my actions will have to speak louder than my words.

They are my purpose for redemption, if I help them, if I make their life slightly better, that might give me the opportunity of be more human, of healing my own wounds and demons.

I hold Aidan on my arms, walking to the car and siting him on the car seat, he giggles as I struggle to tight him up, Ruby easily fasten Naima's and turns around the car to do the same with him, I walk to her door, hold it open and jump into my seat.

I try to enjoy the situation, knowing that somehow I'm making their life somewhat better. That changes nothing, this is a bigger reason to push them away from my life, I realise we are four broken souls.

And just for that, once I help them with this shopping I should walk away and never turn back.

The sound of the engine makes the kids giggle and the emotions of moments ago disappears, awakening new ones as the back of my hand brushes Ruby's skirt when I change gears.

She was checking on the kids and her leg was far too close to the space in between us. My eyes move from our contact to her eyes, fixed on mine, her lips parted and her breath is slow, proving I was right; she feels the same way I do.

You can't react to me, you shouldn't!

I move my hand away, missing her. I shake my neck, exhaling the pressure on my chest and intoxicating myself with her scent.

Far too close to avoid the effect she has on me.

Deep breaths Samuel, is just for few hours.

I adjust myself on the seat, join the other cars driving around and focus on the road, kicked out of my own body when she turns to check on the kids, resting her hand on my biceps.

Please don't let go.

The smallest touch coming from her means the world to me, it is wrong, and I don't care. I want her to feel comfortable, to want to be around me.

We will destroy each other the moment I walk away, I can tell that now.

But I will make sure I die the happiest man.

Robotically following her directions we arrive at a local

party store. The front window is packed with balloons, cake stands, banners—anything you might need for a party. It's a crowded road, but I find a parking on the side road.

"Let's start the shopping," I cheer at the kids, finding two wide smiles on the rear mirror.

Ruby smiles herself and I can't help but study her angelic features one more minute, appreciating the closeness of the car.

I smile when she tilts her head encouraging me to move on.

Ruby gets Naima down, and I help with Aidan, resting him on my side, unsure if he will be glad to hold my hand.

"Hug," Aidan says, his little arms keep pointing up. "Please hug."

I don't think it twice, I will cherish anything they give me today, if Aidan is happy on my arms, I will hold him full time. I bite my lip to hold the smile he build in me with his own smile of triumph.

"Aidan, you need to walk baby," Ruby says, joining us at the other side of the car.

"I'm fine Ruby," I assure.

My chest expands in triumph too, her cheeks turn pink, her bottom lip hides under her teeth and her eyes fly everywhere but on me.

You are to fucking cute angel.

"I think we should go," she whispers, turning and crossing the road heading towards the store.

Minutes later I am full on father duties, pushing a little

trolley with one hand, and holding Aidan in the other arm.

They aren't yours to keep, my hideous mind reminds me.

I chose to ignore those evil thoughts, they won't cloud my day.

I look around as I walk behind Ruby and Naima, holding hands and collecting materials in different aisles.

There are cake stands, paper of different materials and colours, multiple balloons, table cloths and goody bags.

I don't know where she will put all of this stuff in that small apartment.

"Almost done," she says over her shoulder, giving me a cheeky smile, knowing I'm out of my comfort zone.

I might want this woman out of my life for her best, but never out of my pathetic brain, pulling my mobile out I capture her angelic face, her gorgeous backside, every single angle she gives me access to.

After an hour of Ruby explaining what she needs each item for, we are done.

By the till, I place Aidan in the kid's seat, his head rests on his arms as he is asleep and I observe how Naima is scrubbing her eyes too.

I empty the trolley, packing everything up and filling the trolley with bags.

Ruby has Naima on her arms, eyes close, slow breath. Both of the kids are done for the moment, I try to work as fast as I can. Holding Aidan in my arms again, heading to the car and resting him on his car seat, Ruby does the same.

I walk back to the trolley and unload the shopping into the trunk, taking a few deep breaths to decompress my chest.

Ruby joins me, and I lost track of what I was doing, thinking, or the reason of my own existence.

Silence grow thick and uncomfortable around us, Ruby collect the empty trolley, taking it back with the others.

My hands rest on the trunk, my head low and my breath is short.

She doesn't go to her seat, she returns to me, I turn my head and melt when her soft hand rests on my forearm.

My air is hers, her warmth is mine, I can feel her far too deep.

Her eyes travel across my face as she whispers, "before I forget, thank you so much for this amazing day," her cheeks blush and a strip of her hair falls out of her braid.

I hold it, brushing it behind her ear, letting my fingertips follow all the way down her neck, over her collarbone, through her throat, drawing a fire line over her jaw and resting on her cheek, observing how she trembles under my touch—her face moves with my hand, I hold her waist with my other arm and pull her up, our noses touch, her hands resting on my biceps.

"You are more than welcome," I say, letting my breath brush her pink cheeks.

What are you doing Samuel?

Her palms release my arms, travelling up to my shoulders, over my neck, up to my jaw.

My eyes close as she plays with my stubble, my entire body is on fire and a soft moan leave her delicious lips when her core meet my hardness—*I need to stop this, before is too late.*

I feel how she draw a warm line to my nape, curling her fingers on my waves on my nape, her other fingertips brush my lips, they part and my tongue brushes the tip, my waves fist around her palm, and a trembling moan leaves her lips.

I rest my forehead on hers, I can't breathe, I turn and place her on the trunk, standing in between her thighs and I open my eyes.

Too fucking late!

I pull her closer, her groin meet my arousal and her lips devour mines.

There is no warning, no words, our tongues are on a personal fight, her lips are softer and way more delicious that I imagine, my hips roll, her back arch and my waves receive another pull.

But my entire world pause when she pulls back—*I need more!*

She looks into my eyes and I understand it's not them been pull into my darkness, it's me falling on the deepest, darkest hole, one where she will torture, enjoy me and use me to climb up, leaving me underground broken and hidden for life, but it will be the sweetest punishment.

Take me there Ruby!

Our forehead join, we caress each other, her fingertip awaken every inch of my body, I have never felt more alive and scared in my life.

I drink her in, caress her, feel her and memories her, when a car honks, "move the fucking car!" the driver shouts.

I take a deep breath, drop a soft kiss on her nose and

lower her. After closing the trunk, I guide her to the passenger door and I walk to mine, ready to continue the shopping adventure.

As I start the car and change the gear, Ruby takes my hand, entwining our fingers, we become one, resting it in between us.

I smile at the cheesy move, one that feels far too good to be the first.

My gazes moves from the road to her in every stop, appreciating all the traffics light these roads have.

"Next exit, turn left twice," she guides.

Her voice is low, velvety, a delicious sound, one that I'm creating.

We arrive in Tesco's car park, empty for an early Sunday morning, Ruby lets me know we will have to wait at least an hour.

Apologising multiple times for it, explaining she thought the previous shopping will took us longer.

She does those things on her own, so I guess do it with two kids and carrying all on your own takes double of the time.

I grin at the thought of one hour with Ruby in the smallest space we are sharing.

My body is aware of the quiet, dark and private space, I discretely readjust myself under my pants, *we can't do this.*

I find a family parking space in a hidden spot.

Bravo Samuel, make it any easier.

I turn off the engine, Ruby's hand turns my face to hers, the low light hides us from the outside, but I can see her angelic face resting on the seat, observing me.

Sick of the middle seat compartment that has been breaking our closeness for long enough, I pull her towards my seat, and place her on top of me.

I push my seat back, making sure we don't disturb the kids in the back.

Her back rests on the door, my fingers play with her braid, my other hand rubs the fabric of her skirt over her thighs.

I am shaking, under her close stare, silences is far too loud around us.

Game over Samuel!

This might be one of the craziest things I ever done in my life, but I can't stay away from her anymore.

I pull her closer, turning her to cradle me, her hands hold the seat over my shoulders, travelling down to my chest, playing my buttons.

She is shaking too, her hands are, and her entire body does too, when draw a line up her thighs, push her skirt higher and hold her hips, pulling her closer and closer.

I don't know who I am anymore, my body is alert, my mind and thoughts are quiet, my throat is dry and I turn into flames when her centre meets my hardness.

My breath is slow, my hands hold her tighter, and she fists the back of my hair, her forehead rests on mine, bitting her bottom lip when a deep moan leave her throat.

I hold her nape and pull her to my mouth, devouring her delicious lips, leaving her breathless moving to her neck, licking, bitting and sucking her flesh until I meet her lobe, her entire body trembles and a deeper pull of my hair and moan on my ear answer my question.

I need to ask, "are you sure?"

"Samuel..." she moan as my blow on the sensitive spot around her ear.

"Answer Ruby," I pressure, licking her neck and receiving another pull of my hair, I rise my hips and her head fall on my shoulder hiding a deeper moan, "you just have to answer," I remind.

I pull her head up and force her to look at me, her lips are moist, her eyes glassy with lust, her breath broken and her heart nearly leaving her chest.

My fingertips trace all the way to her back, finding the edge of the skirt, drawing circles on her round bum, brushing her knickers.

Her back arch, her hips move forward and her centre presses my arousal.

"I can give you more," I assure her on a cocky voice, "I just need an answer."

My tongue brush my bottom lip, desperate for some moist, for her taste.

Her eyes follow my tongue trace and her hips push forward again, moaning and biting her lip to keep it low.

I grip her nape harder that I intend it, but I can see on her eyes she liked it, "answer the question Ruby," I murmur on her lips, pushing her bum lower and giving her a harder rotation of my hips, holding her head in place as she try to let it follow the curl of her spine.

"I want more," she whisper on my lips, I growl in

acceptance and kiss her—raw, carnal, our tongues fights a new battle.

Our bodies rock on each other, sending me to a new level of pleasure. I want her as much as she wants me, and I'm not willing to let her go.

I move under her top, she is not wearing any bra, I cup her breast, drawing circles and enjoy the way she tries to hold herself.

She is busy unbuttoning my shirt, I am far too busy kissing her and feeling the reactions her body has to me, eager to explore her deeper.

Trembling when her palms come in contact with my bare chest, tracing fire under my skin, reaching my belt.

I holder her tighter as she undoes my belt, buttons, and zipper quickly.

Her fingertips hold the waistband of my boxers and pull it away, exposing my hard as rock cock, our kiss breaks, her gaze falls to where her hand embraces me, expanding the drop of cum resting on the head around, this is the best torture I ever experienced, her long fingers curls around my throbbing erection and start working me, slow, precise, and firm.

My hand moves lower, brushing her wet knickers, circling her clit over the soft fabric, pushing it aside, and meeting something even softer.

I can feel how wet she is becoming just by the softest touch on her clit, getting ready for me, until a drop fall on my palm, followed by a deep moan hidden on my lips, I spread her wetness around her entrance, introducing my fingers painfully slowly. Her walls squeeze and suck them, making my hardness grow.

After a few more slow movements, her movements speed up, her hips ride my palm, I break our kiss, forcing her to look at me, dying a million times when I see her eyes.

Her walls shuck me deeper, her hips ride me faster, her hand works me faster, we are both too close.

I reach for a cloth on the side of the door, placing it on top of the tip of my ready to explode erection.

My hand travel on her front, in between us, finding her clit, applying some pressure and drawing circles.

Her lips fall on mine, hiding her screams, and my growls as we let go, staying there until our breath steady.

Her head falls on my shoulder, brushing my torso, I suck her release, finding another cloth, softly cleaning her, sliding the knickers back in place. Cleaning my own release, covering my once more, hard cock.

That will have to wait.

Once I make sure we are both clean, I caress her nape, playing with her messy hair, kissing her crown, and brushing the exposed skin.

"Ma..." Aidan whispers, bringing us back to reality.

Before she runs away, I give her a deep kiss.

She moves back to her seat, adjusting her clothes and fixing her hair before he is fully awake.

I can't take my eyes away from her, of the way her cheeks blush, or the way her eyes look my way and she tries to hide a wide smile.

I'm in the deepest trouble I have ever been.

Willing to lose myself under this angelic creature touch again.

Aware this won't be my first and last time with her.

The day is not yet finish after all.

Chapter Eight

Ruby

I am confused, overwhelmed, and scared.

When I look on my right, I see a hot and dangerous as hell man, someone that I know little about, but that makes me feel alive and, in a place, where I belong.

The first time I saw him something inside me remember a forgotten memory, the first time he steps close my entire being dance an unknown melody, and now, the first time I broke every boundary or promise I ever done to myself with regard to men, I stand in a thin rope with two opposites end, really similar, with different outcomes.

Giving me three choices, follow my mind and what I think will be the correct and safe, follow my instinct inside the unknown and explore a new world, or follow my heart, lose my balance and hope for a soft fall where things could be good after all.

"Mama," Naima voice brings be back to the present moment, to a small space where four broken souls hide in the darkness of a parking space.

Giving me the answer to my doubts. I chose my children, the correct path, the safe new journey I start building for us, where we need nobody but each other to find happiness.

I turn to the kids, sadly smiling, knowing that the experience I just had on Samuel's arms, the way I burn and come back to life in his hold can never be mine again.

Naima drowsy eyes study me, I give her a small nod and she does it in return.

It's unbelievable how much a six years old can understand me inside our secret silence, most certainly I can't tell her what is happening inside me at the moment.

"Ready for more shopping?" Samuel asks. "I sure am!"

I step out of the car, helping the children, letting Aidan hold Naima's hand, when I notice Samuel haven't move.

If I wasn't focus, this close, I would have missed how his body tense, his hands fist his waves, his head shakes, his eyes shut, and he comes back like he wasn't here all along.

I turn pretending it didn't happen, letting the kids run to the lift as we walk closely.

"Who would like a drink at Sarah's café?" I ask.

She is our neighbor, who works at the little stand by the entrance of the store. The kids head there as we exit the lift, cheerfully calling her, I give her a small wave and tense when her jaw hits the floor.

For a simple instant, I have forgotten the tall, gorgeous

man that walks inches away from me.

I frown at the thought of how natural and easy his presence feels, a new reminder that something inside me knew him before I even know he existed.

You are losing your mind.

It will be absurd to think, worst say it, I don't believe in soul-mates, past lives, meant to be couples.

Samuel whisper order brings me back to reality and I step forward to build a space in between us, one that allows me to breathe and think.

"Morning," I say, blushing and shaking my head to the only woman I can trust my secrets and children too.

"Morning, guys! So nice to see you here," she says, raising her eyebrows.

I met her when we move, she is Korean, in her mid-thirties, and was in the apartment building for a year before we arrive. We went through similar things, but she suffered the most, because that monster took her children away.

And even when Louise have worked endlessly to get them back, nobody will give her back the time they've been apart.

"May I have a juice?" Aidan asks, he can be a talkative big boy when he needs something, "please, Sarah," he ends, gifting me with the cutest smile.

"Anything for you, big boy," she winks back.

"We will have two kids' juice, a Power for me and a Super Boost for Samuel," I say, pointing to him behind us.

"Right away!" She says, giving me a cheeky grin.

I move aside, pay and collect the drinks, giving Sarah a

'we talk later' look so she will stop digging a hole in my head to get all the information she wants.

I collect a trolley, set Aidan on the seat and head inside the store, walking away of Sarah and Samuel's gaze burning my skin.

If I think one more second about all the reckless decisions and thing I've done in the past twenty-four hours, my head will explode.

There is no justification to my behavior, I can't put all the blame over him, I didn't stop him at the game when he curled his arms around me multiple times, I didn't return to my seat after I return the trolley, and I didn't avoid the dark, empty parking, sleepy kids' scenario.

It's all on me, I let curiosity win once more.

I just had the best sexual experience of my life, *YES!*

My body is screaming for more since he pulls out, *YES!*

The smartest and most mature side of my brain is telling me to run away from this Adonis, *YES!*

But I aware it won't happen that easily, at least not yet.

That might be what he thought on that transition moment he had back in the car. He must have realized what a big mistake this can be.

We are complete strangers, he is irresistible, women turn around when he walks by them, men tight their muscles to look as big as he does, I am keeping my hands busy so I quit the temptation of exploring him any deeper.

For what I touched, seen and felt, there is not an inch to complain about. But it is not about the cover, that is just the attractive shell hiding a Samuel that won't be easy to get to know, that will hide away if I don't force it to come out.

Considering the list of questions, I want and should ask to hear that version of himself, to see the darkness coming fully to the surface, I realized we are done with the aisles, the trolley is filled and time has slipped through my overthinking mind.

God damn you Samuel Irresistible Smith!

I head to the till, joining Martha's queue, and letting the children unload the trolley with me.

Samuel's gaze is fixed on me, studying me like he has before, as I let my shield stand in between us, keeping him where is safe for us both–away from each other.

"Morning, Ruby," Martha greets, looking in between Samuel and I.

Great, one more person in my inner circle to judge me.

"Morning, Martha," we all answer.

"It's this week's order delivered?"

Once a week, every local store receives a fresh batch of chocolate cookies, to be labeled and sold at their bakeries.

It has been so far the best way for easy money and a good new customer's flow.

As they keep my brand name in the bag so everyone knows who make them and where they can find me.

"Tomorrow as usual," I confirm.

"I have an order, but don't worry, will text you to confirm. We have a little meet up coming up."

"Anytime," I say, paying and walking away from her questioning expression and Samuel's presence.

Even when I have to load the car and seat next to him,

on the way to one last place.

The best market in town of delicatessen products, that will make the difference in Stella's menu.

I keep my head facing the window all the way there, letting the silence grow thicker and uncomfortable.

That way I might push him far, to where I should have let him stay, but I couldn't resist it.

Samuel parks at the assigned space and help one more time with Aidan, who enjoys the arm hold and the world from up there too.

I hold Naima hand and head to the entrance, far busier than I expected, Samuel stands close, as I study the best route to avoid the crowd stalls.

"Let's go this way," Samuel says, holding my spare hand and taking us in between stalls to a quieter area.

Naima doesn't miss the way he is holding me, how his fingers push in between mine and they entwined.

My body shakes at the simple touch, giving Naima that sensation too, she smiles and my chest aches when she hugs me, approving the madness that I have turned my life into.

We visit some stalls, test new ingredients and grab some nibbles for the kids. Samuel knows a lot about high-quality food, and even if I know little of him, you just have to see his clothes and car. He has money—he has lived a different lifestyle than us, and just for now I won't question it.

His knowledge on multiple things, his care for the kids, his attention to detail re-reading my list multiple times to make sure I have it all and even more just in case, all of that has helped more than words can explain.

Around a two hours later, we walk back to the car, Samuel gave up of my hand when he saw there was no way he could hold a third bag and Aidan on the same arm without dropping my hand first. But he didn't miss the opportunity to step close, rest his hand on my lower back, or whisper his opinion on different ingredients on that raspy voice that has me melting all day.

I walk to my door after helping Naima on her seat to find him holding it for me, he has done that all day, gorgeous and a gentleman. *What are you playing at Samuel?*

"Before I forget," he murmurs on my ear, "thanks for the day," he says kissing my cheek.

Making my entire body shake, while a triumphant smile grows on his delicious lips.

We drive away, heading to Miguel's store, today is closed, but he was happy for me to drop all the type of cardboard, paper and banners I bought.

I get back to the car and let Samuel take us back to the apartment, as Naima does the last thing I was expecting to happen.

"That's going to be our house soon," she says, as we drive by the cottage, *"one step closer to heaven,"* she sings.

Why Naima?! I mentally hide away and burn in hell.

I exhale loudly and look back at her over my shoulder, in my mind I was planning all the ways to push Samuel away, take him out of our lives and enjoy our fresh start, that now my sweet daughter has revealed, he knows where to find us.

Something changes on Samuel's expression, when I turn to face forward. A thick frown grows in between his brows and his head tilts.

"What was that?" he asks.

"Mama just bought that little cottage and I like to call it *one step closer the heaven!*" She explains.

"*Heaven*," he mumbles, "what do you like about that big house?" he asks.

I look at him, realizing the question is for me.

"When we moved to the neighborhood, the house was for sale. I saw the pictures online, it's a dream come true on the world of properties, far too big and over budget," I explain seen the house by the rear mirror, "dreams are free."

"What did you like the most?"

I pause, considering why would he ask too much about a property is clear we would never be able to afford. It's will be excessively big and empty for just us three. That is the type of house only large families should have.

The fact that nobody has ever ask me why I consider that place heaven makes me want to express it all at once.

"The kitchen is bigger than my apartment, the master bedroom has a full wall facing the park, but the biggest room is the one facing the cottage, that will be a great room for children, it has a Jack and Jill bathroom, a closet, and a what looks like two rooms in one. I would transform it into a bedroom and toy room." I say, dreaming of a life that can't be mine, "if I lived there," I giggle nervously.

"Bedroom and toy room. That is a great idea. What

else?"

"About that room?" I ask, he nods, "there is an arch in the center of the room, I will paint a rainbow in both sides, and colorful walls on the toy room area."

"Rainbow?"

"Naima is my rainbow baby," I say, nibbling my bottom lip at my stupid revelation.

Turning to the window and ending the conversations before I spill all my deepest secrets.

That is Samuel's strength over me, he can make me say things I can easily hide from others.

And once more, he's the one hiding himself from me.

It's 3 p.m. as we walk inside the apartment, unloading all the shopping and warming up dinner.

Samuel has helped to take everything out of the car and filling up cupboards to ease up the multiple new ingredients.

"Apologies, we don't have much space."

"And I am horrible organizing spaces," he jokes and we both laugh.

"Dinner will be ready in ten," I say, pilling what I will need to start baking for the stores later on.

"You want me to stay?" he asks, I drop my head, shaking my stupid mind.

What was I thinking? He has to go!

"Can't let you go on an empty stomach," I say before I think.

What in the hell are you doing Ruby?!

The deep frown grows in between his brows, his steps are slow, his turquoise gems paralyze me while his fresh scent intoxicates me, making me tremble when the sweetness of his face oil overpowers me.

"Let me help you," he whispers.

If I am doing this, I need him at least three feet away.

"Hands! Wash them," I order, pointing to the sink, walking back and giving the distance I need so I can think.

"Bossy cook," he murmurs on a delighted voice.

I dry my hands as I study every inch of his figure, the tightness of his denim over his thighs, the curve of his ass, the flex of his muscles when he moves under the thin fabric of his shirt, the waves brushing his nape, the curls that frame his temples, the straight line of his nose, the fullness of his lips–

I freeze when I meet his eyes, his head tilts, and the corner of his lips rise.

Stop looking at him Ruby!

"When you are in my kitchen," I say, turning and getting busy with ingredients, "I am in charge." I whisper, feeling his body standing behind me.

His tallness frames me, his warmness melts me, and his breath on the small gap of my neck as he whispers in my ear shakes every cell on my body.

"How can I help?" he asks, trapping me in between his arms as his hands rest in the island.

My head tilts exposing my neck, biting my lip while his soft breath gives me goosebumps.

Please step away, we can't do this.

I take a step back, he does front, and I shut my eyes when I fill him grinning in my most sensitive spot behind my ear.

Well aware of every move he is taking, "I am under your control," he whispers kissing my nape.

"I doubt that," I moan back.

"Your wishes are my command," he blows a line down my shoulder.

Please don't touch me!

My head falls back on his shoulder, turning to meet him, gasping when his arm holds me closer to his body, molding together as one.

I turn and face him, drawing with my fingertips the shape of his hair, his face, jawline, the clean cut of his stubble, the bridge that frames his lips, the straight line of his brows and the soft long lashes that brush his cheek.

"Kiss me," he orders.

"I thought I was in control," I whisper, his eyes open and I melt under the darkness that now covers his gaze.

"You want me to beg?" he asks, raising a brow, my lip hides behind my teeth and my cheek burn.

His arm tightens around my waistline, pulling me up the island, his hips spread my legs, his body steps closer and his hand pulls me to the edge.

"Ruby, I beg you," he whispers, twisting my hair on my finger, brushing my cheek, jaw, throat and stopping at the edge of my top, "kiss me," he ends.

My hands brush his waves away exposing his handsome face, fisting at his nape and pulling his head back, moving forward, keeping him at the exact distance where I could let go of everything and devour his irresistible lips, or mark a line of where limits are.

"I wouldn't like anything more than kiss you," I say, on a slow, control, deep voice, "but–" I pause, letting the oven end my statement.

I smile as he grunts, stepping back and giving me space to prepare the counter so I can serve dinner.

"Can you get the tray out?" I ask, handing the oven gloves, collecting my mobile that rings inside my handbag.

Samuel nods, I frown, something has changed in him, and I am sure it has nothing to do with me not kissing him.

"Is everything alright?" I ask, my mobile rings once more and Louise name bright up in the screen.

"I promise Scott to pick him up after the shopping," he says.

That is what his nephew said after he arranged this help/meet up.

"I get it," I say, signaling to my mobile, taking that as an easy way to let him go.

Samuel looks around, I guess considering something we both know is for the best.

"Mama, can Scott come for dinner?" Naima asks, reminding me of what was happening a few instants ago, at a short distance from my kids.

"We don't want to both–"

"There is plenty of food, you can bring him," I say, bringing the mobile to my ear and answering the third call in a row.

I walk to the bedroom, leaving the kids to take care of the table, aware they should not be listening to this conversation.

"Good evening, Louise," I say on a shaky voice, her persistent calls can only be bad news.

"I just received the email," she pauses, building my anxiety, "the documents are ready, and will be at my desk tomorrow," she is giving me the news in drops, tearing my skin slowly, "Advik will be transferred in a week."

The bedroom spins around, cold sweat runs down my spine, my lungs lose the little air that was left and I fall on my knees.

What are we going to do?

"A week," I murmur, on the last hope she will correct me.

"We need to–"

"Thank you for your call," I say, hanging up, covering my face with the bed covers and screaming the life out of me.

Pushing the anger and fear aside, I do what has always been planned, message, the only person who will make sure Advik never hurts my kids again. *My protector:*

He will be out in less than a week, have everything ready.

I clear my face, fix my braid and head to Sarah's for spare chair, while the kids wash their hands, finding Samuel and Scott at the doorstep.

"Hello Scott," I say, clearing my throat and pushing

everything aside, "please come in. Dinner is ready."

"Thanks for having us Ruby," Scott says, politely pointing for me to guide them inside.

Naima jumps to greet him as I text Sarah for the chairs, I won't be able to pick up myself now.

Everyone washes hands and help with the last touch ups of the table when another knock gets everyone's attention.

"Those are our spare chairs," I point at the door.

Sarah's shocked face meets my cocktail of emotions one.

"*Amiga*! You better call me tomorrow."

I nod, hugging her, letting her brush my back, study my eyes, I close them to pull the tears in and shake my head, Sarah nods, kissing my cheek, brushing my arm and walking to her apartment above us.

She is the only person I can share with the entire experience with Advik and not feel judge or suffer their pitiless.

But right now, with Samuel, Scott and the kids here I need to keep it together.

I take a deep breath closing the door, resting my forehead on the wood piece, gaining the strength to pretend in front of my baby boy, who barely understands what is happening around him, my smart big girl, a little gentleman and a man that can read my mind faster than hear my words.

I turn, jumping on the spot when I see Samuel at the door frame. "I didn't mean to startle you," he says.

I shake my head, and fake a smile together with an

awkward giggle that anyone will notice is fake, but the mixture of emotions that runs through me at the moment is confusing and scary.

He is observing me, his gaze moving around my entire frame and I tense.

"Is everything okay?" He asks, searching for my eyes.

Holding the chair up I turn to walk past, but he doesn't let me go that easily, taking them aside and lowering himself so we can be eye to eye.

There are no words coming out of those lips that minutes ago I was so desperate to kiss, but his thoughts are screaming loud enough.

The deep frown grows in between his brows, and I lower my head and look away, avoiding him, aware that his words, or worst touch, will shutter me, and I will lose the little control I had built up all these months.

His knuckles push softly my jaw up as he moves closer, I hold my breath, resting my hand over his, guiding him around my neck, up to my cheek, and closing my eyes with my head resting over his palm, that cover the full side of my face.

Taking in how good does it feel his touch over me, proving to myself once more that is not just my dreams or imagination.

There is a world where a man can respect, care and love a woman, share a loud silence, connect and unite each other until become one.

And that it's what hurts the most, knowing that exits and it can't never be mine.

His lips rest over mine, his warm breath fills my lungs, and for this instant, at this moment, I let go of everything, taking what I wanted for the past few hours, his lips over me once more.

My feet leave the ground, my legs curl around his waist, and my back rest on the wall, my hands hold his shoulders and his cup my face, our lips claim each other, with a hunger and a desire of connecting until the limit of turning into one form.

I miss him the second he pulls back, my feet touch the ground, and he steps back.

"The kids are waiting," I say, reminding myself of the real world.

Dinner moves along easy, the kids are leading the conversation, I keep myself busy helping Aidan, and Samuel attention is on them for once, giving me the opportunity of breathing and thinking.

Pushing the fact that this dinner will be the second and last meal I share with them, realizing I am not the only one losing in this room.

The way Naima is around Scott and Samuel is a different version of what I am used to, she smiles more, speaks about anything and everything, maintains eyes contact, asks questions, unafraid of the other person reaction or thoughts.

They are her first friends, until now, she has built a close connection with Sarah and Miguel, treating them as family, as the closest version to an aunty and a grandfather she has ever known.

My chest compresses at that though, the memory of my parents, the idea that my children might live a life where they don't exist, and my parents will end their days, if they are still alive after all this time, without knowing if I am alive or unaware of their grandchildren.

As my vision blur, and I struggle to hold my tears, I push my chair back, heading to the kitchen and put away the lasagna empty tray and my plate.

Samuel's gaze burns my back, "I will come back with dessert," I say, moving around and smiling when Naima brings the dirty plates to the sink and collect the clean pile, I had ready.

"Are you a cook or a baker?" Samuel asks, taking a full spoon of cake, closing his eyes as he swallows, "this is *Spectacular.*"

"Baking has always been my passion, I practice a few appetizers with the kids, close friends, everyone came back with good feedbacks, so I decided to incorporated to the business."

Samuel nods, licking his lips after he drops a clean spoon over the empty plate.

"I wish my sister found you, she was desperate for someone who could take care of this little gentleman birthday."

"Your birthday is coming soon?" Naima asks.

"Twenty-second of July."

"That is after the party I am organizing, but I was planning on a little summer break after it," I explain clearing the table.

"Don't worry she found someone already, for sure not at as good as you, but she is happy about it," Samuel explains, helping me with the table, sending the kids to wash their hands and play.

Clearing up the island, I prepare all the ingredients for the testing I have tomorrow with Stella, she hasn't asked for anything in specific, I just want her to know what I can offer on terms of sweets while I figure out something up to her standards with all the new ingredients for the savories.

"Can I help before we leave?" Samuel asks.

I shake my head, aware that his handsome gentleman hasn't taken care of a kitchen before.

"I can take care of it."

"Ruby," he calls stepping closer, "let me help you," he begs on a whisper.

"It's been a long day," I politely say.

Aware that a part of me needs to push him away, he is not safe around us, Scott should be attached to us neither.

And the thought of anyone but us been in danger for stepping into our lives now that the monster is about to be set free.

My hands shake at the thought, I can't think fast enough and Samuel closeness is confusing me.

"Thank you for the day," he says, hiding his hands away.

My chest becomes heavy and my eyes fill with tears, I can't be feeling this way from someone I just met.

But at the same time, he has treated me on a way I haven't been treated before, giving me a sense of security, happiness, comfort, things that I didn't learn when I should, and that now hurts to let go of.

I have to let him go.

"I want to stay," he whispers.

Oh, please Samuel run away, before is too late.

I move around, ignoring how he is following me, towering me on a way to make me know he is not giving up that easily, he might need the proximity as much as I need it.

"I don't want to go," he says, close to my ear, standing behind me.

"Stay," I beg.

What the fuck RUBY!!!

His hands hold my waist, turning me, my hands land on his shoulder and I let him take to that new secret place, where the world as I know doesn't exist.

Chapter Nine

Samuel

I pull her up to my chest, her hands holding my shoulders, our lips as close as possible without touching, yet.

I let her brush my shoulders, chest and arms, she is leading the way, we are moving at her own pace, and I am okay with it, I wouldn't ask for anything she isn't ready to give.

But I won't let go of her that easily.

"I won't leave you," I whisper.

What are doing Samuel?!

Her arms curl around my neck, her lips rest on mine and I let go of every doubt, of anything but us.

I won't let anything happen to them, I will protect them, I will give them the space, safe space and security that they need.

"I need to work," she whispers.

I put her back to her feet, pushing her to the counter, towering her and making her aware what her smile is doing to me.

"You are such a bad influence, Samuel."

The way my name sounds on her lips is angel bells for my ears, I kiss her again, holding her closer.

Growling in disapproval when she pushes me into a stool by the island.

"Sit here," she orders, giving me a soft kiss on the cheek.

You need to stop this asap Samuel.

Her fingers lose up the plait, her feet toss the sandals to the side and her lips mumble a song.

Holding it in place Samuel.

My hands hold my chin, I observe every move, I study every inch of her form, I devour her with my lust, and drink her with my anxious despair.

We should be worlds apart for our emotional sake, I've just promised I am not going away, and every minute I spend with her is clear that they will have to remove me from her side.

I am terrified, the little boy inside me is lost, way worse that I was decades ago.

Wear the shell of a full-grown man never took away the insecurities, fears and loneliness.

A part of me tells me this is my place, that I found her because we needed each other, but there is the other side, the one that reminds me how toxic holding to something that doesn't belong to you can be.

She can't be mine, there is a past that she is still linger with, one that could change this all in an instant.

That is what frightens me, lose what I want, what I need.

And that is Ruby, and so is her children.

I took the camera from the car on the way back, I adjust the lens, focus on her and snap a few great shoots while she does what I can see is her passion.

The gym, fast cars and bikes is my escape, cooking is Ruby's, specially baking.

Wake up Samuel! She can be the last business we been looking for.

I hold on to that thought, sometimes I have great ideas, and before I give it a second thought, I pull out my mobile, record a short video and send it to Helena and Matteo, the only two people I can fully trust and be myself around.

Subject; I present you our special edition cover.

It doesn't take long before my mobile screams, I silence it.

Letting her work, I move to the carpet with the kids. We laugh, play cards and domino—but a few seconds into an extra round of the game, I have three kids sleeping on the floor.

I lay next to them, I let my thoughts do their work, analysing the past few days.

Is insane to think that someone I randomly found in London Friday that I accidentally pop into at the park Saturday and my nephew push me to take for shopping today, is stuck into me this deep.

I don't fucking recognise myself.

I was the one he walks away, I never needed anybody in my life.

I grew on a drama free world around women.

I can't be this attached to her.

I need to let her go.

I will hurt them and on the way end what is left of me.

A soft snore from the kids brings me back to her apartment, I stand and walk back to the kitchen to let her know they are sleeping.

It's time to say my goodbyes and get out of her life for good.

As I reach the kitchen, I see the most delicious picture.

Her hair is on that messy way that I found so fucking sexy, her tongue brushes her lip, a cute frown rests in between her brows and her body moves while her hands kneading some dough.

"Come here," she whispers, and so I do, standing behind her, smelling her. She smells delicious, like a bakery first thing in the morning.

Fuck off woman! You are putting a delicious spell on me.

My body moves faster that my minds, my arms curl around her waist, my chin rests on her shoulder and I draw circles on her tummy, over the top fabric wakening her nipples, and across her collarbone, kissing her neck as I hold it in place.

The surrounding scent, the warmth of the room, the comfort of her body resting on my chest, the soft giggles and the way our bodies turn into one bring tears to my eyes and my poor damaged heart beats harder than ever. After all this year's felling empty and lonely, right now, in this moment and apartment, on her arms, *I feel at home.*

I rest my forehead on her shoulder and breath through

the pain of my broken soul assembling more pieces together.

Why are you doing this to me Ruby?

Her hands pause, she turns, pushing me out of my new favourite place, "this needs to rest in the fridge," she says.

The small space and my long arms play on my advantage, I pull the door open, place the bowl inside and kick it close.

Her hands rest on my chest, I cup her face, my forehead falls into hers and I inhale her, my bottom lip hides under my teeth and I forced myself to compose and act natural.

She doesn't need to see how fucked up I am. She has enough.

Her eyes close, her head fall to my palm and I hold her closer.

"Open your eyes Ruby," I whisper and she does, making me tremble.

Her fingers brush my chest, stopping in the centre, her palm rest over my heart, beating harder under her contact.

I observe how she take in every beat as if it's her own, replacing it for her ear.

Her head moves with the rise of my chest and her entire body calms under the drums of my broken heart, my hands brush her back, feeling her heart matches mine.

"Home," she whispers so low, that if I wasn't this close, and so lost into her I would have miss it.

I bite my lip, looking to the ceiling, pushing my tears back where they belong, she feels at home on my arms too.

I don't deserve this.

I need to run! Hide and forget her!

There is only one way that will happen, I need to make sure she wants to push me away too.

"The kids are sleeping on the floor," I say, on my deep, rough voice that she hasn't heard yet.

I need to show her my worst side, one that she definitely will not like around her children, her body stiffens, shivers and step away.

I stand there, towering her.

Letting her rush to the other room, taking Aidan and walking away.

"I need to take Scott home." I whisper on a painful voice before she leaves the room.

Miserably failed to keep my tough guy attitude up with her.

I care for her, she matters to me, I can't be that son of a bitch with her.

Ruby doesn't say a word, she walks away with a change on her expression.

Please hate me, send me away.

For an unknown and stupid reason, I wait for her to return to pick up Naima.

She has changed, her petite figure now covered with an oversize T-shirt, exposing her legs, far too sexy for what I in vision this moment should be.

Gosh, this woman is teasing me.

"I could be back," I say, biting my bottom lip, as she bends to pick up Naima.

What the fuck are you doing SAMUEL?! I thought we were

running away!

"That would be nice," she whispers and my entire being is back alive.

I can't run, she has trapped me.

"See you in twenty." I say rushing out of the apartment with Scott is in my arms.

I can't wait to be back.

I seat Scott in Naima's car seat, securing him before I drive as fast as I can, the roads are empty and quiet.

Stella opens the door as I enter the driveway, collecting Scott from my arms.

"In a rush?" she asks using her mum voice on me.

Please, give me a break.

"Have a lovely week Stella," I cut off the conversation using my nasty tone.

"Samuel?!" she growls through her teeth.

I turn and jump on my car, she can't talk to me like that, what are we now, best pals sharing secrets?

Minutes later, I am back at Ruby's, she opens, walks away and I follow her like a hungry animal.

She points at the stool, and as good boy I do as she orders, repositioning myself that is desperately screaming for her.

Fuck me that T-shirt!

The white material is so thin that I can see every inch of her body.

Pulling my hair off, I wait for her to place another bowl in the fridge, and ground myself when she walks straight to me—there is no more time to lose.

Let's do it, baby!

I hold her as she jumps on my arms, her thighs curl my waist, her hands directly to my buttons and mine under her T-shirt, confirming my previous thoughts.

She's not wearing anything under it.

I am going to lose myself on you, woman.

I claim her lips, I bite and suck her bottom lip in between mine, I inhale every moan that her gorgeous lips release.

There is hunger and need.

I let go of her, dropping my shirt to the floor, returning to her soft body, touching every inch of her, memorising how good does she feels and how her skin reacts to my touch.

Her palms mimic my moves, there is not area on my torso that her fingertips haven't explore yet.

I hold her closer, catching a delicious cry when her centre meets my hardness under my jeans.

So, fucking perfect!

Her hands move to my belt, and flashbacks of the car come to me.

I stand, resting her on the island as she helps to pull my trousers off, brushing my arse, while I kick my shoes aside.

Exposing my entire being to this angel.

Feeling vulnerable.

Her hands cup my jaw, locking her eyes on me, brushing my stubble with her thumbs, reassuring me, or so I feel.

I step back, gripping the edge of the t-shirt, brushing

her thighs, hips, breast, arms and locking my hands on her and the fabric falls aside.

I want to study her body, but she has me hypnotise with her eyes, my hands travel down, exploring what my eyes can't do yet.

Gosh! Isn't she the most beautiful creature I ever seen.

I hold her hips, pushing her to the edge, her back curls when her centre meets my arousal, moaning softly, dropping her head back.

Take it easy Samuel, she matters.

I hold her nape, her eyes back to me, I kiss her softly, holding her, reassuring both of us this moment matters.

"Eyes on me," I whisper, her broken breath brush my cheek and I grin.

Brushing her centre, spreading her wetness, kissing her once more, teasing her clit and pussy, I focus on controlling my desire for this angel.

I fill her up with two fingers, drawing circles, her walls suck me in, dripping on my palm and warming up.

My thumb pressure her clit, her head falls back and I pull her back up, gripping her hair, keeping her where I need, looking at me while I make her come undone.

Taking in what I couldn't in the car.

The best view I could have.

Her chest expands, her bottom lip hides under her teeth and I grin as I plunge her with three fingers, finding her sweetest spot, bringing her to the limits and I inviting her to release herself on my hold.

"Come for me baby," I whisper on her lips.

Her moans echo around us, her walls suck me deeper, I draw a few more circles and I pull away, spreading her release over her nipples and bottom lip.

Devouring each of them tasting her delicious cum.

Her nipples harden up under my tongue, her lips swollen of my own attack over them, and I step closer.

My throbbing cock brush her wetness and we both moan in need.

"Are you sure?" I ask, her nod is quick, her heels push me closer and with an easy move I enter her slowly.

So, fucking warm and delicious, so tight and welcome, so perfect.

Her legs curl around my waist tighter, her arms around my shoulders, her forehead rests on my cheek, and I hold her there, close, secure, and with the need of making her feel safe.

Because I feel I am home.

We remain like that, there is no rush, time stops around us, nothing exists in her arms and I want her to feel the same.

"I am not leaving," I whisper on her neck.

Her body melts under my words, I pull her to the edge, barely touching the island, her hands fall to the surface, holding herself, her legs spread on the stools by my side and I pull back.

Her back curls as I empty her, resting just the tip inside her.

I hold one of her hands, resting it on my shoulder, the other over my heart.

Mines hold her hips, I have her, she won't move unless I let her.

I push forwards, my head falls back, her hand pulls my head back down, requesting what I did before.

"Eyes on me, Sam."

Sam.

I reach the deepest, hold there and with a soft nod, move slowly, building up her climax, her hips rotate, inviting me to thrusting her harder, to fuck her, I won't, I am enjoying way too much this moment.

"Sam," she cries, as I hit her core.

I repeat it, this time faster and deeper, smiling as she moans louder, pushing my chest and pulling my hair.

"Again," she whispers, I do what she wants.

Over and over again, bringing her to the limit of desperation, I know she wants me faster, harder, but I won't give it until she begs for it.

"Sam," she cries once more, I smirk and plunge her faster.

Building a strength, I didn't know possible to control myself and the release that I can feel way too close.

"I need more," she begs.

"I know baby," I whisper in her ears, "do you want more?"

"Yes," she says.

"Say it."

"I want more, I need more, please, Sam–"

Before she finishes, I thrust her hard, deep and fast.

Her nails pull my flesh away, her teeth bite my shoulder

and I growl on her neck.

"I–"

I won't let her say a word more, I pull back, locking my gaze with her once more, my grip tightens in her hips, I will leave marks, and I don't care.

Not while I thrust her like the animal I am, not while she cries my name, not while her palms hold my heart scared of letting it fall and the other caress my face and hair.

A brutal moment has been turned into something meaningful.

I thrust her harder and her walls suck me deeper, sweat drips around us, the room turn warmer, spinning around, I am dizzy, focus on her blue oceans.

"Sam," she cries, reaching the limit.

"Not yet baby," I say, thrusting faster and harder.

My throat burns as I growl, my lungs lose all the air I had held, and with a few more thrusts we reach our climax together.

The heaviness over my shoulders dissipates, the pain on my chest ceases and even I just empty myself inside her, without protection like a fucking bastard, I never felt fuller.

"We didn't use–"

"It's fine," she assures, I nod.

Kissing her, not just on the lips, but in every inch of her angelical face.

I smile at her giggles, taking her hand from my chest and kissing her knuckles, her palm, and resting it on my cheek.

My eyes close and I let her hold me, my head falls on

her chest, her fingers play with my hair and her lips kiss me softly as I take in her embracement.

Didn't I say it already? *I found home.*

"Hungry?" She asks, after a lifetime holding me on her arms.

A lion roaring in my stomach answers for me.

"Give me two minutes," she says, softly pushing me, pulling out of her, and jumping down.

I feel cold, lost and empty, I want her close again.

Expressing my disagreement when the T-shirt covers her body, she walks around the kitchen collecting ingredients and utensils.

I can't take my eyes away from her, she is dancing around making me fall deeper on her spell.

What have you done to me?

While something gets ready on the pan, she is transferring trays from the fridge to the oven.

I grab my boxers from the floor and walk closer.

"Working?" I ask.

Her cheeks flash pink and my heart jumps into my throat. She is the cutest, most special person I've ever known.

"I have a sample tasting tomorrow," she says with a tinkle of nervousness.

"Is it a big deal?"

"They want me to do the entire party," she sounds anxious. "I'm trying to get organised but am a little overwhelmed."

"What can I help you with?"

I am helpless, I have no clue how to take care of a house or a kitchen. Ruby matters to me, and if there anything I can do to take that overwhelm feeling away from her, I will do it without question.

Ruby laughs, looking at my body cover in just boxers. Guiding me to the corner near the fridge, where the entire pile of trays is ready to be washed.

Me? Washing dishes?

My arrogance flies away with a small look into her beautiful blue eyes, she needs help, and I genuinely want to help her.

I take care of all what is around me, turn and do the same across the small space, glimpsing two plates cover where I made love to her far too long ago.

I miss her, even at this short distance.

My chest contracts at how much it will hurt dressed up and walk away from her once she invites me to leave.

"Done with the cleaning," I say, drying my hands, "what else?" I ask, watching her placing yellow sponge cakes in the fridge.

"Let's eat," she smiles, but it doesn't reach her eyes.

Something is happening, is clear, no words can take that thought away from me, I can't put the finger to it, but is there.

I step closer, hold her up, she can't run or avoid me, I hold her chin and make her look into my eyes, "whatever it is," my voice shakes, she cups my face, and I close my eyes for an instant, "I will always be here for the three of you."

How can you promise that, sir?

Her bottom lip wobbles, she nibbles it, trying to hide it, and fails, so she kisses me. It's slow, soft, painful in many ways.

She can't be thinking of pushing me away, I am not going anywhere, never.

I sit on the stool, and rest her on my lap, studying her face, holding my words, scared my irrational thinking, will scared her.

I need her to know that this wasn't just sex, that today wasn't just a favour, I want to be part of her life, I want to mean to her what she means to me.

Her lips kiss my cheek and we both laugh when my tummy grumbles.

"Let's eat baby," I sit her next to me, my legs spread over her stool, so she is as close as I need her to be.

We eat in silence, I make a couple of questions about her cooking skills and she does about my posh life as she likes to call it.

I learn her mother back in Texas taught her how to do half of what I tasted so far, and she learned that money doesn't buy happiness or love.

There is something that been bothering me all day, I have considered it, I have analysed it, I have suggested to my friends, but I haven't said a word to her, and without her approval there is no way it can happen.

I don't need Ruby to tell me they are struggling financially and emotionally.

She wouldn't be in this house if she could give the children a simple fully rented apartment, this place is given to her by the council, so she has to accept whatever is given.

She has worked hard in transformed it into a house, but I can't let that continue the way it is.

I won't be crazily buying her a castle, even I know she deserves it.

But I can help her in another way.

"Ruby, what would you think of being part of my next edition?"

"For the magazine you work?" She asks, cleaning her lips.

"I own the company," I say, chewing.

"You do? I thought–"

"Scott and Naima were talking, I didn't correct him," I say.

"What is your magazine about?" she asks, accepting the not clarification at the park.

"Big and small brands, the party or events of the season, interviews, fashion, beauty, gastronomy, a little bit of everything."

"Why me?" She asks, surprise. "I'm not a celebrity."

"Not only celebrities can be in our magazine. This one is the 100th edition."

I say proudly, not elaborating the fact that on that same day I will officially become the owner of the empire, that things will change, or worse explain where have I been all these years since my parents' disappearance.

She doesn't need to know all of that, is irrelevant.

"We want to promote new entrepreneurs."

"Am I an entrepreneur?"

"Well, you are starting a business from home. You do all the jobs that make this work with kids, so I could think of you as more of a mompreneur, but yes you are."

"What do you need me to do?"

I can hear the shyness and nervous behind her words, *she is too fucking cute.*

"To be honest, just one more picture as I spent the entire day creating all the content needed."

"You don't need me to do a big photoshoot, interview, or stuff like that?" She asks disappointed.

"I want this edition to be natural—serious, boring stuff will come later on, believe me. Is that a, yes?"

I pull her closer, her gaze falls in between us and the room turns cold, she is distant, uncomfortable.

I am as close as I can be and haven't felt her more distant before.

There is something that I said, it must be that, my world is far too much for her, and I stupidly scared her.

Learn to keep your mouth shut!

"What happens Ruby?" I ask.

Her eyes meet mine, she is here physically, not mentally or emotionally, in that she is miles away.

"Do it, take your last picture," she murmurs.

Jumping down from the stool, swinging in between her feet, rolling the edge of her t-shirt in her fingers.

"I will go and change."

"It's for the cover, so feel free to put your best," I smile, forced as is the one she gives me.

I get dressed too.

I don't want to leave, didn't want to since she accept me by her side.

But I lost her, something I said, something I did, or I didn't say or did.

I scared her, and there is no way back.

It's clear on her body language, on the darkness of her eyes and the forced smile she can't fake.

I walk to the car, collect my bag with the laptop and camera, transferring the files of what I took before, setting everything up.

"You look gorgeous," I say when she walks back wearing a tight, white and blue flowered dress, with off the shoulder straps.

Her long black waves fall on her back, away from her face that she has applied some make up, I can see the redness where before a bright white surrounded her blue oceans.

"Just be you," I explain, "continue cooking," I take a few shoots of her hands over the pastries, when she mixes a new bowl, her concentration over the work she is doing and then comes the best one, "look at me," I order, so she does.

Her cheek blush at my words, the spark on her eyes pushes the darkness aside and the side of her lips raise on a small genuine smile.

"You are too beautiful."

I let the camera on the counter, walking to her, holding her waist and bringing her closer.

"Rub–"

"Ma," Aidan voice brings us back to reality, Ruby rush

away.

No words, no looking over her shoulder, and I don't blame her.

They are her world, I am just, who I am?

I take the moment as the best to leave, writing a simple note, collecting my things and walking out as quiet as I can.

I will see you tomorrow x

I put all my hopes in those five words.

The ball is on her yard, is her move, and I will wait for as long as I shall life for her to come back.

I drive away, calling Helena and Matteo in my driveway.

"Samuel Smith!!!!" Helena screams.

"*Fratello*, she is an angel." Matteo is as delighted as I am. "Helena, don't be jealous. She is perfect."

"I just need you to be focused with your beautiful brain and the head on top of your shoulders." She argues.

In the office she is polite and nice to me, but out of it she is all sassy and straightforward, who needs bullshit from anyone when Helena can give you reality in one go?

"She is perfect. Everyone will love her food and her personality when they meet her." I assure them.

"Are we doing a press release?" Helena asks, taking notes.

I laugh when Natasha walks behind her, startling Helena.

"Hi boys!" we wave. "If you don't mind, I will take this

beauty to bed."

Matteo laughs. and I cover my mouth as I do it, too.

"Please do. I will see everyone tomorrow morning at 8 a.m. sharp!" I say.

Everyone disconnects, and I head inside.

Rosita walks out of the kitchen as I close the front door.

"Don't say anything."

I cut her before she can even greet me, I am back in my space, here I can be and do what I want, nobody judges me, nobody cares.

The fact that this is my most vulnerable place, make it the most dangerous right now. One word and all my guarded walls will fall like a domino.

There is too much and nothing to say at once.

I could share how good it felt to spent the day with them, but I could share how much it hurts to visit heaven and be kicked back to hell in a matter of hours.

No words will change what is happening.

"I need a shower."

"I heard the news," Rosita says from the bottom of the stairs, I turn to her, "you found the cover entrepreneur *hijito.*"

"I followed the advice." I assure.

"For once," she says, I can hear the sarcasm on her tone, but I ignore it.

"*Buenas noches,*" I say, walking down the steps that separate us and kissing her cheek.

"*Dios te bendiga mi hijito,*" she answers, drawing the cross over my forehead and chest.

I take two steps at the time and hide away on my room,
my mourning and most tortuous chapter has begun.

Chapter Ten

Ruby

The small old clock on my night table hits 5 a.m., I'm wide awake—I doubt I will ever be able to sleep again, knowing Advik will be out in a week.

However, seeing how quickly things have changed in the past few days, I can't help but be petrified knowing Advik could be out any minute now.

Getting out of bed, I head straight to the shower, sad to wash away Samuel's touch and kisses, but my anger and sadness need to be washed away too.

By 5:30 a.m. I'm in the kitchen, a fresh coffee in my hand, while I go through today's schedule.

Last night I prepared a few samples of cake, dough, and cupcakes. I just need to add the filling that been resting overnight in the fridge.

Playing some soft music, pulling my hair up I let go of my thoughts and I let my hands lead the way.

By 9 a.m., after we taste the cakes for breakfast, I send he kids to play, to give me the time to clean, and prepare the appointment with Stella.

Giving me the time to mold the last figures I want her to approve, after I send a quick text to Miguel reminding him, I will need the invitations and samples here soon.

Knowing that the hard work of banners, decoration and invitations is taken care by him and his elaborate machines, take a big weight away from my shoulders.

For once I need to accept the help and understand I can't always do it all myself, *'I am good with food, he is good with paper,'* I remind myself.

After a couple of hours with the last touch ups on the designs, I enjoy some cards game Naima has invented when a soft knock announces a visitor.

Miguel is at the other side with a large box filled with my work.

"*Buen día* Ruby," he greets stepping inside, "niños," he smiles to the kids as I guide him to the kitchen.

I organize a sample of each and let him place the rest on a free corner at the end of the room.

"Now that I am here, I want to share something with you."

"What is that?"

"The Mayor ask me to do the banners and flyers and I thought this will be the perfect opportunity for your business to get officially presented to the community," he says, handing me a flyer of a town event.

Summer Fair

In collaboration with Three Angles Church, The Children's Shelter, and Blue Valley Council.

Join us for our famous Summer Fair, enjoy the kids' games and activities, try our best local business food, and help us raise money for the children in need.

Friday 15th of July, from 10 a.m. to 6 p.m.

At Bluebell Park, near the recreation area.

"This is incredible, *señor* Miguel."

"I knew you would be interested in taking part," he says and nods.

What?!

"Take part? I was thinking you want me to assist. How could I be ready for two events on such a short notice?" I ask.

"Ruby, you need to promote your business, and it's for the children," he says, determined to convince me.

"I have the birthday party, the store orders. How can I organize everything? That's madness," I say, letting the panic shows on my voice.

"They don't need nothing fancy, I will help you with the business banner, cards, you just have to bake slightly extra of what your normally do for the shops."

"Why I always let you trap me into everything?"

"Because if it wasn't for me, you will still fill with doubts baking for me and Sarah."

"Thank you."

"I will let them know you agree," he says, "do you need help to deliver this?" he asks pointing to the store orders, resting at the end of the counter.

"We could go after the tasting," I say.

"None sense, I can easily do it with the car," he says, holding the boxes and walking away. "Bye *niños!*" he exclaims, walking away.

A few hours later, after Stella's tasting, I cook lunch, and organize my overflowed month of July. I head to the garden to play with the kids.

The warm sun forced me to open the umbrella to hide my pale skin, the kid's laughter and imagination distracts me, thinking how much our lives has changed in just few months.

And letting the happy overwhelm of the new things coming our way become my priority, who knew that worry about all the good things could be this satisfactory.

Happiness doesn't last long, startled when the doorbell announces an uninvited guest.

Nobody comes to our apartment, unless they have a collection slot. It's school and working hours, the road is empty and everyone I was expecting has already come.

"I will check the door, stay here," I tell the kids as I head to the front door.

There is a short lady accompanied by a tall, good-looking gentleman. Two strangers that don't look lost at all.

"Samuel sent us," the man says.

I hold the door, unsure if what he is saying it's truth,

"please open the door," he says.

"Ruby, he gave us your address, please open the door," the lady says, calling me by name.

I open the door cautiously, tensing as I come face to face, copying their smile.

"Afternoon Ruby," she says, "Samuel is at the city, he wanted us to come and talked to you," she explains.

"Please, this way," I say, walking to the kitchen.

"Nice apartment," she says.

"Would y'all like some ice coffee or maybe lemonade?" I ask.

"Matteo will appreciate an espresso and I," she pauses, pointing at herself, "Rosita, will be glad to have some lemonade."

I look over my shoulder to the kids, who have listened and stayed in the garden.

"Do you mind if I join them?" Matteo asks, pointing that the garden, I nod, and he walks out, easily turning into their new playmate.

I frown, uneasy at the thought of how open the children are becoming to strangers and how dangerous that can be.

"You might wonder what we are doing here," Rosita says.

I turn to her, offering to take a seat on the dining table as we share the fresh drink and cookies.

"This is delicious," she points out trying the lemonade. "Samuel will be stuck in the city for the rest of the week," she explains.

He is putting the needed distance between us, he is

doing what I know it will have been hard for me. *Then why is she here?*

"You don't have to come and talk for him."

"You never exchanged numbers, and he had to—"

"He could have added it to this," I accuse holding up his late-night note.

"Ruby, I can see your life," she says, resting her hand over mine, "your situation is delicate, complicated even," she continues, "Samuel does not know what he is doing."

"You don't have to justify him."

"I am not sure how much he has shared, but this is all new for him," she says, pointing at me, kids, house, everywhere.

"He has shared nothing," I clarify.

He is hiding things.

"I can't do this. We have enough on our plates," I say, standing and nibbling my lip, letting all the good he gave me turn into an anxious feeling of what a fool I have been.

Of course, there is a story behind that man, he is probably married or in a complicated relationship, have a bunch of kids, and I was his little village fling.

"Samuel has always struggled with his thoughts and emotions."

"I am not asking for anything," I point out, making her away I have no intentions of him becoming nothing to us.

Hurting my ego at the idea of been his one-night-stand, the easy woman in distress to take advantage of and toss aside, or worst, keep content so he can have me anytime he is around.

"He lost everyone except me and his sister at a young age—that broke him into millions of pieces," she says with a shaky tone, "I've been picking all up for over twenty years. It has been exhausting—I'm not complaining, just explaining."

I stand by the island, keeping my safety distance, looking at the kids, hurting myself more at the thought of how much they like him and how devastated will be to tell them we have been used.

"Then you appear in his life," she continues, "for an instant, I thought all my hard work would be crushed again. But Ruby, in two days, you have put more pieces together than I could in over a decade."

"Happy to help," I say, letting the sarcasm sink in before she says another word.

"He is walking on dangerous path here. The only thing we need from you is to be patient and prepared," she says.

"I think I am not understanding this," I point around.

The cards are turn the wrong way, I thought he was the one helping and supporting us, when he was actually using us to heal his own wounds. Fantastic, I couldn't feel more used even if he tries any harder.

"When Samuel loves you, the world becomes colorful. It keeps spinning so fast you can't focus much, but then he holds you and everything gets better."

Love? I met him 48h ago.

"I saw that boy born," she says melancholic. "Since the day I held him for the first time I could feel how special he was. I was there the day he broke, and all turned dark around him."

"Mama, can we play paint with Matteo?" Naima asks, taking me away from the information I'm trying to process.

"Of course, just show him where to find everything," I say, refilling Rosita's lemonade, and taking the seat next to her again.

"You might not understand it right now, but you are the light in his darkness. I just need to know he is your safe place too, otherwise we need to stop this now," she says.

I tilt my head, questioning if he sent them, or this is them stepping up and taking control of something they think Samuel can't manage on his own.

"Rosita, things aren't that easy with us," I say.

"*Mi hijita,* I can see your apartment, your approach to strangers, the darkness in your eyes. I can smell a broken soul miles away," she says, "Samuel doesn't know how to communicate, he is attentive and care for who matter to him, there is where you need to step up, teach him how to talk and open up, share who he really is."

"I think this is a conversation I should have with him, I appreciate your visit, but involve more people won't be good for anybody."

"I understand, may I have your number so he can contact you?"

I stand, collecting a business card from the shelve and walking to the garden, politely inviting Matteo to leave.

Naima soft nod makes me aware that she understands they have to leave and that everything will be better if they do.

Hours have passed since they left, and my phone hasn't received any unknown number calls or messages.

Rosita might have shared my thoughts and words, making Samuel take the correct approach and step away from our lives for good.

As I prepare the ingredients over the counter and set the table for dinner, I turn off the volume, set it facing down on the counter and take him out of my mind.

He is, he was, and he will forever be a stranger.

Punishing my pie letting the past three days play in my mind, or even further the past week. Everything started that morning in London.

If I wasn't that upset and decided to take the kids to the park for a minute of distraction and freedom for me, I will have never cross paths with him. The train station was round the corner from the court room and Miguel was waiting my call to pick up us from the station on the nearby village.

I let my emotions take the best of me.

That was a mistake, but the park was an evil twist of destiny, unless he found me, he followed me.

That is impossible, Scott lives here, it took Samuel minutes to pick him up and return last night.

"Mama!" Naima exclaims, startling me, "someone is at the door," she says, bringing my attention to the soft knock.

Sarah is at the other side, persistently knocking, giving me a worry look when I open.

"Why are you ignoring my calls?"

"You call?"

"Yes, I did, multiple times," she says inviting herself in.

"What happens?"

"Hello kids," she waves at them on the way to the kitchen, turning on the kettle, grabbing two mugs and serving some of the relaxing tea she homemade, "they are on the way."

I pause for an instant, unsure of exactly what we are talking about, my world has expanded since I let Samuel in on a way that I am unclear how many people could be knocking at my door to talk about him tomorrow.

"The kids?" I ask as she nibbles her lip, she nods and I jump on her arms, giggling and screaming in delight of the news, "I can't believe it!"

"Is not that easy," she says, pushing me slightly away.

"What do you mean?"

"They will be in the country soon," she pauses, her chin wobbles and my heart aches for her pain, "they will be sent to a center–"

"What short of center? they have to come to their mother."

"They don't remember me Ruby, it's been many years, they were babies remember?"

The thought twists my stomach and makes me feel sick. Her children where around Naima and Aidan's age when her ex-husband nearly end her life and run away with them back to Asia, hiding away for long enough that everyone that could help thought they were death, after all they were vanished for over a year before they were found on a small town in the mountains living under different names, but not he. That bastard kept his identity, his ego was bigger than the damage he made on Sarah's and her children's lives.

I won't deny that has been one of my greatest fears with Advik, that he will take the kids away, with or without ending my life, move along that inexplicable punishment he endure on me since the moment I met him.

The idea of Naima and Aidan been away from me, or worst, forgetting who I am hurts much more than any wound I have ever had on me.

"There must be something they can do, they don't deserve to be sent to a place on their own, they are still babies and need their mom," a thick tear rolls down her round face, "I am sorry, I didn't mean it–"

"It's the truth, but that doesn't mean it doesn't hurt," she says.

"What about one of these centers where there are orphans and women in need, you will share the same space, get to see each other until they are ready."

"Louise says there are fully booked."

"That bitch," I mutter on a low voice.

"Ruby," Sarah exclaims, "is everything okay?"

I shake my head, pointing at the kids, silently assuring there is much to talk that they can't be present for.

"Turn on your mobile, call me after bedtime," she says, kissing my cheek, waving goodbye to the kids and walking away.

"I will prepare the bath," I tell the kids, letting them

finish their dinner, grabbing my mobile and heading to the bathroom.

There are at least ten miss calls from Sarah, with an extensive number of messages begging me to answer the phone and door.

A message from Miguel confirming my spot at the Summer Fair, Martha's order for her crochet meeting next Sunday, with a possible collection on Saturday morning, and an alarming amount of miss calls, every ten minutes sharp, for two hours and a simple message from an unknown number.

I know we shouldn't do this again, I just need to know the children and you are fine.
Please, I beg you, at least reply to this.

He doesn't have to add his name to let me know is him— Samuel Smith.

I rest the mobile on the mirror self, preparing the bath and considering what to do next.

I could reply, let him know we are alright, take that worries away from him, and block his number.

I could ignore it completely and move ahead, holding on the memories of what we had, and we could never be mine.

The ringtone of the mobile startle me, a different unknown number pops in the screen, I doubt for a moment, realizing, before Samuel, or Louise call with Advik news, I had always answered my calls at the first ring, ready to welcome new customers, now, I analyze fearful all the things that happen to me.

I take a deep breath, clear my throat and answer the call.

"Ruby Sweet Dreams, Ruby speaking, how can I help you?"

I can hear the breath of someone at the other side of the line, my body shakes, panic fills my veins, and cold sweat runs down my spine.

I hung up, holding my chest with my heads, applying pressure for my lungs and heart to function before I pass out, my hands hold the edge of the bathtub I fall on my knees, screaming as the mobile rings again, a different number, with trembling hands I check it, trying to remember if that is the same number Samuel message me from.

This time I turn off the water, close the bathroom door, answering the call, holding my breath and waiting for that other person to speak first.

"Hello?" his raspy voice makes my entire body tremble.

"Hi," I answer in relief, tears overflowing my eyes, letting out a heavy exhale.

"How was your day?" he asks, acting as if this was our regular routine.

Shaking away my emotions from minutes ago, I turn back on the water, head to the open room to let them know they can get into the bath and clear up the dinner while I clear my throat to talk with him.

"Productive, yours?" I ask, faking an emotion I don't feel.

"Spectacular! I've worked all day editing a gorgeous angel picture, How was your tasting?"

"Spectacular! She loved it all," I answer mimicking his tone.

"Kids?" He asks.

"Bath."

"You?"

"Kitchen."

"Baking?" he asks on a seductive tone.

"Cleaning, actually. You?"

"In the car."

"You shouldn't drive and be on your phone at the same time."

"I am not driving."

"Oh, that is good then."

"I am unsure."

"Of what exactly?"

"Of where to go next."

"I see."

"I'm exhausted, ready to craw in bed and end the day," he says, pausing chuckling and taking a deep breath, "I can't go home, the builders have invaded every single room, I could sleep in the garage," he explains, making me giggle at his bad joke.

"I'm sure you have many other houses," I point out, aware of the fact that whatever house he owns in the neighbourhood, is an addition to at least another in a different location, or he could be in a hotel easily.

"Yeah, but they are too far from where I want to be," he

says casually.

"And where that will be?" I ask, nibbling my lip anxiously, "the kids are calling me," I say, following Naima's voice, "I need to go."

I hung up before I walk inside the bathroom, facing two sleepy faces, helping them to brush their teeth, changing to pj's and tucking them into bed without a bedtime story needed.

I stay there, brushing their little curls, their soft cheeks and letting my heavy breath and heartbeats match theirs.

After I fix the bathroom, I take a shower, change into a maxiskirt I head back to the kitchen, finishing clearing all up and double checking my schedule to-do list for the upcoming days when my mobile rings from where I left it by the corridor cupboard when I walked to the bathroom earlier.

Sarah's name announces a message.

What can I do to get a new counselor? Louise is not helping, her vague excuses and little care for me and the kids is unacceptable!

I know how she feels, Louise has done the same to me, but I can't tell Sarah that, she has far too much on her plate as it is, I do not need her to be worry about us.

I need to find out that too, we can apply together and maybe apply some pressure to the council to check her lack of help and emotion towards the one in need.

The three dots take long enough before another text arrives at the same time that a call from what I believe is Samuel's number.

I will check it out, see you in the morning to discuss it more.
Love you sweet, night night xx.

With a simple 'night-night', I answer the call and wait for the other side of the line to speak first.

"Hello again," he cheekily says, I can see the smile on his words.

"Hello."

"What are you doing?"

"Finishing the kitchen."

"Kids?"

"In bed, you?"

"In the car."

"Should we discuss the driving and phone calls again?"

"Not at all, I haven't move," the thought of him waiting for a call back for over half an hour since I hung up, makes me feel guilty, "I was just thinking."

"To which one of your mansions should you go to sleep tonight?"

"Despite what you think, I am downsizing on the type of properties I live on," he says, confirming my suspicions, he is far wealthier than I thought.

"There must be one that has the best bed to rest, a great bath to have a relaxing time, I don't know, never had that issue."

"I don't want the best bed or a great bath."

"And what do you want, Samuel?"

There is silence at his end, only his breath makes me aware he is still there.

A soft knock brings me out of the thoughts of him not answering my question where awakening in me.

Maybe he does have someone waiting for him elsewhere, something complicated, someone that misses him as much as I do.

"Someone is at the door," I say, breaking the silence.

"Don't hung up," he begs, I frown and walk to the front door, muting the call as I open the door.

My feet leave the ground, my back hits the wall and the room spins, intoxicated by my new favorite fresh scent, mixed with the sweetness of his stubble that travels across my neck, up to my ear.

"Have I startled you?" he asks in a whisper, I nod, trembling when his lips brush the sensitive spot in between my neck and my ear, "my most sincere apologies," he whispers.

"I thought you were in the car," I say, brushing his waves, biting my bottom lip as his travel around my jaw until they rest a breath away from mine.

"I've been parked at your front door for far too long," holding his face back, I tilt my head, studying his expression, understanding what he is saying is the truth, "I didn't know if you were busy, or if you wanted me here."

"And here you are startling me, walking in unannounced," I point out.

My feet land on the ground, Samuel steps back, brushing his waves back, his eyes travel around the room, never meeting me, I can hear these thoughts screaming all at once.

Giving him the time to decide his next more, not regretting pointing out that his actions weren't correct.

He can't show up at my door just like that, he can't push himself in that way either, and most definitely he should jump on me like a hungry beast and expect me to take it all in at once easily.

"I should leave," he says, turning and heading out before I can think things through, leaving me there, standing on the corridor with a messed-up head and an unsure heaviness on my chest.

A full week has passed, filled with sleepless nights, not because Samuel has walked away from us faster that he walked in. That passed through my mind a few times, working in the night reminded me of that night. The one where nothing existed but us.

Now, that doesn't matter anymore.

Carrying the last boxes inside the cottage does. Things change that weekend, my entire life ended as I knew it and a new one started, one where we own the cottage that Miguel has helped me for the past couple of days to fill up with the few belongings we had at the apartment.

I terribly miss the kids that has been for now over three days with Sarah so I could focus on packing and moving without disrupting their schedules much.

"There is nothing else in the car, mi hijita," Miguel says, placing the last box in what soon will be our family room.

"Thank you."

"Ruby, you and your kids are my only family, I will do anything for you. I should be the one thanking you, for sharing this big moment in your life with me."

Miguel lost her daughter to a terrible illness shortly after we move, I never got the opportunity to meet her, but he believes I was sent to support him over the lost, and give him a reason to move forward.

After couple of hours helping to unpack, I sent him away to enjoy the rest of the Saturday afternoon, is his only day off, and even when I know he loves to keep himself busy, I want to be doing this on my own too.

I haven't been alone before, my life has been a spiral of been the little cowgirl and daughter of, to be the wife and prisoner of, to be the mother and protector of.

There has never been a time when I was just Ruby, when I just belonged to myself and I could for once make a decision without thinking on anybody else, as simple as what I want for dinner tonight, me, on my own, at the floor of our new home.

With a second thought, I hold the house key and I walk outside, smiling at the beauty of our front garden, a path of multicolor flowers that on one end takes you to the park main gate, on the other, at my back, takes me through an orange door, inside the cutest little home I ever image I will call home one day.

I let the little wind of the early July mark my path, I let go of all my thoughts, the good, the bad and the ugly. I move for once in a spontaneous way, without destination or hopes. Just me.

The park is busy as I walk through the trees, across the path and after a while, back by the lake.

That same lake that weeks ago brought Samuel to us, I pause, closing my eyes and letting the wind clean the air inside me, and calm the knot building inside my tummy.

That was his purpose in life, help us, he did, twice, and now he is where a part of me wishes he always stayed, away from us as a complete stranger.

A cold breeze makes me tremble, I cross my arms around me, rubbing my arms for some warm feeling, opening my eyes, to find I am the only one feeling it.

I turn around, searching in between all the groups of people having a nice time under the sun, near the lake, for that could make me feel that way.

All my senses come up on alert, I can't see anything that should make me feel this way, choosing to return home, ignoring it all, it must have been my own imagination.

But it wasn't, now I can see it across the road, standing by my little gravel pathway, surrounded by flowers, with a black shirt open at the top, revealing his pecs line, sleeves rolled up exposing his olive skin and muscly arms, tight denims that molding in the thickness of his thighs and biker boots.

With a small glimpse at his dangerously handsome face, I cross the road, heading to him on the determination that he should move, and let me past.

The world stops as I approach him, and a bouquet of sunflowers pops out from behind him.

I step back, my blood turns ice, my head hurts, the air on my lungs escape my body on a panic sight, and every wound that Advik ever put on me, internal or external, every scar that hasn't healed, or disappear come back to life, burning my skin, bringing all those moments when I let him hurt me, disrespect me, abuse of his mental and physical power over me.

My knees wobble, threatening to lose the little strength I feel inside me, and let me fall into the dark hole where he had me imprisoned for over a decade.

Just when I feel everything was over, all my courage, healing journey, will power of move forward could be lost, he holds me.

Samuel arms embrace me, bringing me close to him, holding me on his chest, where I let my pain leave my body on a raw cry, burning my throat, inhaling his fresh scent, curling my arms at his back, fisting his shirt, giving him the opportunity to bring me back to where I was before I saw those flowers.

"What are you doing here?" I ask him, resting my forehead on his chest.

"I needed to see you."

My head falls back, my eyes locks with his, hearing

every thought that pass through his mind, scaring the hell out of me, understanding that he wasn't the knight in shiny armor trying to rescue me, I was the hope to his darkness.

"You left," I remind him.

"There is a said. *If you love something, let it go. If it comes back to your, it's yours forever. And, if it doesn't then it was never meant to be.*"

"You came to my house, not–"

"I saw you by the lake."

"How did you?–"

"Naima said you will move here soon. I just tried my luck."

His boldness brings me back to reality, this snaps of multi personalities that live inside one same body, and that is what makes him irresistible and dangerous.

"I brought you–"

I step further as he places the bouquet in between us.

"I don't want the flowers, good day Samuel."

"Ruby," he calls as I walk down the path to the front door, "please don't push me away," he begs.

Holding the round handle, I take a deep breath letting his plead sink in. Understanding he is out of his bloody mind.

"You left," I remind him, turning to face him, resting my back on the door.

"I miss you Ruby, I made a mistake," he says, stepping closer, "I shouldn't have come without telling you, and I shouldn't have left," his wide frame towers me, his forearms rest on the side of my head, and his body lowers until our nose touch, brushing the tip of each with the other, "tell me you didn't miss me."

"I didn't miss you," I lie, and the corner of his lip's trembles.

"Tell me you haven't thought about me."

"You are the last thing on my mind," his bottom lip disappears in between his teeth by the corner.

"Tell me your body doesn't remember me."

My body shakes at his words, he grins and I close my eyes for an instant, inhaling his sweet face oil scent, melting on the spot, "remember what?" I tease him.

"Let me touch," he begs in a whisper, my head falls back to the door, and his fingertips draw a line from my neck, across my jaw, down my collarbone, resting at the buttons of my top.

My breath turns heavy, my heart hits my ribcage so harsh that I feel it will come out, my eyes shut, and my hands hold the door, refusing to touch him and lose the little control I have over me.

"I missed you so badly. I couldn't live or exist without you around. Ruby, I don't know what you have done to me. The memories of those days together, that night in your arms, they haunt me day in and day out. I need you to take me out of this misery," he begs.

I listen, feel and let every word sink in. His guard has fallen, a new version of Samuel stands in front of me, a hidden and deeper version is talking over the tough man I met before.

My body response faster than my mind, my hands

caress his face, his chest, my arms curl around his waist and our body connect before I can understand what I am doing. Jumping on his arms holding his shoulders.

The door opens behind me, and Samuel takes us inside, pushing my back against the other side of the door, giving me once more the control over the first steps towards something I've been craving for all his days.

Holding his nape, I rest my lips over his, taking in the wave of cold and hot sensations that travels from my lips down to my center.

My small invitation is all what he needs to press his hips, making me cry when his arousal brushes mine.

"Tell me to slow down," he mumbles, biting my bottom lip.

"I need you Sam," I cry on a moan.

His head shakes, his hips rub harder against me and I giggle at his grunting noises.

"You owe me a week," he says, pulling his head back, pointing at my face, "I will give you what you need now, and you will give me–"

He pauses, looking around for an instant, his deep frown grows in between his brows and he looks back at me.

"Where are the kids?"

"At Sarah's until Monday morning," I say, making his expression change for a mischievous smirk and a dark spark in his eyes.

"I have you for the rest of the weekend?" I nod at his question, "What a lucky bastard I am," he mumbles, devouring my neck, lips, working on the buttons of my top, and the short, holding my waste as he pulls them down, curling my legs around him again, now that only his jeans are standing in between us.

My top falls next, giving him full access to my body, his fingertips draw fire lines across my skin until he caresses me from the front and the back at once, my arms and legs tighten around him, dropping my head back when his warm touch draws circles on my clit and throbbing center.

"Eyes on me Ruby," he demands, introducing slowly one, and then two fingers inside me.

My walls tighten around him, I force my eyes to open, my head to fall forward, and I lock my gaze on his. Jumping inside that space where only Samuel and I exist, where words aren't need, and no past, or future matters, just this moment when we give each other what we need without doubt or fears.

My chest raises, my breath breaks, and my core tightens.

"Let it go, baby," he whispers in my lips.

Devouring the moans that my body release as I reach my climax, melting over his palms, caressing his waves, his thick beard, working on the buttons of his shirt.

Brushing my palms across his pecs and shoulders, pushing the material away from him, resting half way, smiling at his refusal of letting me go, drawing circles on my clit and across my walls, waking up a new climax.

My hands work, what my body can't, his jeans, pushing him away so he can lose them up.

"You need to move," I moan as he shakes his head and

applies more pressure over my most sensitive spots.

"Ruby," he grunts.

"Move," I giggle, "stop been so–"

The ring tone of my mobile interrupts me, taking me back to reality, instinct works faster than anything else.

I push Samuel away, holding my shirt up to cover my body, and I rush to the living room. Sarah's name bright on the screen, I clear my voice and answer.

"Hello mama," Naima calls at the other end.

"Hello baby, how is everything with aunty Sarah?"

"We just helped her make homemade pizza, and cleaning the little mess, Aidan is seated in front of the oven controlling it doesn't burn and I just finish setting up the table."

"That sounds fantastic!"

"What are you doing?" she asks, I look over my shoulder, where Samuel stands in his boxers.

"I was unpacking, but you just remind me about dinner, thank you."

"I wish we could be there helping."

"This is boring baby, I wish I could be there eating pizza with you," I say, walking to the kitchen, grunting at the empty fridge.

"Can we help with our rooms?"

"Of course, I will just bring your boxes inside, so on Monday you just have to unpack."

"Thank you, mama."

"I love you baby, night night."

"We love you mama," they both say at unison, bringing

tears to my eyes.

I rest the mobile on the kitchen counter, taking a deep breath, dropping my head on Samuel chest, as he curls his around my waist.

"It's normal that you miss them."

"I've never done it before."

"I have a little idea," he whispers, resting his chin over my shoulder, I turn my head and wait to listen it, "I am dying to lose myself inside you," he points out, turning me and bringing me up in the counter. "The kids can't come back because of this," he points out at the room filled with boxes, I nod and he does too, "if I force myself to keep my hands busy with other things that your body. Gosh, I hate the idea already," he says, dropping his head, making me giggle. "We can put everything back in place faster, and they might be able to come sooner, yes! That takes away many hours I could spend slowly worshipping you, but it makes you happy, what makes me happy too."

"You will do that for me?"

"Angel, I have a lifetime for that, I am not going anywhere. But I can see how much you need them back."

Nibbling my bottom lip, curling my arms around his shoulders, I push him closer, embracing him, sharing a silence filled with grace and appreciation.

"Get dressed," he says defeated, "I swear to God this is killing me," he says letting me walk away so I can grab a clean maxi shirt and join him back in the kitchen.

"Nearly all the boxes are in the rooms where they belong," I explain.

"Dinner is on the way, tell me what goes up here, and you can do the bottom ones," he says pointing at the cupboards that cover the top of the kitchen.

This is one of my favorite rooms, not because I love cooking, but because has a rustic touch, vintage cupboards, a large, deep sink that reminds me the one at the farm, and a cute corner dining table with a bench around it on a U shape.

I point at the boxes that have all the materials or tools that I can keep away, as they aren't used frequently, and I fill up the bottom ones.

Smiling every time he kisses my cheek on the way for another box, or holds my waist to move me out of the way so he can put something in place.

Before dinner arrives, we are done with the kitchen. Samuel sets up the table and I walk to the door to collect what I now know its Chinese food.

The thought that this is the first meal at this house, the first takeaway, the first time Samuel is here, the first time I feel back at home, many overwhelming emotions that can't take a smile away from me.

"I can bring Rosita and some of the boys around tomorrow, they can help with the rest and maybe have the kids back by the afternoon."

"Have you seen all of this? I have cupboards to assemble, decoration to hang on, it's too many things to be done in what? twelve hours?"

"You understand I am standing in between what is a responsibility and what is a live or death need right?"

"Responsibility?" I ask, exercising Rosita request of helping Samuel communicating.

"Unpacking and getting Naima and Aidan back to you before sunrise, if possible," he explains, filling his mouth with some fried rice.

"Life or death need?"

"You, me, no clothes, the world outside doesn't exist kind of moment, multiple showers to wash away the sweat, you know what I mean," he says, sending a wink my way, that hits my cheeks on the right spot to make them burn up.

"Do I?" I tease him, dropping my fork and biting my nail, tilting my head, devouring every inch of his bare chest.

"You are so beautiful, it hurts," he confesses.

"You are so delicious it hurts," I confess, and he smiles.

"I'm full," he says pushing his plate forward.

"Are you?" I ask pointing out my bottom lip on an attempt of looking sad.

"Are you teasing me, angel?"

"Am I?" I ask.

I have no idea what has gone into me, with Samuel, alone, this close, I am a new version of myself, a confident woman, aware that the Adonis seating across the table is holding himself in place to avoid jumping over me as his prey.

Shuffling out of the bench, I walk to his side, grinning as he pushes the dishes away and the table until it hits my side of the bench, giving me enough space to straddle him.

"And I thought I could be your dessert," I tease him, sitting over his arousal, holding my breath, dropping back my head as a wave of pleasure travels across my body, "would you be my dessert," I whisper on his ear, rolling my hips over him, moaning and holding his shoulder tighter.

"I'm all your baby," he says, kissing my neck, grunting when I stop him from unbuttoning my shirt.

"You said you are full," I remind him, standing and kneeling in front of him, replacing his disapproval face, for pure desire.

"You don't hav–" he tries to say, pausing as I caress his thickness, holding the elastic of his tranks and releasing him.

Pushing my insecurities away, I let my body lead the way, my thumb spread a drop that rests at the tip, my knees to hold me at the perfect height, my tongue to taste his full length and my lips to kiss, suck and devour him with a hunger that I doubt will ever me satiated.

My own pants become wet with every mumble that comes out of his lips, with the way he caresses, fists and holds my head in place, encouraging me to take him deeper, harder, faster, until my own moans match his grunts, his hands hold my head in place, rotating his hips, my nails sink on his thigh and the other grips him tighter, welcoming his cum down my throat as I let my own one drip down my thighs.

Licking the remaining's of his release, I stand, letting Samuel pull my shirt over my head, brushing a fire trail down my body, and smirking as he reaches my wet pants, raising and eyebrow, pulling them down, I straddle him before he can make the next move.

"I don't have to wonder if you are ready for me," he says, grinning.

"I am always ready when you are around," I whisper in his ear, holding his throbbing dick and bringing into my wetness, my hips take control, lowering and circling around.

Samuel's hand holds my hip and my breast tight as I do so, both increasing the wave of pleasure traveling in between us.

Holding the back of the bench for support, I ride him in need, reaching the full climax that I build up when he was filling my mouth to my throat.

"I want you from behind," he begs, holding me up and turning me around.

Coldness hits my bare skin, my muscle tense and the grunt mixed with a painful cry that comes from behind me brings me back to reality.

I know what Samuel is facing, my darkness, my past, my wounds, the memory of the night I die and came back to life.

"Please don't say anything," I beg.

"Ruby–"

"Samuel, please," I say, holding my shirt from the floor and walking away.

"Wait!" he exclaims rushing behind me, catch me in the family room. "Ruby, talk to me."

the shirt hides my skin, but doesn't prevent his gaze from burning me through the material.

"Angel, I beg you," my head shakes, "I need to know!"

he says anxiously in between teeth, "I deserve to know!"

I turn, facing him, ready to confront the fact that my past, my live that doesn't involve him is none of his business and I have no obligation on explaining anything. After all, we are just feeding each other's needs.

Chapter Eleven

Samuel

The mix of emotions travelling across her angelical face makes me back up.

I didn't need to be a genius to know Ruby holds a heavy past over her shoulders. I knew that since that afternoon after the park.

I saw it in the children's behaviour, in her silence, and I found a lot more in all the days I spent away from her.

I know she is married. I know about the horrible things he did to them, and I know where those scars that cross side to side on her back down until her thighs come from.

Knowing and seen it is a completely different world.

"I apologies," I say, stepping closer, offering my hands that I need her to take, so I know she will have me, and never let me go.

"I think is time for you to go."

"No!" I exclaim, "Ruby, please, don't push me away."

"This is a–"

"It is not! I shouldn't have reacted like that, I apologies," I say, holding my hand on my chest, "we don't have to talk about it, just don't push me away."

"I want to be on my own," she says.

"Refuse me, but not the help I am offering for the kids."

"Samuel–"

"Get change, I will call the boys," I say, walking back to the table, pulling up my tranks and collecting my clothes at the foyer as she heads upstairs, as I hear the shower running, I head to *Little Castle*, taking everyone with me with no explanation. "Remember," I call Rosita, Matteo, Jackson, Logan and Calvin, "she doesn't know I live there," I point to the side, "or that Stella is my sister."

"*Mi hijito*–"

"One thing at the time Rosita, she needs these boxes done before the sun is out, then we can open the Pandora box," I point out, leading everyone inside the cottage.

Calvin gets rid of all the empty boxes, Jackson moves two or three around following what says on the outside, Matteo helps build up furniture and Rosita and I head upstairs.

She helps fill up a cupboard in the hallway, while I wait for Ruby to exit her ensuite bathroom.

"You startle me," she says, walking around me on a little towel, dripping water over the carpet.

"Everyone is downstairs," I say, raising my shoulders at her cute frown, "done before sunrise, remember?" I ask.

"You always get what you want the way you want right?"

she asks, taking some knickers and a summer dress out of her luggage.

"If that was true, you will be covered in our mixed sweat, out of breath, moaning my name," I explain, "but here I am, watching how you dress up, frown and refuse me."

"I didn't refuse you, it was all the way around."

"What? I am not sure we are talking about the same."

"I won't answer your noisy questions, I won't feed your ego and your need of knowing everything without reciprocating."

"I am not nosy."

"This," she points in between us, "is pure neediness and lust. I do appreciate the help and support. But I am not your charity work of the month, I am not yours to be fixed," she says walking to the door, "in fact, if there is someone who has to be fixed, that will be you," she points out, walking away, leaving me confused and irritated.

Ruby is the first woman refusing me, pushing me so easily away, clearly speaking up her thoughts.

I can't say is the first one honest or sassy, I had Stella and Helena for that. They are regular women in my life. Ruby is someone I want and need in my life. Someone I feel the urge to protect and please so she won't go anywhere else.

Storming out of the bedroom, I head downstairs looking for her, "Mi hijito deep breaths," Rosita reminds me as I walk passed by. I shake my head, pushing my demons aside, reminding me that 'A nobody talks to me that way,' and 'B I love her'.

I pause halfway on the stairs, holding the rail before I fall on the step. My head spins, my chest contracts, and the air leaves my lung.

I love Ruby. What the bloody fuck?!

My stupid mind is trying to calm my anger, that is all, I can't love her, there is no way I have those feelings towards her. *We just met. I am damaged. She refuses me. She is married to someone else.* The overflow of reminders why this is madness makes the room spins around.

I desire her, that is absolutely clear, the thought of her turns me on, I like her, the sweetness that she spreads with her cooking, when she talks, or by simple existing, I admire her, for the courage of fighting back, and not giving up.

"You love her," Rosita says from the top of the stairs.

I turn to face her, tears flood my eyes, I shut them and shake my head. *That is impossible.*

"Have you ever heard about *the spell of the turquoise*?" she asks, stepping down and meeting me a step above me, I shake my head. "Many years ago, your grandfather told me a tale. That your grandmother put a spell on him by a simple look," softly giggling, she pauses, "it sounds ridiculous, but I've seen it with my own eyes." I frown at the story she is trying to say, "the day Sebastian lay eyes on Sammy, the world pause, nothing existed but them, just like the movies," she continues, brushing my waves back, "I've seen it with Stella, and now with you."

"That is ridiculous," I say, standing and rushing down, pausing at the foot of the stairs, "if that was true, she wouldn't refuse me."

"Have you considered that she's scared and confused as you are?"

"I need some fresh air."

Stepping outside, heading to the main road, brushing my hands on my waves and taking a well needed deep breath.

Chuckling at my absurd perception of life before Ruby.

Everything magnified and covered in this thick, suffocating darkness.

I couldn't hear, see, or care for others.

Nothing mattered but keep me alive, scared of the destiny that awaits for me on the other side.

Fucking burning in hell that is for sure.

I didn't invite her in, but I didn't pull her in either.

Circumstances have put her inside my world, and now is all a tangled mess. I try to help her that day, and as much as I was intrigued, I knew it was a once in a lifetime encounter, one that will remain with me. But I didn't know she was the business I found for Stella, neither that she will be at the park and Scott will choose to play with Naima and Aidan. Or that we will let those little monsters turn our lives upside down.

I am responsible for not knowing how to keep my eyes away from her, my hands hidden in my pocket, my lips sealed, and my dick on my pants.

That is something I won't deny.

Anyone with two eyes will fall to their knees for her, is not just how fucking beautiful she is. Is her personality, that inside that scared shell, is gorgeous, unique, and I refuse to let it go.

"I thought you left," Ruby's voice brings me back.

"Just taking some fresh air," I say, turning, keeping my burning gaze low, afraid if I look at her, I might lose the little strength left in me.

"Thank you–"

"I am sorry–"

We say at unison, her giggle makes me look straight at her, nibbling my bottom lip to hold the silly tears that are burning my eyes.

"I am not good with people."

"I can see that," she assures, letting me step closer, hold her hand, kiss her palm and rest it on my cheek.

My eyes close, letting her caress bring me back to the space where just us matter.

"I am comfortable in my darkness, it helps me," I say, holding her waist and bringing her closer, "but your just keep pulling me out."

"I can't fall on your darkness Sam, I need you to understand that."

"I love when you call me that," I whisper resting my cheek over hers.

"What? Sam?" she whispers back, I grunt and she giggles.

"I am sorry, angel."

"You have said that a lot lately."

"And understand this young lady," I say pulling back, resting my index on her cute nose, "I don't apologies."

"What a privilege woman I am," she says, on that sassy tone that makes me want to take her in and finished what we couldn't before.

"Let's get in, I want them out of here soon, you owe me something," I mumble on her neck, smirking at the low moan that comes with her exhalation, followed by a louder one when I press my arousal into her low tummy.

"Not happening," she teases, stepping back, holding the distance, "I am busy."

"I will keep you busier once they left," I tease her back.

"Sam," she sings as I step forward, grinning as she steps back.

"Yes, angel?"

"I am in control," she reminds.

"You were," she frowns and I lick my bottom lip like a hungry beast, "we are not starting, we are finishing."

Her blue oceans roll and a tired sigh leave her delicious lips.

"Dissatisfied, angel?" I ask, shaking my head to control the urge of holding her and take her here and now, when her shoulders raise, her lips pout and she turns away rush behind her, holding the front door, pressing her front against it and mine over hers, "I will make you forget your name, and where you are. You are going to scream my name more times that you will get to call it when I am not, over, under, beside, or inside you."

"Sam," she moans on a whisper.

"Yes. Angel," I whisper, pushing her hair aside, blowing a trace behind her ear and pressing my throbbing dick

199

against her round arse.

"We have to stop," she begs, pressing herself against me, holding the door, dropping her head forward.

"Why, Angel? Tell me why? I might do it," I say, brushing her shoulder, holding her neck and placing her head over my shoulder so I have a better access over her expose neck.

"We are in the street–"

"We are at your front door."

"There are people inside—"

"They won't come out."

"Sam," she moans, when my fingertips travel from her knee, under her dress until I reach her soft and soaking panties.

"You are so fucking wet," I grunt on her neck, biting her skin, covering her mouth as I caress her clit over the material, "do you trust me, Ruby?" I ask, pulling my hand away.

Missing her closeness, stepping back and waiting for an answer. I am breathless, blind with lust, and determine to show this woman all what she can have only if she asks nicely.

Her chest raises rapidly, her cheeks blushed, matching her cherry lips moist and parted. I nibble my bottom lip, remembering how good did it look and feel filling her mouth, having those full lips around me.

Times slows down, her lust turns into something else, something I can't put my finger on, my body becomes cold, and I found myself walking past her and inside the house.

"Sam," she calls from the door, "please–"

I turn back to her, embracing her, kissing the top of her head and brushing my palms on her back.

"I am not going anywhere, we have a lifetime for that," I assure, cupping her angelical face in my palms, kissing her nose and walking to the family room.

The couch is finished, there is a walled covered with a large bookshelf that Logan is filling up.

Matteo is assembling a tower of boxes, that by the box resting next to it, tells me will be the kids toys space.

Standing there, seen how this little cottage becomes a home to Ruby and the kids makes me wonder if this is what Stella meant when she paid that fortune for Scott's party. If that was her little contribution to make sure they had a life they deserve and will have been nearly impossible to achieve on their own.

"Calv and Jacks are up with the beds," Matteo mumbles, drilling the cupboard to the wall, "and those belong upstairs," he says, pointing at a box filled with soft toys.

"Did Ruby tell you that?"

"No, she listened to our suggestion on how to organise the rooms. Kids need some toys upstairs too, and she needs a room she can have people over too," he explains, "are you going to move, or go back home?" he asks exasperated of seen me doing nothing.

"Mr Black and Decker, *vaffanculo*."

"*Succhiami il cazzo, fratello*."

"Is that Italian?" asks Ruby, walking in.

"Matteo is from Rome," Logan says, closing down an

empty box and opening another filled with more books.

"And where are you from?"

"Logan, my name is Logan, and I am Scottish like this bastard," he says pointing at me with his chin.

"You don't sound Scottish," she says, brushing my arm and giving me a bright smile, "neither do I Texan, right? I guess it goes away with the years of been far from home," she says, closing her eye and pushing aside what I want to think was a good old memory.

"Enough chitchat," I cut everyone off, aware that if I give them five more minutes around her, they will spell the entire tea about my family tree, she is not ready for that one yet.

"I will check on Rosita," she says, walking upstairs.

I wait until I hear the cracking of the wood floor in the corridor.

"You can't hide who you are forever," Matteo warns me.

"I am not hiding shit," I assure, opening a box with some blankets and pillows.

"Did you tell her who your sister it? Where do you live? Who your family is? Why there is no record of your past anywhere?"

"What are you fucking trying to prove?" I ask, dropping the box and confronting him.

"You can't lie to her," he says, stepping closer.

"Is that a threat?"

"You better tell her before she finds out."

"Or what?"

"She will walk away, and for what I heard and see, she is

not the type of women that will rush back to you, or take you back that easily."

"Everything is under control."

"Stop manipulating her with your fucking dick and used your brain. I made sure many years ago you didn't sink it in alcohol or fired it with drugs."

"Do you need a prize?"

"For saving your fucking life? No thank you. I need you to respect the life I help you to have today."

"I am not doing anything wrong."

"Tell me you have managed to share more than two sentences without laying a hand over her."

"What is your fucking point?"

"Appreciate what you have around, she is not you to keep–"

"I will never let her come back to him."

"That is not your choice," he says, marking every word like fire on my skin.

My nostrils flare, my fist grows on my side, my feet ground on the wood floor, and my muscle tense as rage builds in my system.

Forcing myself to turn, I walk out of the house, head to *Little Castle,* heading to my bedroom for some running shorts and trainers, burning the day down at the gym.

My muscles ache, my skin turns burgundy, a pool of sweat rests under me, and I can't catch my breath. But my head is clear.

Washing everything off, changing into joggers and a T-shirt, I head downstairs, nodding to Calvin hiding behind his laptop by the kitchen counter.

"All done at Ruby's?"

"I left Jackson fixing the lights and Rosita helping with wall stickers, for the rest it's all done. Matteo left to dump the boxes and told me to inform you he is taking a break."

"He is fucking kidding me, right? We are heading to London tomorrow."

"He is not coming boss."

"Bastard!"

Collecting what I need from the freezer I head to Ruby's, crossing path with Rosita and Jackson, who gives a questioning look to what I'm holding in my hand. Smirking I head to the front door, knocking softly, hiding my little surprise.

"Hello," she greets me with a surprise smile.

"Did you miss me?" I ask, biting my bottom lip.

"I was busy, so I barely thought about–" I step forward, throwing her over my shoulder, grinning at her little squeak from the fast move, and I head upstairs.

"Tell me those bastards finished the bed."

"They did," she giggles, sneaking her hand under my joggers, "put me down," she exclaims, squeezing my arse.

"You are not in control, angel."

"Sam!" she cries, as I drop her over the mattress.

A mixture of excitement and that thing I've seen before travel across her face.

"Too harsh?" I ask, reminding my animal instinct of her backstory.

"I am fine," she confirms breathless.

"Dress off, or I will ripe it," I order.

Her cute frown lands in between her brows and I shake my head.

"It's fine, I promise, and no way! it's one of my favourites."

"My favourite one is you absolutely naked, and you have not given that to me in many hours, so? young lady, what will it be?" I tease raising an eyebrow.

"I adore submissive Samuel," she says, kneeling in the bed, moving closer to me, standing on the edge, "but dominant Samuel is far hotter."

"You haven't seen anything yet, angel."

"Will you show me?" she asks, dropping her dress on the floor, resting her hands under my T-shirt, caressing my abdomen.

"Do you trust me, Ruby?" I ask once more.

Her eyes locks with mine, her head tilts, her lips hide under her teeth and her nails awakens my entire body as she runs them across my torso.

"I want to," she assures.

I nod, not fully content with her answer, not giving up that at least we are one step ahead that we were hours ago by the front door.

"I will earn your trust, and for that I need to know where the limit lays."

"I don't know," she assures, letting her innocence lay in front of us.

"What about this, you pick a word," I explain, bending closer to her lips, "any word," I whisper, moving to her ear, "you let me show you my darkness," I say slowly over her neck, "you can stop me at any time by saying that word."

"A word to stop you," she repeats, I nod on her neck, kissing a trail up to her ear, "what about if I want more?" she asks, my teeth bite the spot right behind her ear, growling in hunger, her giggles light up the fire inside me, "*sunflower*, as my stop word. *Cookie*, as my need of more word."

If wasn't clear before it is now, she hates those type of flowers, and I stupidly shown up with a full bouquet. Now that doesn't matter.

"I love the selection," I point out, moving back, towering over her, "sweet as you, something I'm looking forward for you to plead for really soon."

"What is that?" she asks at my little surprise.

"A little thought I had while I burn my horniness at the gym, but since the flavour is your safe word, I guess it lost the spike."

"You want to eat cookie dough ice-cream? In bed?" she asks, confused.

"Angel your innocence turns me on so much," I assure, popping the lit off, scooping some with two fingers and place it over her lips, "open," I order, "do not swallow," I warn her, resting her tongue out, holding the ice-cream while I take my clothes off.

It wasn't on my fantasy, but I don't stop her, when she moves closer, dropping the cold chunk over my hard cock and suck it with hunger, building a wave of pleasure that takes me out of my body.

"Bloody hell, Ruby," I mumble, brushing her cheek,

locking my gaze on hers, placing another chunk as she pulls back, and enjoying how it disappears under her top lip.

As her mumble moans become louder, her body rotates with her mouth, I reach the back of her throat and she place my hand over her head, fisting her hair and pushing her closer, I let go, filling her mouth with another mixture of ice-cream and cum.

Observing how she sucks every drop left inside me, cleaning the corner of her plump cherry lips, and giving me a look of pure lust.

"That was *Spectacular*," she teases, resting back over the mattress, spreading her legs, running her hands across her body, reaching her breast and massaging them, closing her eyes, and moaning as she gives herself some self-pleasure.

Tilting the jar, I let the melting liquid fall over her tummy, her eyes open wide and she cries in surprise.

"Do, not, fucking, move," I warn her, a small nod of approval makes me fall over her, spreading the coldness over her warm pale skin, as I suck and bite every corner of her torso without touching her breasts that she keeps massaging.

Licking her skin until I meet her knickers, I ripe them apart, exposing her pink sensitive skin, ginning at my next move.

Resting my forehead on hers, I order her, "touch yourself for me," that fucking unknown expression cross her eyes, "you never done if before," I say, burning as she sweetly bite her lip and shakes her head, "I will guide you," I assure, falling to the side, holding her right hand, slowly brushing her skin until we reach the small pubic section, encouraging two fingers to her wet pussy and her thumb to rest over her swollen clit, drawing circles, and applying the pleasure she needs by a simple look on her gorgeous face. "Just keep it like that, angel."

I climb on top of her, caressing what I have covered in cream before, holding my groin over the back of her hand, thrusting her fingers inside her, "feel how your body welcomes you," I whisper in her lips, pulling back and slowly pushing her fingers in again, "let your body adjust."

I keep moving slow until I feel the pressure of her hand, in need for more, making me push her hand deeper and faster inside her.

"Build it up," I say, introducing my fingers on her mouth, matching the speed of her hand, "there is one place I haven't claim yet," I murmur in her ear, fucking her mouth deeper, and pushing my hips forward, rotating them, applying extra pressure on her hold, "just welcome me," I explain, bringing my wet fingers to her tight soft arse, drawing a circle, building a stronger friction over the fingers that are inside her pussy and moaning on my lips. "I told you to welcome me," I warn her.

Pushing my hips forward her body relaxes, letting me work her on, massaging her walls, enjoying how she melts under the pleasure that we are both giving to her, holding the tip of my throbbing cock on her tight hold, I enter her slowly, encouraging her hand to work her pussy and clit faster, inviting me until I reach the deepest.

"Sam," she moans, dropping her head back.

"Take your time, angel," I still letting her adjust, roll her hips, and tease herself closer to her climax, "that's it," I mumble, licking my bottom lip, matching the rhythm of her hips, thrusting harder as he walls pull me deeper, holding my hands over hers to match my own pace, teasing her nipples, dropping my head back and growling as we both reach the release, I was needed of for way too many days.

Gently pulling her hand and my hard cock out of her, I fall over her, kissing her flushed skin, letting the small strokes of her hands bring me to a sleepy stage, where I finally find my peace.

Coldness kicks me out of my dream world, drowsy, my eyes can't open, my body trembles, it's so fucking cold, my hand searches for the cover, that are over me already.

I know what is not with me–Ruby.

I jump too fast out of the spot that I fall on the floor, I look around, I need to find her, before my panic grows, I smile, because I can smell her.

The wildflowers, the fresh coffee and this morning, cookies.

Memories of the past few hours awaken the hungry beast inside me, searching for my prey.

I walk downstairs, slowly into the kitchen, observing how her hips move to the sound of loud music, under an oversize t-shirt, her hair is wet, pulled up on a sexy bun, barefoot.

I bite my lip, my palm adjusts my arousal and I plan my

approach, so I can eat her alive.

"Good morning, Sam," she says in between mumbles as the song ends.

"Morning, angel," I whisper walking closer.

"One or two shots?" she asks holding a mug on her hands.

"Two shots please."

I stop right behind her, observing how she kneads some dough, how her body mould it and make it be a part of her.

"Is this for the birthday?" I ask, moving closer, resting my chin on her shoulder, my arms frame her.

Tell her is Scott's

My mind reminds me, I shake it away and draw kisses on her shoulder.

"Nope," she says, cheerfully, "they are for the stores. Señor Miguel will collect them this afternoon."

"Should I be worry about Señor Miguel?" I ask, tickling her. I move up when she turn, kissing my cheek and placing a biscuit on my mouth, winking at the playful feeding me treatment.

The biscuit melts on my tongue, I haven't taste anything this good in ages.

Her eyes light up as I moan taking another bite, "do you like it?" I nod and she smiles widely, "Rosita bought you a large box of them."

"This is *Spectacular*," I mumble, finishing the remain of it, sucking her fingers to clear away the chocolate that was there, and prove the point of how turn on I am.

I move closer, towering her, holding her up and hiding

on her neck.

"You didn't answer," I remind her, not letting of a conversation that involves other man.

"He is like a father to me, an abuelo to the kids, Ruby Sweet Dreams wouldn't exist without his help," she explains, rolling the dough, pushing me back with her perky bump and heading to the fridge, "he loans me the money to get the materials, I was scared how quick I could return that money, now feel ages ago."

"It's normal to be scared of success.."

"You don't seem scared of anything."

"I have learned to hide my emotions from the world."

"Is that what you are doing with me?"

"No of course–" I pause, cut off by the ring of her mobile.

"Sorry, it's Sarah," she says, picking up, "Hey, yes, everything is ready, are you on the way?" she pauses, "walking by the park, perfect."

I stand there, on tranks, my arms folded under my chest, waiting for an explanation as she rushes away, returning with my clothes and a dress for herself.

"I am so sorry, but you have to leave. Come back, please, later on if you prefer with Scott, I don't know. But they are on the way, and I can't have them find you here, like this," she explains pointing at my body, I look down and tilt my head. "Sam, please, we have to talk this through, I am not sure of anything, it's not time–"

"I am not your one-night-stand, I am not the man feeding your needs, I am not the person you burn your emotions on."

"See, you are taking all of this wrong," she says anxiously, "please go before they see you."

"I am wounded and offended."

"Go, shower, change and come back!" she laughs, pushing me while I resist leaving.

I can see the kids in the other side of the main road when I walk out, but there is something she doesn't know, we share the same land, hiding by the back of the cottage I enter *Little Castle* by the back door, the one that hold the boys' rooms.

"Boss," Calvin greets me, waking out of his room, "caught in the moment?"

"Why everyone seems to be spying on me?"

"She told us the kids will be there for breakfast, maybe she forgot to let you know," he says, walking ahead of me, "I have work to do for the Gala," he yells, heading out of the front door.

Rosita is in the kitchen having some coffee as I walk in.

"Buen día."

"Buen día, how is everything?"

"Matteo is MIA, or that is how Jackson describe it. He is at Stella's helping with something to do with cameras. Helena is at the edge of a panic attack because you are ignoring your mobile, and someone at the office needs you back in London for a meeting."

"Welcome home Samuel, I am good, thank you for asking, how are you?" I mumble, saying what I wish she would have told me.

"Stop been a malcriado, and get ready, I have to be in London in an hour."

"I am not going, Ruby is waiting for me."

"Samuel, SaStel needs you. You made a promise to Ste–"

"Take that spoil brat to London and make her take care of the office and those idiots, I have better things to do."

"She won't be here forever, your legacy will."

"You know what? Why don't you find my *fratello*, and stay with him wherever he is hiding, so you all stop telling me how to live my life."

"Stella was right."

Without letting her say another word, I head upstairs, consider the trip to London. Not for work, the last meeting was a disaster. They hated the idea of using Ruby on the cover, Helena offered and alternative, I took it far too personal and now we are in no communication terms.

I don't want her in there just because she is gorgeous and I am crazy about her, I believe she deserves it. The others have a bunch of workers by their side, or a tone of growth on social media. She has herself, and this small community for support.

After all the changes, a few days in the city will be fun for the kids, they aren't at school yet, so they can enjoy the warm weather on a not so crowded stage.

And I get to spend more time with Ruby, proving to myself if I am blindly obsessed with her, needy for her touch or falling for her like a school boy.

Eager to know what they think about it, I change and

head back to the cottage, crossing path with Thomas's boys, who are finishing the last touch ups. That should be done by the end of the week.

Once more the reason why a little trip to the city will be great, I will let the boys work on an empty house, and have something to surprise Ruby with when we come back.

Am I ready to tell her all the truth?

Pushing that thought aside as I reach her front door, I take a deep breath and knock, welcome by a smiley Ruby, and two cheerful little humans, talking at the same time, sharing all the new things the house has.

"Please come in," she says.

Letting the kids lead the way, I turn, steal a kiss from her and head to the family room, where Naima invites me to seat on the new couch while she explains all what the boys build for them and all the new things Ruby got them.

"I supposed say you love the new house is an understatement."

"What is under... I don't know how to say that word," Naima says, making me smile at her innocence.

"I mean, you more than love the house?" I ask.

"This is *our* house, you know that?" she asks, remarking the word that means everything to her.

"Your mama told me."

"She said you helped with all of this?" she asks, pointing around.

"I have some little helpers."

"The man that visited mama the other day?" she asks. I look at Ruby, who reminds me of Rosita and Matteo visit.

214

Keeping to myself the fact that I specifically told them not to get involved, they did, just to find out who Ruby really was. Stella's party organiser.

But neither did I ask Calvin to run a full check on her past, he could just find out about the marriage, and some GPs informs of home visits for some domestic injuries.

Not enough to make me change my mind of the things I will do to that bastard if I had him in front of me.

Lost on my thoughts, I nod when Ruby explains to them why there is people working for me and the type of work they do.

"Can we have a bodyguard mama?" Naima asks, Ruby turns pale, avoiding to look at me.

"I heard they build up something in the garden, have you seen that already?" I ask, standing, breaking the conversation and taking they attention into something kids should worry about.

Ruby stands there, I can hear her mind screaming at miles per hour.

"Is everything alright?" I ask, holding her hands on mine.

"Sorry, they can sometimes say thinks without thinking."

"I can let you borrow one of them if you want to, they are not as fun as they look, but kids can torture it for a while, I wonder who will look better with all that make up and accessories you got for Naima."

"Do you need them?"

I let her question sink in, aware this is not just coming

from a curious thought, but the idea of me needed to be as protected as she needed to be.

"They are like my brothers, and had helped me throughout the years."

"You are not answering my question," she says.

"I come from a powerful family, with power comes danger."

"Have you ever been in danger?"

"Without knowing it, since the day I born," her brows raise, her expression turns cold.

"My priority is to keep the kids safe–"

"They will never be safer than when I am around."

"That comes from the man that walks around the world with tough looking guys."

"It's all a façe."

"An intimidating façe."

"What are you trying to say?"

"That I am not sure we will be safe inside your world."

"Don't be inside my world, I don't want you there–"

"And why is that?"

"Because my life is a shit show, your is special, angel, please stop this nonsense."

"Samuel–"

"Didn't you have orders to finish?" I ask, cutting the conversation that I am well aware where it will end, "may I play with them, and once you finish, I have a little surprise."

"I don't like surprises–"

"You will love this one," I assure, kissing her cheek.

Interrupted by the ringtone of her mobile, the room

turns cold, Ruby turns pale, her eyes open wide, and I see her trembling as I walk away, regretting been thankful a call interrupt her pushing me away once more.

I don't miss either how she shakes her head and snaps out of that trance, all while she thinks I have walked away, and in the contrary I am hidden by the door frame.

Giving her some time and space, I join the kids in the garden, listening to Aidan endless talk about his new trucks and dinosaurs, reminding me a lot about Scott, and his passion for them too. And sitting with Naima in a bench that make me look like a giant, where she is colouring a new book.

"Do you want to paint?" she asks. I nod and she smiles brightly. "Thank you, Samuel," she whispers, handing me some paper and crayons.

I observe the way her body tense, the shake on her little hands, the nibble on her bottom lip. This poor child has been through so much in such a brief life.

I didn't have an easy life myself, but I was a teenager when things went south, I was eighteen when I run away and ruin my life.

"You are more than welcome," I say.

Looking over her shoulder, through the back door that she has kept open so I can now just see her floating around the kitchen, but moving at the rhythm of the music she is playing. I want to stand, curl my arms around her and feel the way her hips turn as she dances, devouring her neck that is exposed by her sexy bun, and intoxicating myself with her sweet scent.

I am in big trouble.

Conscious of how good I am hiding emotions, pushing people away and lock myself inside my own darkness.

I thought I could do the same with her, take it slow, letting her lead the way, and think things before acting.

So far, I have done the absolute opposite, I am blindly obsessed, the idea of her pushing me away takes the air out of my lungs and hurt as daggers.

"Mama won't tell me. I think there's something going on," she says, looking over her shoulder at Aidan and behind me to Ruby. "There's something going on with Advik."

I frown at that name, have heard it before, and by the way her little body shakes, reminding me of Calvin's digging—he is the bastard that harmed them.

"I will protect you," I move my hand forward slowly, resting it palm up and waiting for her to accept it.

If I learn something on the with them, is that things have to be done on their terms.

Her little, trembling hand rests over mine. "No matter what, you are safe with me," I assure, gazing up when Ruby's ringtone stops the music she was listening to, this time she picks up.

Her frame tense, and shakes, her skin is nearly transparent, her hands search for the counter, but her legs are faster than her arms, her body bend, and I rush on her direction, jumping to hold her just before her head hits the floor.

There is a voice coming from the other side of the line,

holding the mobile to my ear I listen.

"I'm so sorry, Ruby. His safety became a priority over yours–" the woman at the other end says.

There is no need of listen anything else she has to say. I hung up, place the mobile on the counter, hold Ruby in my arms and take her to the bedroom, resting her head on the pillows and seating by her side.

"Naima, be a big girl and get a glass of water, please," I say to a petrified child, "everything is okay, big boy," I say holding Aidan on my arms as he jumps on my lap, hiding his little face on my neck and sobbing in fear.

I walk to the bathroom, grab a face towel with so water and return to the bedroom, brushing her forehead with it brings her back to us.

"Baby, it's me," I whisper.

Her gorgeous blue oceans are now red as fire, her deep frown pops in between her brows, and with a forced smile, I bring her to sit, her arms hold my shoulders, I look at her, holding the closeness as I inhale her fear.

"I'm sorry, I don't know what happened–"

Not tolerating a lie more, I cut her off. "I heard the conversation–" I pause as Naima walks in with a shaky glass of water in her hands

"Mama are you okay?"

"Yes, sorry baby, I haven't eaten very well all weekend," she lies, "I didn't mean to scare you."

"Your mom has worked really hard lately, what do you way if we take a little break, just a few days in the city?" I ask Naima, feeling how Ruby body tenses, not appreciating my curve ball. But after all she is the one holding secrets, hiding things, pushing me away when they need me closer the most.

"Are we going to London?" Naima asks Ruby, turning back to me. Aidan pulls his head out of my neck, his little face red and wet.

Brushing my thumb under his eyes, I caress his cheeks, "would you like to go to the zoo or the aquarium?" I ask him.

"Animals?" he asks.

"Better! We can go to the science museum. They have dinosaurs, cars, airplanes."

"Mama, plezzzeee," he begs.

I turn to Ruby, her gaze drills a hole in my centre, and I smile triumphant, I have the kids on my side, they don't want to stay here, where she will hide, live in fear and kick me out the second Aidan jumps out of my arms.

In London we will be in my territory, there will be no escape for her, and neither for me.

She will have to answer my questions, and I will show her my deepest secrets, under my terms, on the correct circumstances.

"We can't go for a day, I can't take a day off."

"Kids, why don't you go and prepare some clothes, I have to talk to you mama," I encourage them to walk way, closing the door ajar, turning to a woman that can manage to made me madly angry and in love with her at once.

"We are not going to London," she assures, stepping out of bed and walking closer, "You give orders to all those men, I get it, they feed your big ego. I do not follow what you say."

"Why can't you just appreciate what I offer you?"

"I don't need you."

I step back, running my fingers in frustration over my waves.

"I don't need you either," I point out. "I want you, I want the kids, I want what I feel when I am around you, I want to be the man you let me be."

"Samuel, we can't do this–"

"Why? What is wrong with what we are doing?"

"You heard the conversation."

"You don't get it, do you?" I say stepping closer, towering her, desperately wanting to bring her to my arms before I say what I want to say, afraid she will push me away, reject me, chose him, or her loneliness and pain over me. "Ruby, I–"

"Mama," Naima knocks the door, I step back and open for her, "can we spend few days in London, please," she begs.

"Samuel is busy, baby, we can't–"

"Samuel is the boss, Samuel is in break for you three," I correct Ruby.

"Can you?" Naima asks.

"Are you sure?" Ruby asks.

I grin at the amusement of one and the surprise of the other, "now get we choose, the apartment in Belgravia, or a countryside house in Surrey?" I ask, receiving confusing frowns, "forget it, you are making me feel weird now."

"Have you packed?" Ruby asks Naima, she shakes her

head, rushing to my side, curling her arms on my waste, hugging me and running away.

"That," Ruby says, pointing at the door, "is why this," now she is pointing in between us, "should be happening."

"I am not talking about this, pack, we are leaving," I say standing closer to her gorgeous face, "I have some calls to do."

Chapter Twelve

Ruby

Fifteen years ago, Shepperton, TX

The sun is down when I walk back to make sure I fed all the animals, and they are warm and secure. I don't want to run behind cows in the darkness ever again in my life.

Coming to a halt when I hear a noise in the stables, where I was minutes ago, where Moon and Dalia were down for the night. I can hear Dad back in the house, at the same time that a movement makes a clacking noise inside.

I grab a rake and walk towards the noise that has now increases. It might be a cat, a rat, a damn snake. *Oh gosh, why me?!*

It's not an animal, it's *toilet boy*.

Wasn't I clear in the morning, was my warning not enough for him do understand he wasn't welcome.

I did what I have to do last night, I helped, now was his time to leave, but he didn't.

"Upsy," he says, grinning.

"What is wrong with you?" I mutter in between teeth, "I could have been my father. You would smile like that, you will be underground by now!"

"But the universe sends you." That smile again. "Right?" he whispers, getting closer.

"Stop right there!" I exclaim, raising the rake, and God help me, I will use it on this stupid boy.

The smile doesn't faint when his arms raise where I can see them, and he walks closer. "I just need a place to stay until I find a way out."

"I get it, but this farm can't be that place."

"Will you let me out there, like this?" he points at his dirt clothes.

"You should have been more careful with your belongings."

"Where is the Texan kindness everyone talks about?"

"This is Shepperton. This is my farm."

"I get it, appreciate it," he says, turning and walking to the door.

"Where are you going?"

"Do you care?"

"You can't walk out just like that−"

"Are you offering a better option?"

"The local bus leaves tomorrow morning to the city, you can use that," I say, pointing at his puppy eyes, "to get a lift, or the Sheriff will help you."

"You rather get me arrested?"

"Are you making me choose between my father and

you?" I ask sarcastically.

"Can I stay for the night? I will catch that bus in the morning."

"The next one leaves in a week, so you better not miss it."

"Can I ask one more thing?" my brow raise, tired of helping him, "I would like to clean up, change. I don't think they will let someone smelling as cow travel all the way to the city."

"Is this what backpacking involves? Everyone giving you everything for free?"

"Isn't it call kindness?"

"Not when you are forcing the person to do so."

"Me, asking for a backet of water and some clothes is forcing you?" he asks, stepping closer.

With a courage coming out of nowhere I step closer, squaring my shoulders, ready to put this boy in the place he belongs.

"You, giving me no choice but to let you sleep here one more night is forcing me."

"I thought a sweet girl like you," he says, stepping closer, "will care more for others."

"You are confusing kindness with stupidity."

"I was—"

"You will get water and clothes," I say, holding a backet in the wall and handing it to him.

Without another word I walk inside the house. Dad is sleeping on the armchair, the TV is turned on with some short of sport channel, and mama is in her bedroom getting ready to bed, I head to the bathroom, collecting some soap, toothbrush and paste, a large towel from the cupboard in the corridor and working on how will I get clothes.

Dad heavy snore reminds me he won't move unless mama help him out, and that will give me five minutes in their bedroom.

"Mama," I call, resting my face on the door frame, "papa will wake up the whole town if you don't move him," I say, giggling as a louder snore leaving his wide chest.

"I know, give me two minutes," I nod, heading to the kitchen, grabbing some water, looking over my shoulders for the moment she steps out. I rush, taking some old jeans and shirt from the back of the cupboard where I know are the things that can't fit him anymore or that are too old.

Hiding everything in my bedroom, I head to the shower, washing off the day, covering myself with a summer dress and letting the late summer night fresh air dry my hair as I walk back to the stables with all the gathers.

Toilet boy, now shirtless, exposing his toasted torso, turns to me as I walk in.

"You look beautiful," he points out, "do have some soap?" he asks, I hold it forward, tensing when he holds my whole hand to grab it, grinning by the burn that now covers my cheeks.

"This might not fit, but better than nothing," I point out, resting dad's clothes over a wood panel.

"Thank you," he mumbles, brushing his teeth, clearing his mouth and throwing an entire bucket of water over him.

For an unknown reason, I can't take my eyes away from

him, traveling from the back of his head, down his slim back, following the trail of the drops.

"It feels good," he says, walking closer and holding the towel that I forgot was on my arms, "I am Advik."

"Ruby," I whisper, holding my breath. He is way too close, but I don't move away, just hold still.

"Listen Ruby, I know this is a difficult, way too weird situation," he says, stepping closer, "I appreciate cry much the help, and the last thing I want," he whispers, moving some hair behind my ear, leaving a tickling feeling on the way, "is to cost you any problem."

"My father will be here in the morning."

"I will be out of you way before the sun comes out," he whispers, intoxicating me with his musky scent, mixed with soap and minty toothpaste.

My gaze falls in between us, "I have to come back," I say, trembling as his fingertips push my chin up.

"Thank you, Ruby," he whispers, I can feel the warmth of his body, the water dripping in between us, "you are very beautiful."

"Thank you," I say, dropping my face, pulled up by his fingertips once more.

"Don't do that."

"What?"

"Hide yourself from me," he says, holding my waistline, pulling me closer and stealing a kiss from me.

My first kiss, at the stables, with an absolute stranger.

His arms curl around my back, pulling me closer, sharing the warmth of his bare chest and the remaining drops of water that were falling from his hair, my arms rest on my sides, not sure if this is the moment I should let this boy take something that was mine to choose who I gave it to, or I should push his and show him how to respect a young lady.

My feet steps back, but my torso doesn't follow as he pulls me closer, y hands rest over his chest and I push him back, breaking the little connection our lips were sharing.

"That was inappropriate," I say, brushing my lips with the back of my hand, "you don't have to wait until the morning," I say stepping back, "change and leave, you aren't welcome here."

I rush back into the house, angry and fluttered at what just happened, understanding now what my parents always say about boys, thinking they can take what they want when they want.

Chapter Thirteen

Ruby

I walk to the window, observing Samuel in the garden, irritated towards someone at the other side of the phone, walking in circles, pulling his waves back as he speaks.

I am unsure what Louise said once I fainted, but I can remember what she told me.

Advik was released, I knew that, ahead of time, I was ready for that too, but not to hear he has escaped from the social center they assigned him to and it's nowhere to be found.

I knew he wouldn't give up. He has a mission since the day he met me, and he won't stop until he fulfills it.

My forehead rests on the fresh window, my eyes close and I try my best to control the range of emotions that travel inside my veins. I head downstairs, collecting my mobile from the counter, and hiding from Samuel, I text the only person that can help us–*my protector.*

He has escaped. We will be out of Blue Valley for a few days, have everything ready.

I message Sarah letting her know about our little trip to the city, hiding the real reason. She has to focus on her own family.

"Mama," Naima calls, as I walk inside my bedroom. "Can we talk?" she asks, in a tone that no child should have towards their parents.

"Of course, baby."

I sit on the bed, waiting for her to join me, tensing when I see her expression change.

"The call, was that–Advik?" she asks, spitting his name out like poison, I nod and she swallows hard. "Does that mean–"

"No, nothing changes."

"Do you love him?" she asks, I frown and relax as she points to the garden with her chin.

"It's complicated."

"I love the way he looks at you, the way he talks, the way he loves you."

"He doesn't–"

"He loves you, mama, in a way I've never seen in–" she pauses. "Sarah says that is the way a man should love a woman."

"Did you spoke about this with Sarah?"

"I asked her, what a happy family looks like, how will it look when some cares for you–"

"Naima–"

"You don't love him," she points out, nodding, understanding that things can't just be black or white.

For God shake, she is a child.

"Tell him, you always say honesty is really important. Go down there, and tell him,"

"You can't hurt his feelings? or admit yours?"

"When have you grown this much?"

"The day I understood that one day it could be just Aidan and me, and I wouldn't be the big sister anymore, but all what he has left that care for him."

"Naima–"

"I will be in my bedroom."

I set there, observing how my nearly seven years old daughter teach me another lesson in live, opening my eyes to something I had been thinking of, something that confuses and scares me at the same time.

Do I even know how love someone feels like?

I don't. I followed a complete stranger around the world because he will give me something I would have never experienced on my own. He was manipulative and a narcissist, that confused my young mind.

I am not fifteen anymore, and Samuel has not a single similarity with that bastard that made my life hell on earth.

He is powerful and carries over his shoulder a dark, heavy past. But when he lets his guard down for an instant, when something that I say or do touches a tricky spot in his soul and mind, then I can see the young man that was broken into the man he is today.

I look over the window, letting a tear roll down my cheek, unannounced, but ready to fall when I see Samuel seated on the grass, his elbow rest on his knees, his face hidden on his palms.

I rush downstairs to him, pulling his hands away, straddling him, letting his face hide on my neck, brushing his waves, and kissing his temple.

"Take us away," I beg, letting our bodies become one, silently letting my tears roll down my cheeks as Samuel's roll down my chest.

We stay there, on each other's arms, sharing a silence that speaks better than any word we can say until the voice of a man calls Samuel from behind me. I look over my shoulder to find Logan standing there.

"They are waiting at the front," she says, pointing behind him, I frown and he gives me a compassionate smile. "Samuel asked for help with the packing. There is a van at the front."

"Can you go in by the kitchen? We are coming."

"Of course, ma'am."

"Ruby, please," I correct him, who nods and walks in.

"Don't be too friendly with them," Samuel mutters on my neck.

"They look more friendly than you do," I point out, receiving a little squeeze on my hip.

Pushing him away, I stand, offering my hands out, curling my arms around his waist and heading inside the house.

We reach London in the late afternoon, Rosita welcomes us on an apartment, just on the same road Samuel and I met, what feels now, a lifetime ago.

Walking in an over-the-top apartment. Everything is black and white here, slightly bore for my taste, but that match Samuel perfectly.

The foyer has a marble shiny floor, that heads to a long corridor with matching stairs to the top floor, and multiple white doors to different part of the apartment.

The kids follow Rosita to the end of the house. Logan and Jackson head upstairs, and I follow Samuel through another door, walking into a family room.

There are white velvet couches set under the window that faces the main road, the wall opposite the door has a large fake fireplace, with a frame that matches the ones holding images of all over the world across the entire room.

"We barely use this room," Samuel points out, holding my hand and taking me to an office at the other side of the corridor, "I hide here when I don't want to stay in the office," he explains, walking to the end of the corridor into a gym.

"Let me guess, the room you use the most," I say, brushing my hand over his muscular arm, blushing at his hard stare.

"It was indeed."

"Was?" I ask, letting him take me upstairs, where he points at Rosita bedroom, walking inside one with twin beds for the kids, and pulling me to the one with the largest door, "your bedroom?"

Leaving the door ajar, he invites me to walk past him, whispering in my ear, "our bedroom," I brush his torso as I walk by, and step inside a room that takes the space of the entire front of the apartment.

A closet with what I can see is mostly rows of suits, on the side. A bright bathroom on the opposite end, a large bed takes a big part of the room, white satin covers rest on the top, a black desk on the opposite corner and a dresser on the opposite wall.

"Why everything needs to be black or white with you?"

"Boring?"

"Simple and mysterious."

"Is that what I am to you?" he asks, resting his chin on my shoulder, curling his arm around my waistline.

"That is what you try to be to others," I point out.

His lips rests on my shoulder, traveling up to my near, "only what you think of me matters."

"Can we go for a walk?" I ask, feeling as if I keep inhaling heavy air, one that doesn't let my mind think clear.

"I can take you around the neighbourhood."

"Isn't this area famous for the rows of same type of houses that only difference each other are the numbers at the front?"

"Belgravia has more to offer than just houses."

"I can't wait to find out."

We walk down, inside the kitchen that takes my breath away, white marble counters, a large island on the center, a dining table on the corner heading to the back garden, the same I saw through the gym window walls before.

"Where would you like this, Ruby?" Rosita asks, snapping me out of my shock.

"I don't want to take you space–" Rosita cuts me off, opening one door after another of empty cupboards.

"Samuel only sleeps here, and I spend a lot of time at my friend's house," she explains.

"What were you planning for dinner?" I ask Samuel.

"That is what we will figure out on our walk."

"We are not getting a take-away."

"We are–"

"Ruby and I will cook," Rosita says.

"Have it your way," Samuel says, "kids, who wants to go shopping?" he asks.

Heading out, I tense when Samuel holds my hand, my eyes fixed on the kids, who give me a sweet smile, helping me relax and for the first time in a very long time enjoy the moment.

The sun is down by the time we head back from a walk in the park, some ice-cream and bags filled with vegetables, fruit and meat that could feed me and the kids for a month, but Samuel point out will be a one-time intake for him and the boys.

Rosita and I are busy cooking with the children laugh in the background, echoing around the house, changing the heavy aura that we have all carried around the past few hours.

"You are better at this that I am," Rosita points out as I peel some carrots.

"I used to help my mother since I can remember."

"Where are you exactly from Ruby?" Rosita asks.

"My mom is Mexican, my dad is from Texas," I say. "That's where I was born, in a little town call Shepperton." I smile, remembering home, my parents, my animals. "you wouldn't be able to see anyone for miles. It was peaceful, but I was really busy taking care of the animals all day."

My heart hurts!

That is all I can remember since I have memory, running around the wheat fields, feeding animals, cleaning stables, riding, having an amazing life that I appreciated little as a teenager.

"Samuel grew up in place like that too, was more a castle than a farm," she points out, I roll my eyes and we both giggle.

"I can't picture Samuel cleaning stables."

"He had a horse, they hate each other, that animal wouldn't let him ride it, and I think is because he could feel how strong Samuel's spirit it, how wild, uncontrollable even."

"Bona sera," Matteo says, walking to Rosita, kissing her cheek and giving me a bright smile.

I smile back, observing the closeness that exist between them all, Rosita is like the mother that they all lack. They are all grown men that without her probably will live surrounded by mess and take away boxes.

"Where is he?" he asks, testing a sauce I was working on, "sorry, old habits," he says, popping his finger out of his mouth.

"*Malcriado*, get out of here."

"Ros, be nice to me, I'm hungry."

"Nobody feed you these days?"

"Her food smells too good," he says, pointing at me, winking and making me blush.

"Eyes off her Casanova, Samuel will kill you," Rosita points out, pushing him aside, grinning at my reaction.

I am not blind, every man that works for Samuel fall on the category of man any woman will turn around to observe them passed by.

They all have a similar height, Jackson is the tallest and with the widest shape, intimidating brown eyes, and grumpy expression, but an absolute kind gentleman.

Logan's built on pure muscle, they all are, after all the boss has gym available handy for everyone. Long blonde waves that he keeps on a high bun, following the line to a fully growth beard and deep bright green eyes to complete the beauty in him.

Matteo features are similar to Samuel's. Charcoal hair, stubble, toasted skin, in Matteo from the sun, but he doesn't have my Adonis turquoise pools, his are light brown. He has the straightforward charm, where Sam has the mysterious aura.

And then is Calvin, the youngest, with blonde short hair, freckles spread over his nose and soft blue eyes. He is really polite and sweet with the kids.

"Samuel?"

"Family room with the kids," Rosita says, placing the bread in the oven.

"Ci vediamo," he says, winking and walking away.

"What did he said?"

"Ignore him, he argues with Samuel, and is just trying to provoke him."

"But Samuel is not here."

"Espera un momento," she says, I wait as she says.

A door closes in the corridor, I can hear the loud murmurs but not understand a word, and as Rosita says, I turn to find Samuel and Matteo standing by the door.

"why is this rat in my house?" Sam asks, I raise a brow, surprises at the way he talks about his supposed best friend.

"Ruby invites me for dinner," Matteo says, resting his back on the doorframe behind Samuel, sending me another wink.

And proving what Rosita was talking about, my cheeks turn to flames at his gesture, I nibble my bottom lip and turn away from them.

"Stay away from her!" Samuel exclaims, I shut my eyes waiting for a fight to start, but I can only hear Matteo's laugh.

I turn and found something I wasn't expecting, just two friends standing side by side as if nothing happens.

"Eyes on the food missy," Samuel warns, I giggle and Rosita brush my arm assuring me everything is fine.

"Ruby was telling me about a farm she grew in," Rosita says, I look petrified at her, receiving an apologetic pair of brown eyes.

"Samuel used to live in a farm," Matteo tease.

"My house bigger than your entire town," Samuel teases back.

"When did you come here?" Matteo asks.

I drop the knife I was using, bringing the tray of vegetables and turning on the kettle, we can have a tea, maybe that will end the talk or I could change the topic.

"Your parents must miss the kids a lot," Matteo says, opening a bag of nuts and filling his mouth.

I smile when Rosita walks closer and take it away from him, he complains and I giggle at how a full grown-up man can be so childish.

"Did the kids enjoy visiting the farm you grew up in?" Rosita asks, preparing the plates and cutleries.

"They—" I pause, taking a deep breath, cold sweat runs down my spine, and no matter that we are four people in a big room, I can hear Samuel heavy breath, and the way his thoughts work faster than my words can.

"They don't know the kids exist," Matteo finished for me. "Holy shit. That's bad."

"Matteo," Rosita complains.

"You didn't know," I say nervously.

"Nowadays everything is done electronic anyway, my best friend calls her daughter in Australia every evening," I nod, wishing that was too the case.

The kettle startles me. I look up and freeze when I meet Samuel's gaze, when the pain as he learns about my past travel from his mind to his eyes and down to his chest.

"*Santo Cielo*," Rosita gasps, covering her mouth. "They don't know if you are still alive."

My teeth sink at the inside of my cheeks, letting the metallic taste of blood travel through my mouth, my eyes don't leave Samuel's glassy ones, his deep frown grows in between his brows and his palm runs nervously through his waves.

"Ruby, my most sincere apology. I didn't know, we didn't. But is never late for a call."

"It's too late for that," I whisper, dropping my head.

Rosita embraces me as she speaks, "it's never late to start over. We all deserve a second chance," she says.

"I don't know if they are still there, alive, waiting for me—"

"A mother will always wait for her child to come back."

"You left just a few years ago," Matteo says, assuming I left before Naima was born, but that wasn't the case.

"I left fifteen years ago," I whisper, and the room become silence, I can listen to their hearts humming on their chests.

"Holy shit!" Matteo spit, nearly choking.

Rosita steps back, and Samuel jumps down from the stool he was sit it on.

"I thought—"

"That I left because I got pregnant with Naima?" Matteo nods, "I was pregnant shortly after that, but that baby wasn't the kids you know today."

"Ruby—" Rosita cries.

"You don't have to say nothing else," Matteo says.

"I made a mistake, and that is a consequence I will have to live with all my life. I left my simple life because a complete stranger promises me a world I wouldn't be able to have, not with the culture I grew up with, not on my own.

He fooled me for a few months. I was so naive and stupid thinking I was living a fairytale, newlyweds and expecting a baby," a thick tear rolls down Samuel's cheek, dissipating on this beard. "With the same rage and force he gave me the miracle of life, he took it away from me, over and over again. I just wanted to die, leave this cruel world, and be at peace with my babies. But that wasn't in his plans, I don't know why he let me have Naima and Aidan, after he constantly did that to me for years. But if wasn't for them, I would have gave up on life many years ago."

"Ruby. That is heartbreaking." Rosita whispers.

"It doesn't hurt anymore," I assure her. "And after all, I won."

Samuel's brow raises, probably questioning how could I be victorious when I let a man murder our children inside me for nearly a decade.

"I die with my first baby," I pause, nibbling my bottom lip, "he killed who I was, so I will submit to his will."

"Couldn't you—" Matteo pauses when the door opens.

Naima and Aidan storm in, followed by Logan and Jackson. I look away and the thickest silence grows in the room.

"Niños, let's wash our hands." Rosita says, taking them away.

"I will take care of the dinner," Jackson says.

Samuel steps closer, but I turn around, avoiding him and I run upstairs, hiding in the bathroom, releasing the cascade of tears that I hold back while I was opening my past to them.

A soft knock startle me, "I am sorry," Samuel says at the other side of the door.

"Why would you be? I didn't tell you."

"I am sorry I couldn't find you sooner," he says, turning the knob, I crawl forward and let him open the door, resting my back on the other side of the doorframe, "I couldn't find you, because I couldn't find myself either."

"This is not your fault. You didn't know me, I doubt you could find me, please Samuel," I whisper, resting to his lap and hiding on his chest, "I just want to forget."

"Let me help you rewrite the present, a better future, where our past has no space."

"I wish it was that easy."

"Give us the opportunity, my angel," he whispers, embracing me as I let my past roll down my cheeks, leaving me empty, like my memories do not exist, and today, a new life starts, one where it doesn't matter what happened before.

"Can I tell you a little dream I had once," I say, once I had control over my voice and breath.

"Of course, angel."

"It was before the kids born. I was on my own, that night I could sleep because I knew he wasn't coming back until the next day," I explain, feeling how he tense under me, "I haven't had a dream in a very long time, I was ready to give up, that dream change it all. I found myself walking through a little path filled with flowers heading to an orange door, I enter this gorgeous house, with the scent of wildflowers, there was a tray of fresh cookies resting in the kitchen, but what called my attention was the giggle of children and the growling of a man playing in the garden with them, he was the beast, the little girl was dressed as a princess and the little boy had a horse mask and trotting around them," I giggle at the memory. "I couldn't see any of their faces, but I will never forget how real it felt, and how much Naima and Aidan resemble the features of the kids in my dream."

"The house was the cottage, the children were your children, what about the man?"

"He was as tall as a tower, strong like a beast, toasted caramel skin, charcoal waves, warm smile. But you know what shocked me the most?"

"What was that?" He asks, not really happy with where the story is going, and the way I am describing the man of my dreams, the one that together with those kids changed my way to fight for live forever.

"This was the only feature I could see in his face, everything was a blur. I only see it when he stopped playing, turned, and walked to me. I was intimidated at first, but I didn't step back, or cover my body afraid of him," I explain, caressing his gorgeous face, smiling at his impatience. "It was his eyes, I've never seen that color on someone's eyes before, they were deep, hypnotic, full of life, joy and love. Those eyes changed my life."

"Should I be jealous now?"

"No, you shouldn't," I assure him. "A few weeks ago, I went to court, they couldn't apply for a divorce as no certificates were found, I was scared, confused, devastated. I started walking without destination, and when I was about to lose all the strength that was left inside me, when my own daughter could feel my pain and cry the tears I was scared to set free. I found those eyes."

I pause, looking up to those eyes. Samuel's frown deep in between his thick brows, tilting his head at my words.

"I was the man inside your dream?" he asks, I nod. Resting my lips over his, softly letting the words I am not ready to say, travel across our skin. "How is that possible?"

"I don't know. How could I dream of my children before I have them? With the same body features? How could I dream of the cottage without been there before?"

"That is why you didn't feel scared of me? why you didn't react the way the kids did when I touched you?"

"I have no way to explain things, I only know that on my lowest, three of you and that cottage gave me the hope of a better future."

"Come here," he says, bringing me closer to his chest, kissing me.

Chapter Fourteen

Samuel

I help her out of the shower, cover her gorgeous body with a bathrobe and sadly let her go.

There is nothing I wouldn't love more than lose myself in her body once more. But after spending the week travelling around the city. Visiting all the places London has to offer.

Today I have to take her shopping, for the Gala tomorrow. The event of the year. the reason the city is fully booked with celebrities, well-known people, fans that have travelled from any place around the world to get a glimpse of their favourite actor, singer, influencer as they enter SaStel.

For me this day marks the century of my grandparents passing, despite people believes that this is the launch of the first magazine. After all, it is easier sometimes to let people write history their way, that give them a chance to twist it for their benefit.

For Ruby it's the day her business will be launched worldwide. An opportunity to grow what I know is already a successful business.

For the children, will be a fun trip to the countryside. They will travel to Surrey with Rosita, and that is where we will all spend the rest of the weekend. Returning to Blue Valley on Monday.

Walking downstairs with a clear mind after a fresh shower, I nibble my bottom lip when I see Ruby. She is wearing a dress I saw on a shop we passed by the other day, and had Helena purchasing it immediately.

The material adjusts to her curves like a second layer of skin, the heels enhance the way her long legs and perky bump look.

"Brunch is on the table," she teases, pointing to where everyone is devouring whatever is that she has cooked and baked this morning.

"I want something else," I whisper in her ear, biting her lobe and jumping back as she pinches my skin.

"Behave," she warns me.

"Kids, I have two plans for you while I suffer the horror of going shopping with mama," I fake, complaining and rolling my eyes. I can't wait to sit, see her naked changing gowns, in a private room, I shake my head and focus. "You can go with Nana Rosita to her friend's house, there is a party going on, or to the park, feed ducks, ice-cream, blablabla?"

"We haven't been invited to that party," Naima says.

"You have, *mi niña,* only if you want to."

I look over my shoulder when Naima sends a silent question on Ruby's direction, they look at each other for a moment and they both smile.

"We need to get a gift," Naima points out.

"Bring a box of cookies please."

"*Mi niña*, if I do that, you will have them ordering more every week," Rosita says, brushing Ruby's arm, "and I already have a gift," she explains walking away and returning with a birthday bag.

"Matteo you are with them, Jackson you are with us," they nod and I turn to Calvin, "Helena is burning my mobile, can you see what is all the fuss about?" He nods and I return to my gorgeous angel who is waiting for me ready to start the fun part of the day.

Minutes later, and rejecting Stella's call for the third time in less than an hour, I follow Ruby inside Harrods, when a uniformed gentleman holds the heavy doors for us, holding her hand, I head to the department I need, making Ruby tip toe to keep up.

As we enter the women's department, I spot the gowns and I head there, welcome by the stylist I hired.

"Ms Ruby, welcome, I'm Leticia, your consultant today."

We follow her into a private room, I take a seat on the red velvet couch and Ruby stands on the pedestal in front of me.

My elbows rest on the back, one leg on the knee of the other and my tongue brushes my bottom lip in anticipation. Watching how she runs her palms along her curves, finding my gaze on the mirror, I can see the lust in her eyes, feel the warmth of her body, and scent her arousal mixed with floral perfume.

I rose and walk closer, pulling my hand that was about to touch her when Leticia came back, I turn growling in my breath while Ruby giggles.

She was doing it on purpose and she will pay for this.

"Ms Ruby, we weren't sure what your style preference was. Mr Smith just mentioned your love for colour and flower prints."

"We will keep all the pastels, the light grey, and the white gown," I answer, "you can take the others away while," I look back to my angel, devouring her with my eyes, "Ms Ruby tries them."

Taking my seat back, I wait until Leticia leaves, pointing with my chin to the gowns, so she does what I've been waiting all morning.

Adjusting my crotch as she steps down, walking slowly my way, raising her dress, straddling me and holding my chin up.

"Do you mind some privacy?"

"You are fucking kidding me."

"I need you to wait outside," she orders, standing and pointing at the thick curtain that hides us from the shoppers out there.

"I will go, but you and your sexy arse owe me one," I wink, "choose the one you love the most but will never wear, that is the correct one."

My mobile rings once more than I walk away from Ruby, Stella's name bright up once more, and looking over my shoulder, putting enough distance between us and signing to Jackson to keep an eye, I connect the call.

"I've been calling all morning," she shouts at the other end.

"Afternoon Stella, I am good, thanks for asking, how is Scott? Good? Great. How about Mr Wrinkles?—"

"Fuck you Samuel!" She shouts again.

"If you are going to keep that attitude I rather you call Helena, or message, I don't have time for this. You can also do there your tantrums."

"You are a piece of shit,—"

"Okay, enough," I say, hanging up and taking the time Ruby is inside to have a look at the updates on the event.

It doesn't take long before Helena is at the other side of the phone ready for round two of women tantrums this afternoon.

"Why can't you listen to others than just your stupid voice?"

"Nice to talk to you, yes I am fine thank you."

"Cut the crap, Samuel. Why can't you talk to Stella?"

"She was shouting, anyway she talked to you, now. What does she wants?"

"Scott."

"What with him?"

"Send someone to pick him up so she can go to the gala."

"Are there not babysitters available?"

"Are you for real? After all you are suggesting that? You know she can't, and if you don't help, they will come and pick him up."

"Family time, he needs to spend sometimes with them too."

"You are the biggest piece of shit I ever met."

"Second time in less than an hour, please find another nickname, that one is boring."

"Are you coming to the office? Or are the family holidays getting extended?"

"You don't like her, I get it. It's not your choice to make, anyway."

"I don't know her, but I know since she appeared you have forgotten what matter."

"You have no idea what you are talking about."

"Even a blind can see your focus is on her and her needs."

"Jealousy doesn't suit you," I say, looking over my shoulder, "I have all of you to do your job, something else?"

The line cuts off before she answers, I look at the screen and hide my mobile away when I see Ruby walking my way.

It's not the time or the moment to open my own family secrets, nothing will change if she knows or doesn't know who my sister is. And it's clear I need to keep her away from Helena.

"Which one did you choose?" I ask, curling my arm around her waist.

"You will have to wait and see."

"Time to go," I say, pulling her close to me and taking

her across the road to SaStel building.

As we approach she pulls me back, "is this where you work?"

"These are my offices, indeed."

"Why are we here?"

"I have something to collect."

without giving her any more explanation, I bring us to my office floor, walking past all the workers that are extending their stay in the office and that irritates me, they should all have gone home by now.

"Working hours end at 2 p.m. today!" I exclaim on my way down the corridor. Helena is not by her desk when I open the door to let Ruby enter, and for that I am glad. she would have eat Ruby alive.

"This is your office?" She asks walking around, taking in the view from the window wall, fixing her gaze on me as she brushes her fingertips at the top of my chair, "Mr Smith's CEO of SaStel magazine. You kept that for a while."

"Does it matter if I own the company or I print the pictures?" I ask, her brows raise and I grin, "come here."

"You can come too," she points out.

"Miss Rao, you and your pretty mouth have misbehave too much today."

"What are you going to do about it?" She asks, sitting on my chair.

"You look irresistible in that dress, in that chair,—"

"What are you going to do about it?" She teases.

Walking slowly, considering my every move, I reach her, turning the chair to face the outside view, running my thumb over her jawline, holding her chin, and bending to brush my nose with her.

"You are not ready for that—"

"Are you sure about it?" She asks. I would love to show Ruby all what I could give her, the places I could take her with a simple touch, in my territory.

But I can't do it yet, not after what I've learned from her past. Making me sick to my stomach that I have even given her some dominant, rough intercourses. She agreed, but I will never know if she did it to please me, because she was blind with lust, or because her mind has built this coping mechanism where she accepts things she can zoom away from and act as if nothing is wrong.

"We need to discuss the safe words for that," I say, kissing the tip of her nose.

I step back when she pushes me back and walks around the room, observing my reaction, nibbling her bottom lip, as her mind works something out.

"Do we need them?" She asks, tapping her chin, "I don't want to use one for you to move forward. a safe word should be a sign that I just need you to stop. But will I really want you to stop?"

"Ruby—"

"I am just saying. I will understand the use of them with a stranger, someone you don't know much. I mean we only know each other for under a month, but—"

Cutting her little monologue, I hold her up, hitting her back against the wall, devouring her neck, pulling her dress up, grabbing her perky bump on my grip, spreading her cheeks and accessing her pussy from behind, over her lace knickers.

No warning, no permission, nothing but my hunger for her.

Dropping her, I step back, breathing heavily as the beast I am aware I can turn into.

"How did that make you feel?" I ask, studying her pink cheeks, the rash trail my beard has left on her collarbone and neck, the mixture of emotions in her beautiful blue eyes. "Say something."

"I don't know what to say."

"That is why you need a safe word. I can take what I want without you having the chance to stop me. I need you to guide me, draw the limits that maybe with time we can expand—"

"I want to give you what you need."

"I need you Ruby, not your body, not sex, I need your mind, heart and soul."

"I thought—"

"What? That woman has to give the man all what they want?"

"Short of."

"I am not like other man. I am Samuel, *your* Samuel. And me, I don't mind taking things easy, one step at the time, at your pace. Your satisfaction and happiness are mine."

Stepping closer, resting her hands on my chest, then her ear, listening to my hammering heartbeats, I kiss the top of her head. Covering her little body in my arms.

"Let's go home," I say.

Holding her closely, we head down, where Jackson and the car is waiting for us, taking as back to the apartment, that now is empty.

"Thank you Jackson," Ruby says stepping out of the car, "can I ask you a favour?" She asks.

"Of course, what is it?"

"Can you go to that party, where the kids are, and keep an extra eye over them?"

"It will be my pleasure, call me if something comes up," he says, on my direction.

The moment the car pulls away, something changes in my angel's expression, walking slowly inside the apartment, stopping at the centre of the foyer, turning to face me. I close the door behind me, resting my back on the thick wood door.

"We are alone," she points out.

"I've notice."

"Tell me, Mr Smith. What will you do to me now? At this moment when nobody can see or hear us."

"Ruby—" I warn her.

"It's just you and me," she says in a low voice, remarking every word.

Without another word, holding the edge of her dress, she pulls it over her head, revealing just a transparent lace thong.

"I want you to look at me, every inch of me, study it, let your anger boils your blood, run your fingers through every scar if you must. I need you to make peace with my body. I can't take your delicate touch, your eyes shut when my skin reveals something you don't like, and the low light sex so my marks won't take you out of the momentum."

I swallow heavily, conscious that what she is saying is the truth. The first time I touch her, back on the parking, that was a spontaneous move, but I took control over me, at her house after that, we were under the dim lights of her old apartment, covering us in more shades than brightness. Everything changed that night in the cottage, when her backside was exposed, when I saw what that bastard did to her, I couldn't take that away from my mind, push it aside and see her the way I wanted her to be.

I step closer, observing how she rolls her waves on a high sexy bun, standing still, letting me, under the bright light see it all.

"The worst is my back," she says, when I draw a line on a scar I haven't notice before on her hairline.

"Nothing change how I see you," I whisper, finding other at the top of her shoulder.

"It does, because every time you see them, you will remember my past, and I don't want that in between us anymore. I need you to let go as I did."

Her shoulders tense when I stand behind her, the scars are dark pink lines running from her nape to under the curve of her arse.

"Do they hurt?" I ask, holding my fingertips close to the skin.

"The thought of you not touching me because of them, that hurts more," she says, gasping when I run my index across her spine, "do it again," she requests, in a slower motion I repeat the trail.

"You are gorgeous, I am sorry if I made you feel uncomfortable before."

"Mr Smith," she calls in that sensual voice that makes my dick twitch.

"Yes, angel."

"Do you like what you see?" She teases, I step closer, circling my hips on her back, "hands off," she says, and I step back.

Licking my bottom lip at the touch of her soft warm skin, I wait as she turns, holding the edge of my t-shirt, pulling it over my head.

"I like what I see too," she teases, holding my hand and running my fingers over her wet thong.

"Angel—" I warn her.

"Pants off," she requests. I do as she says, taking my tranks with them, followed by the shoes and socks. "I didn't ask for that."

"Easier to take it all out of the way. What now angel?"

"You mentioned earlier," she whispers, stepping closer, letting the heat of our bodies connect, "that I misbehave," I raise a brow, "and I was wondering."

"Ruby—"

"Are we talking about a naughty girl spank on my bump, or restrained and taught a lesson that makes me forget my name."

"Ruby." I warn her once more, feeling how hard I am turning at the thought of what she is offering.

"I want you to spank me."

"No way," I say, resisting as she pulls me to the stair, pushing me to seat, positioning her body over my knees, her perky bump on full display, brushing my waves back, I take a deep breath, bringing my body to a calmer stage, as my throbbing cock, twitches under her tummy.

"I want you to do it three times—"

"No fucking way—"

"You will go from the softest to the hardest you can give."

"This is insane."

Brining her head up, so she can face me, I study her expression.

"We will never know where the limits are until we don't test it."

"I don't want to hurt you."

"It's a spank Samuel—"

"Three."

"Probably the first one I won't feel much, can you please do it?"

Before her head falls forward, with my lips apart making her think I am about to say something else, my palm lands on her skin, my dick response and so does her entire body, curling over me, until her hips pop higher as she gasps. Caressing the pinkish area, I run my other hand through her back, holding her in place before I increase the spank over the other cheek, helping her to don't fall as the sensation travels across her body, moaning out of breath. For the third and final time, I brush her hair, loosing up the bun, fisting her hair on a mass of waves, pulling her head back at the same time that my hand lands at her centre, feeling the wetness under her thong, grunting at the own pleasure that has given me, when I hear her cry in lust.

Holding her up I seat her on my lap, holding her hips, searching for her eyes. Dark, glassy and filled with lust. Her lips are red cherry, moist and parted as she heavily breath.

I tense when her hands hold my dick, placing it at her entry after she pushes her thong aside, and she lowers herself until I fill her to the deepest. Riding me widely, we reach a climax that was threating to happening if I got to spank her more times.

"We aren't done yet," she murmurs on my lips, pulling her back, I study her eyes, "this was just the warm up," she says, standing and running upstairs.

"Angel," I complain when she leaves me there.

"I need to shower first," she whispers at the top of the stairs, "I feel really, dirty," she says, looking at her climax dripping down her thighs.

"I could help you wash up," I offer.

"That would be very nice Mr Smith," she says, as I walk up the steps that separates us, "but for that, you will have to catch me first," she teases, rushing away.

Jumping the steps left two at the time, I throw her over my shoulders, marching inside the bedroom, letting go of her and her giggles over the mattress.

"I thought—"

"I will wash you once we are done."

"Mr Smith are you giving me order now?"

"Your safe word is sunflower, say it clear and loud Angel," she nods and I shake my head, "say it."

"Sunflower!" she trembles at the world, she hates it as much as I do now, but it will make this safer.

"That is my girl. That is the way I will stop anything at any time. Do not play Ruby."

"I won't, I promise," she assures, stepping out of her roleplay.

I walk to the closet room, grabbing two of my favourite thick ties, and a thinner one that I believe has never been used.

Ruby is laying across the mattress as I straddle her, showing the ties, letting her imagination run to where I need her to be.

"Sit up," I order, moving behind her, covering her eyes, making sure she can't see me, "open," I order, placing the other one in between her lips, "hands forward," I order one last time, securing her wrist together, attaching the end to a metal at the end of the bed, grinning at the thought I always had of when I will us that hock shape piece.

I walk back to the bathroom, collecting some sweet body oil she has been using these days, dropping some on her tummy, spreading the liquid around, letting her skin come to life, hearing her moans hidden behind the tie, and biting my lip as she pulls the wrist hold as I approach her thighs.

"Don't pull too hard, you will mark yourself," she nods and I move along, observing how her full body burn for me. Turning her around and doing the same on the other side.

Resting over her, placing my hard cock over her perky bump, I kiss her back, pulling her hair up on a ponytail and whispering on her ear.

"Are you comfortable?" She nods, "the mouth gag is to quiet your screams," I say, pulling her hips up, lowering her shoulder to the mattress and without a second thought, thrusting her to the deepest she can take me. "You were right Angel, we don't need a safe word," I growl, thrusting her harder, taking her mumble moans to build my own ectasis.

Her walls suck me deeper, dripping her climax over me. I pull back, and lick everything away, building a new one that comes to a new release the moment I thrust her with my fingers as my mouth teases her clit.

Freeing her mouth as I feel she has something to say, "yes, angel?"

"I want to see you, touch you, feel you," she begs.

"Not yet," I say, turning her, bringing her to her back, filling her up once more, thrusting harder than ever, torturing her nipples, and clit as I bring us to the release I've needed all day.

Releasing her, I hold her to the shower, take special care on the spank's marks and wrist, applying some oil to take away the redness.

"I am sorry," I whisper, kissing her skin.

"I am fine, can I take five more minutes, I want to wash my hair."

"I will go down and clear up, we don't want the kids to find out what we do when they are out," I explain, walking away, covering myself in running shorts and hiding away any evidence of our recent intercourse.

I am reading the last minutes updates of the gala on the laptop over the kitchen island when everyone walks in. the cheer on the children's voice makes me smile.

"What are you smiling at?" Matteo asks.

"How ugly you are!"

"He is handsome Samuel," Naima points out, "*Tata* Teresa was asking Nana how could mama live with so many *guapos* around," she says, resting the goody bags on my side, climbing the stool and kissing my cheek.

"*Tata* Teresa never met me."

"Nana shows her a photo, and another of Logan, Calvin and mama."

"Really?" I ask Rosita.

"She asks, and she hasn't seen you in many years."

"Tell him the verdict, Naima," Matteo teases.

"*Tata* Teresa said 'how can mama concentrate,' and then she bites mama biscuit like she was really hungry."

"There are never going there anymore," I exclaim, making everyone laugh, "you are a piece of—"

"Sugar!" Ruby exclaims, walking to the kids and cuddling them, giving me a warning look, reminding me of what I was about to say. "How was the party?"

"*Tata* Teresa was so kind, and she was saying 'how—"

"Let's go shopping!" I cut her off, tired of listening to that comment, "I am starving and the fridge is empty thanks to the *guapos* of the house," I say, tickling Naima and holding her on my arms.

"You can't go out like that," she points out.

"May I have five minutes?"

"I need the toilet!" She exclaims.

"Me too," follows Aidan with Ruby.

Finding them on the foyer, I hold Aidan in my arms, Naima hold Ruby and my hand, marching to the main road to grab something for the night.

After all, from tomorrow morning we will move to Surrey and then back to Blue Valley.

"Have you considered this is our last night in Belgravia?" I ask Ruby.

"Is that a big deal?"

"Is the neighbourhood where it all started," I remind her.

"I will miss the scent that has, especially at night," she points out, inhaling the fresh air mixed with flowers that rest on every front door as the traditional road decoration.

"It's okay," I assure Naima, when we take the shortcut through a dark mew. The shop I am looking for is on the opposite side. We are in Belgravia. Nothing happens here.

I can see the people walking by the main road, I can hear the noise of the shops, but as my hair stands on end, I look over my shoulder, a male figure stands there, at the other end, observing us, making me jump out of my skin, when a sensation travels from Naima's hand into my chest.

I look at her and found we are all doing the same, Ruby snaps back, avoiding me, "we need to keep walking." I say, holding Naima up on my arms too.

I walk the short distance to the main road, entering the first shop I see, walking through the aisles, searching for something I know is not here, my sense of security.

"Let's go to the other store," I mumble, Ruby seems as lost as I am.

I am not making it up this, we have all seen it, otherwise Naima wouldn't be trembling, and Ruby wouldn't be in a trance.

Stepping closer, I kiss her temple, her arms curl around my waistline and her forehead rests on my chest.

"We are not doing takeaway," she says, giggling nervously, pushing this aside and getting Naima's curious attention.

"What is takeaway?"

"Unhealthy food that Samuel loves."

"Sam," she calls, "you said is special night."

"It is indeed."

"Mama says you only eat unhealthy food," she says struggling to pronounce the word. I nod and she tap her chin, "what about, is we do a cooking competition?"

"Baby, Sam doesn't know how to–"

"Deal!" I cut her off, "the winner gets to choose what the other has to do as a payback," I tease her.

We both know she will win, and I will have an excuse to not deny another of her exploring fantasises.

"It will be a blind competition," Naima explains, making us laugh loudly, remembering how Ruby was few hours ago, in bed, on display for me to do as I please.

"Can we buy the ingredients together?"

"No!" she exclaims, "Aidan and I will wait outside with one of you, the other gets the ingredients, then we swap and we go home."

The way that simple word comes out of her little voice makes my wounded soul feel warm. For these children, there has never been a safe place, and with all that happened the cottage didn't have the opportunity to become one. That she finds the apartment, or a place where we are all together a *home* for her, that just means the world to me.

"Let's get everything on the other store," I point out, heading to a bigger one, across the road, where we both can find anything we can think of.

Following Naima's instructions, we purchase the ingredients and head back, discussing the rules of the challenge, filled with excitement and joy.

Both of the kids are now walking ahead of us, my arm rests over Ruby's shoulder and her head on my chest, overtaking the kids when Naima hold Aidan closer, freezing on the spot.

"What is–" Ruby tense on my hold too, I look on the direction and all I can see is darkness from the park at the end of the road.

I have taken them through the other walk back to avoid the mews, but that doesn't seem to change the fact that we are been followed.

"Come here," I say holding both of the kids up, "Ruby," I call, snapping out of it, holding my arm we speed up, sprinting as we see the house at the end of the turn we take, pushing the door behind us.

Ruby's back hold it, securing that nobody enters.

Out of breath, trembling, we stand face to face, startled when Rosita walks in the room.

"What happened?" she asks.

Ruby's breath speeds up, her skin turns transparent, her eyes are empty, and her body trembles.

I am confused, and questioning everything that happened since we step out of the house.

"Mi ni–" Rosita hand rests over Naima's shoulder, pulling it back when a painful cry leaves her little chest, her hands run through her dark curls, and her knees give up.

Nobody moves, I doubt we are breathing, watching as child let go of what feels like a lifetime pain out of her chest.

Her forehead rets on the cold marble floor, while her fists hit it, crying louder, turning into a loud sob.

Ruby seats by the door, her gaze fixed on her daughter, while tears wash her cheeks.

Silence grows thicker, Naima pulls herself up, facing Ruby.

"It was him, right?" she asks.

Ruby shakes her head, I frown and kneel, pulling my hands out, inviting her to reach me on the hope that this little gesture might help.

"You've seen it too," Naima says on my direction, my head tilts, unsure if that was the man that ruin their past.

"Naima–"

"Naima, what mama?" she challenges her, "are you

going to lie again?"

"I can't do this," Ruby says, standing, and heading to the kitchen, "we have to get dinner ready."

Naima sprints behind her, all eyes are on her as she let her anger take the control over her.

"Enough!!!" Naima yells, "you can't run anymore!"

"Naima, please," Ruby begs, looking to everyone and lowering her face in embarrassment.

"Please what, mother?" she asks, "he found us," she says, confirming what I suspected, "I won't run. I'm not afraid anymore."

"You don't know what you are saying," she assures, "I will never stop running to protect you and Aidan."

My body tense at the idea of her choosing to run that easily.

"That's it? You gave us this, and now take it away just like that?"

"This was never ours to keep."

I broke into pieces, all my worst nightmares are echoing in my mind, every word she says are sharp daggers stabbing me everywhere.

"Running keeps us alive."

"He will find you, he always does, what about Aidan and I?!"

Ruby shakes her head, is incredible to hear how a little girl understands, and know what is happening that vividly.

"He will finished what he started, he always has his ways," she says as tears wash her cheeks, "what about Aidan and I?" she repeats in between teeth.

"I am trying to protect you," Ruby cries out.

Tuning around, Naima looks at all of us, "we have never been safer that around them," she says, pointing at us, "they are protecting us."

"You can't put this on them."

"He will do anything for you," she says holding my hand, bringing me forward.

"Naima–"

"He loves us all, we are his family too," she says, walking to the boys, climbing to Matteo's lap, holding him the way Aidan is holding Jackson, in need of a safe space, "you can run, we will stay."

"Naima–"

"We are moving to Surrey," I say, finding the strength to talk.

"I'm hungry," Aidan mumbles to Jackson.

"Let me prepare you something," says Rosita, holding him up and walking to the island.

"We can't go," Ruby says.

"We are packing and moving to Surrey immediately, you can come with us, or go somewhere else, but nobody is safe here any longer," I explain, gesturing to Matteo, who takes Naima with us.

Chapter Fifteen

Ruby

Letting fear win over any rational thoughts. I pack all of our belonging, fill up the van with Jackson's help, place the kids in their seats safely and without looking over my shoulders to avoid the devastating scene playing behind me we drive away.

Every tear that rolls down Naima's cheeks is a dagger that stabs me deeper and deeper, with a guilt that I doubt all the way back to Blue Valley if it's mine to hold on to.

After unloading the van, I help the kids into bed and spend the rest of the night seated by the window, observing the town sleeping and waking up.

Pushing any thought out of the way, not ready to comprehend what has happened, when my miserable life reached heaven, and at which point I was pulled back to hell without warming.

Something inside me knew this couldn't last, this was a perfect, delicate and dangerous bubble, we didn't want to see it. Advik was more than ready to remind us where we came from, what was our place.

I might be a coward, other person might have hide under Samuel's money and power and let him do what he wants.

That will take all what I have built these months away from me. I will let once more a man overpower and control me.

Regardless of his intentions.

I going through my own struggles with my past and present wasn't enough, now I have my little girls own anger and sadness to deal with.

She disagrees with my decision on putting space in between Samuel and I, she knows more than a child her age should. She has lived things that many people don't get to live in a lifetime.

But that doesn't mean she knows how to face what is coming for us the way I do.

Founding myself putting all my energy left in trying to make her understand and accept my decision.

But patience is running extremely thin by the afternoon, when I have received nothing but silence, hard stares and some tears.

"We could go to the park," I suggest to Aidan, ignoring Naima's cocktail of emotions, I can't blame her, but this is not my fault either.

I didn't plan to meet Samuel. It was a coincidence. I didn't force him inside our lives. Circumstances brought him closer and closer. And most definitely, I didn't imagine our worst nightmare will follow us to Belgravia, threatening to take what belongs to him.

"Yes, please," Aidan says.

"No, I'm not going," Naima protest.

"I won't take this any longer, you have to know the grown-up world is not the fairy tales from the books. Is actually filled with many more unhappy things that you could imagine."

"I didn't say a word."

"You don't have to, I can see it in the way you avoid me, stare at me, and it is written all over your face. And I won't take it. I am your mother, it is my job to protect you, and I think I haven't done too bad so far."

Her little face rose away from the painting she was messing around for the past hour, her eyes are glassy, and the only thing she has for me is a sharp nod.

"I will get some more water," I say, kissing Aidan's head, walking inside.

I return, opening the new umbrella I bought with the rest of the cupboards, I make sure they are covered, startled when sirens echo across the neighbourhood, and I can hear the murmuring of people at the main road.

"Fire truck?" Aidan asks.

"Those are the ambulance and police car noises," I explain, kissing his chubby cheeks, "mama has some work to catch up on, I will be inside," I walk back inside the kitchen, ready to go back to the life where Samuel doesn't exist and I was settled with my new business and my children.

Holding up the freshly baked cookies, I place them out of the way when Naima and Aidan run inside the house, out of breath, talking at the same time.

"What happened?"

"Scott!" Naima exclaims out of breath, "he is there!"

"In our house?"

"No! Come," she says, rushing away, I follow her by the garden, crossing a small path that connects the cottage with our neighbor front yard, and in a few more steps I am standing in front of my dream house.

"We can't be here," I say, urging them to come back before someone sees us.

"Scott lives here," Naima says, rushing to the front door, ringing the bell.

A cold sweat drips down my spine when Logan opens the front door, brushing his waves back, exposing a red tint that falls down his forearms.

"Ruby?"

"Logan, are you okay?" I ask approaching him, seen what is over his clothes, hands and arms is blood, "kids stay back," I say hiding them behind me.

"It's not–Scott's mother had an accident, we were–"

"Logan, I need more towels," I hear from the inside of the house, "who is at the–" I hold my breath when Scott appears, his clothes are covered too, "Ruby!" he exclaims, rushing to me, curling his arms around my waist, sobbing.

"What happened?"

"I was in the city, Scott called–" Logan explains, "Rosita

is there," he continues, shaking.

"Why don't you clean up and come for a tea?"

"I was helping Scott–"

"I can take care of him, go clean up," I encourage him, seen the agony on his gaze.

We walk back to the cottage, taking a seat on the kitchen island, cleaning Scott's face, hands, and arms.

"If you want to talk about it," I whisper, studying his expression, nibbling my bottom lip, holding back the tears that are burning the back of my eyes.

"I was upstairs getting ready, a babysitter and the people that helps mom get ready for parties was coming," he says, taking a deep breath, holding back his tears, "I heard a noise, I was scared, I hide–"

"There is nothing wrong with that," I embrace him, brushing his back with my palm, trying to reassure he is not responsible for this.

"She was in the floor, her eyes were open," he pauses, sobbing, clearing his throat, "I call Logan, he always helps us."

"You are brave, you helped her, you did what any grown up will have made."

"Is she going to?–"

"I don't know–"

"She will be back in a few days," Logan says, walking in by the back door, "she is strong, she needs to take care of you," he reassures, brushing his dark blonde waves back.

Holding him close to me, keeping my own emotions under control, I look at Logan. He is not telling Scott everything, I can see it on his deep frown, on his glassy, dark eyes, on the way his hands shake, and his feet balance him from side to side.

"Tea?" I offer, Logan shakes his head, "why don't you go there and change?" I offer Scott, holding the clothes that Logan has brought.

"Ruby I didn't know–"

"That my kids will see you?"

"This is the closest place I could take him,--"

"Isn't this Scott's house?" I ask, following the kid's assumption when they came in before.

"It's Samuel's," he says, brushing his face as the words skip his lips, aware that he just told me something he shouldn't.

I step back, my mind running miles per hour, the moments shared, the words said, the secrets kept, the lies.

"Ruby, listen–"

"There is nothing you can say," I cut him off, running my hands through my hair, closing my eyes, forcing my breath to stay under control as I let the betrayal to sink in, marking something inside me that words won't be able to erase it.

"He wanted to tell you," he says, holding out his mobile as it rings in his pocket, "it's Matteo."

"I will get Scott, so you can leave."

"Ruby," he calls, "listen to Matteo, he can explain things."

"The only one who needs to explain anything is Samuel, and he will not do so. There is no point anyway."

Logan nods, waiting for us by the back door as I bring Scott, waving goodbye, taking his offer for a movie night, one that I'm sure it will never happen, but I am not ready to let my own children know yet.

"Scott said that is Samuel's house," Naima says, pointing to his house, "why you didn't tell us?"

"Because I didn't know," I say, swallowing the truth, and making my smart girl know that what I mentioned before is the reality. Grown up life sucks.

A soft knock on the door startles me, reflected in my face as I open the door, founding a tormented Rosita, her eyes are purple, her round face red, and her short frame is trembling as she tries to control her sobbing's.

"Tea?" I offer, opening the door and inviting her inside. "The kids are playing in their room, I was just getting dinner ready," I explain, inviting her to have a seat as I turn on the kettle.

"Logan told me you saw them."

"The kids saw Scott across the bushes,"

"I begged Samuel to tell, that boy never listens," she says, cleaning under her eyes, "I wanted to tell you, everyone did actually."

"Are you justifying him, or the entire household?"

"Ruby, our duty is to make sure he is safe, healthy, not to speak about what goes on inside close doors."

"So as long as the master has a good public image, who cares the things he does."

"Haven't he been kind to you, he loves you Ruby, what

else do you need?"

"What do I need? I think we know two different men."

"Why tell you his full past, where he was, or what he does is so important for you? Can't you just accept him for what he is?"

"And what is that?"

"Someone who cares for you and your kids, someone who wants to help you in your delicate situation, open your eyes," she says, leaving a large envelope in the counter and walking away, "he will be back soon, the door back door is always unlocked, and he will be in the first door on the right by the front door, or the large double doors by the left upstairs."

"Why are you doing this?"

"Because I saw Stella suffering her whole life, and I did nothing about it. Look where it took us," she explains, clearing some more tears away. "Samuel is my change of redemption. If I give him what he wants, I will die in peace."

"I am not a possession, or an object."

"I didn't mean that."

"Good evening Rosita," I invite her to leave.

Turning to the envelope she left, turning it upside down, holding my breath when the content falls out.

It's me, weeks ago, in the old apartment, baking.

It feels like a lifetime ago, like if I am staring at the old me, the weak version of who I used to be.

I brush the picture with my fingertips, drawing my features, reading my business name on the bottom, and SaStel name on the top of my head.

That is Samuel's company, this is Samuel's magazine, holding it tightly to my chest, deep breathing as once more a wave of mix emotions travels across my body.

"What is that, mama?" Naima asks.

"Something I did for Samuel," I say showing them the cover.

"Is that you?" they ask, I nod and Naima asks to have a look at it. "This is Samuel's company," I explain.

Waiting until they find the full article, "can you read it?" Naima asks. I taught her how to read, but I guess this looks like too much compare with children's books.

The name of Ruby Sweet Dreams is the headline of the page, with the subtitle 'mompreneur of the year' on the bottom.

Ruby Sweet Dreams

For many months, the entire team of SaStel was searching for the perfect business to be the headline, the most important part of this 100th edition. They couldn't find it, until one day, the incredible owner of this magazine, Mr. Samuel Smith, was around London when Ms. Rao walked by him. From that instant, he knew she would change his life forever, but wasn't just the special connection that grew in that moment that gave her this first place in England's best small businesses. It was when he met her again and got the privilege of tasting her food, and I quote, "That bite was a piece of heaven, served by an angel."

Who isn't already looking forward to trying her food? I sure am.

She is an American Mum of two, who came to this country pursuing a dream and so far, is getting the entire fairy tale.

She impressed the SaStel team with her hard work, genuine passion, and love for food, which set her as an example.

When you want something, work hard, follow your dreams, and enjoy life.

This might be the first time you've heard Ruby Sweet Dreams' name, but believe us it won't be the last.

This writer has a sweet tooth, and I know many of our readers do too.

I close the magazine, pushing it aside, turning and giving my attention to dinner.

"Are the toys back in pace? Dinner will be ready soon."

"We will do right now," Naima says, holding Aidan hand and walking away, I look their way, not missing how her shoulders fall low.

I hate the article, my image is there, but is filled of appreciation for the fantastic boss they have, not about the small businesses that has collaborate. I haven't read the other interviews. but I am sure they are pretty similar, with the difference that the entire world is aware I am the only one warming up his ego maniac bed.

How naive and stupid I was?

The kids ask for bed earlier than usual, and I appreciate it. Maybe they did it aware that I couldn't wait for this day to finish too.

Finishing the kitchen, and writing some items we will have to go and buy at the shops tomorrow to finish some extra orders of cookies, I harshly throw the pen I was using away when someone knock on the door.

We have moved from none a soul been interested on us, to an open house. Matteo is at the other side, holding my gaze for a while, he chose to talk first.

"May I come in?"

"The kids are sleeping."

"It will take five minutes," I open the door and invite him in, walking back to the kitchen, turning the kettle on and preparing a coffee.

"Why he sent you?"

"He didn't, I want to talk to you."

"About him."

"About you," he says, capturing all my attention with his straightforward approach.

"What you want to–"

"He used you, only sole and complete benefit. That is Samuel. He holds himself in others so he won't sink."

"Why are you telling me this?"

"Because I like you, very much indeed," his words heat up my cheeks, "I won't let him hurt you, but I can't let you break him either."

"You can't break what was already broken to begin with."

"I met Samuel when we were eighteen, nineteen. Little boys, playing the game of grown men. I come from a simple family and I won't deny his money blind me. But I was aware of who I was, and that my life matter most that the temporary masking of pain. He had far too many issues."

"He is old enough to mature and push all of that behind him."

"Samuel was lost until a few months ago, he was mentally unstable, emotionally dead, and he will do anything that made him feel better."

I nod, taking a sip of my coffee, placing a platter of biscuits in between us.

"You have a pure soul, an innocent and kindness inside you that are rare to find. Ruby, you can't save him. But you can't run either," I nod at his words.

Tensing when he stands, walking to me, holding the magazine in his hand, stepping closer, intoxicating me with his citrus scent, the warmth of his body temperature meets mine and I tremble, his fingertip brushes a strand of hair that falls forward as I lower my gaze to his chest, avoiding his deep eyes.

"This is the biggest disrespect I read from someone who claim loving the other," his knuckle pulls my head back, making met his eyes. "You need to tell him, as clear as water, teach him the lesson he won't learn from any of us."

"I rather let things go."

"He will come back, he will use his words, his looks, his talents to make you bend on his knees again," his words remind me of our last submissive-dominant encounter. Making me wonder if he knows what happened that day, "you are gorgeous," he whispers.

I step back, walking to the other side of the counter, breathing clean air, shaking my head, and blushing as he grins.

"Where is he?" I ask.

"The office, I will keep an eye on the kids," he says, sending a wink that warms my cheeks.

These men aren't just dangerous on the looks, but on their personality, capable of make a woman do as they request, killing you slowly with their words and ending you with their touch.

But I won't submit to Samuel, I am not a child anymore, and he needs to know what he did is wrong.

With determination I head to his house, walking in by the back door as Rosita suggested, pushing aside the curiosity of exploring around the house, reaching the front door, opening the door and slapping it behind me.

Ready to confront a man that has never been taught a lesson.

That ends today.

Chapter Sixteen

Samuel

The darkness and silence of the night grows around me, I haven't slept at all. My mind keeps replaying the moment Ruby rush upstairs, packed, grabbed the kids and left.

I could have stopped her, I should have stopped her, but I didn't do it.

I can't force her to stay where she doesn't feel at home, safe and happy. Even when I thought she was. Maybe I was just seen, hearing and feeling what I wanted. Not the reality.

That fiction I build in my mind was easier to handle than reality, life is reminding me of the agony, loneliness and emptiness I lived on before I found her.

I head to the kitchen for some coffee, finding Matteo, Calvin and Jackson having some by the island, shutting as I walk in.

"Do not make me stop you," I say, serving an Americano and standing at the other side of the island.

"We weren't talk—"

"I know what is on your fucking heads, my stupid move, all the 'I told you so,' well now I know them! Happy?"

"You are out of your fucking mind," Matteo says.

"Gracie! Something else?"

"I told you this will happen, she is not yours!"

"He lost her long ago. I found her, I claim her, I fix her, she is mine!"

"Stop talking about her like she is a fucking object!" Matteo exclaims.

"You think your name and money can own the world, and you don't even own you fucking soul." Jackson says.

"She should be here, we could have protected them."

"Samuel," Calvin call, "that bastard found her, she was right, he won't stop, and you just stand there doing nothing."

"You weren't here, so shut the fuck up!"

"But I was, Naima was on my arms when Ruby took them away, Aidan was on Jackson's. All while you stand there quietly, what the fuck!"

"How is okay for you to blame me for this?"

"You are so blind, I can't take it," Matteo says, standing and walking past me.

"Did you contact Logan?" I ask, before he leaves.

"He should stay with Ella," Jackson says.

Grandpa gave Stella that nickname when she was little. I haven't heard it in ages. After all she only allowed her close friends to use it. And Jackson is one of them.

"*Ella*, is doing nothing in Blue Valley. I have the gala, Ruby and the kids on the run and a bastard threatening anyone I care for."

"Why do you need him? The office security takes care of the gala. You Ruby go. And that bastard image is in every private service, police station and bounty hunter that exists in the city," Jackson explains.

"Because I pay him, and I chose where and how do you all have to be."

Jackson chuckles, irritating me, I turn to Matteo who tilts his head and give me a questioning face.

"What is so hard to understand? Calvin in the gala taking care of CCTV. Matteo and Logan with me. Jackson, find Ruby and keep an eye."

"You need me and Logan for the event?"

"I do, there will be so many people, and I want them away."

"You celebrate an event to don't even greet the people that pays your fucking lifestyle," Jackson chuckles.

"Pay me?"

"I am done," he says, standing, joining Matteo by the door.

"One more step and you don't have to come back."

"*Vaffanculo fratello!*" Matteo exclaims, walking away.

"You?" I ask Calvin.

"I will get Logan, and I will call someone to keep an eye on Ruby and Stella.

"Thank you."

"What have you done?" Rosita asks, passing by Calvin and heading inside the kitchen.

"Rosita, it's too early," I assure on a tired voice.

"Can you stop messing it all up?!"

"I am not doing anything!"

"That is the problem, you are not doing anything. You are a spoil baby, wanting all and appreciating nothing."

"I think that is enough."

"Will you kick me out too?"

"I haven't—"

"Invite me to leave, is the same *ridiculo!*"

"I will be in the gym and my bedroom, and be down at lunch time, hopefully you have all move on from this early morning tantrum."

My aching arm rests over my eyes, my mind is drowsy after a long session at the gym, a warm shower, helping me to fall into a weird short of nap, that feels more like my entire life is been played under my lids.

I hear them storming upstairs, hitting the wall with the door and pulling me out of bed before I can understand what is happening.

Is Rosita's cry for help what brings me back, "Samuel!" she screams again.

Matteo hold me up, siting me on the bed, "what the hell have you done."

"Workout until I couldn't walk," I explain, while he walks to the closet, throwing some clothes over me.

"I can't believe I have to fucking change you."

"Like old times *fratello.*"

"Jacks!" Matteo shouts, "bring the shot!"

"What?" I ask, holding my body on him to bring my

joggers up.

"Did you shower on boiling water again?"

"I needed to sleep."

"You are out of your fucking mind."

"Where?" Jackson asks, stepping closer and giving me a shot of adrenaline fresh from our first aid kit.

Holding me in place, it doesn't take long before I feel my whole been going wild. My heart hitting my ribcage so hard it will break my ribs, my brain burns and my blood flows as wildfire across my body.

I growl, holding my best friend, the only man I can trust with my life. I wouldn't be here if it wasn't for him.

But something is happening, he wouldn't be doing this again if we weren't in a situation where my stage doesn't matter, my presence does.

"Listen before you move," he says, "we need to travel to Blue Valley, Logan and Rosita are already on the way," my muscles spasm as the words sink in. Something has happen to Ruby or Stella. And for one or another I am full responsible, "no matter what, I am here *fratello*, do not forget that." I nod, taking a deep breath, straightening my body as they step back.

My body trembles, my muscle tighten as the adrenaline shot awakes my body in a way that isn't human.

"The bikes are ready," Matteo assures, I nod and we all rush downstair, jumping on our bikes, and riding to Blue Valley. As we reach the countryside, Jackson takes the lead, I follow him, exhaling in relief when we ride past Ruby's cottage, gripping the handle as the sirens echo inside the helmet, the road is close, there is a mass of press and neighbours, three cars of police building a circle that keeps an ambulance facing the front of the house.

I jump out of the bike, un-bother of the damage I might have cost it, throwing the helmet aside and rushing inside the house.

Rosita sobbing echoes in my brain, I follow it and find the consequences of all my mistakes, neglection and selfishness laying on the floor surrounded by a pool of blood.

Her blonde curls are tinted in red, and she has lost so much blonde that her olive skin now looks grey.

My body spasm as the shot gives me the last boost that now is mixed with the real sensations my body would be experiencing without it.

I stand there, in silence, holding my breath as the paramedic wrap her arms, and practice CPR on her, her small body shakes with every pumping, and a continuation of flat lines blast burns my brain.

The memories of Grandpa last minutes blur my thoughts, the cries of pain from Stella, the pain I never thought possible to feel.

Time slows down, my chest shutters in pieces as I see the only family I have left, my little sister fighting for her life. Or actually not fighting at all.

Her past, all the things she has been through for the past thirty years run like a movie in front of me, showing me that I wasn't there. Nobody else but me existed, and now I might lose her without having the opportunity of apologising.

And the chance of explaining why she will do this to herself, or worse to Scott.

I snap back to that thought, my nephew, I rush around the house, he and the dog are nowhere to be found.

"Where is Scott?" I ask Matteo at the door.

"Logan took him to *Little Castle*. Scott was the one who call," he says.

With heavy foot I walk back to the kitchen, holding myself in the door frame, when she sound of her heartbeat echoes around us.

I march towards William's office in St Marcus hospital with Rosita following closely.

Our families have known each other since Grandpa went to boarding school with Will's grandpa. His father assisted Stella and my birth. Forcing a friendship that has lasted a lifetime. Turning him in our private doctor.

This won't be the first time Stella has put herself in a situation like this, never taking well care of her health, but who am I to judge, as neither did I.

I lost myself in alcohol way too many times, but never in my forty years of life, have I tried to take my life.

My world is darkness, loneliness, emptiness, but I am more scared of the other side than I am of this life.

Stella has everything anyone will dream of, the perfect life, a family, a world resting under the feet.

That has never seemed enough, and I can't push aside the tinkling at the back of my head, that there is more to this that someone isn't telling me.

Will walks in with a clipboard on his hand.

"Where is she?" Rosita asks, cleaning away the tears.

"She is now in a room, we have sedated her after we give her some fluids, blood and clean her up. She was scared, confused, and disorientated."

"Why she did this?"

"She claims she did nothing to herself."

"She is out of her fucking mind," I exhale, pulling my waves.

"Is not the physical damage," he explains. "The police found an extent amount of medication inside the house. Enough to be illegal without prescription," I raise a brow. "Samuel, I would never prescribe her that type of medication, or worse, hide it from you," he is telling the truth, and that scares me the most.

"Someone did, and look what happened. She need to be locked up, taken away from Scott–"

"You can't lock her up for this, I can speak with a friend of mine, she is a therapist, that might help her to open up and tell us more of what happened–"

"You want her around us? Alone with Scott? She could harm him." Rosita says alarmed.

"I believe her inner circle is more harmful that she can be to any of you."

"He is eight, his mother was sinking in blood in the kitchen floor, auto-medicating herself—"

"I run some tests on her before I came, she is clean Samuel, she didn't take that medication, what will help her when she needs to file a police report, but there was something in her blood. That should scare you, and be a warning that makes you want to protect anyone around you," he says, handing me the folder he walked in with, "she was positive in Rohypnol," a ringing nose inside my ears makes my mind confused, my head burns. This cannot be happening.

"That is—"

"A drug that rapist used to attack their victims," Will says, explaining it to Rosita, "she might be right, someone gave her the drug."

"Was she?" I ask.

"No, just the cuts on her arms."

"This is too much," I say, pulling my waves away and resting my elbows on my thighs. "Scott won't see her until she is clean."

"She will stay here for the weekend, that way she can rest, you can make arrangements for what the next move will be, but she needs you Samuel–"

"I am one fucking call away!" I yell.

"Sometimes that call is the hardest move a person can afford to do," William assures.

"I can't be her fucking babysitter."

"Where was her security?"

"Are you putting this shit on me?" I stand, holding my anger to don't storm right on top of him.

"When will you understand her life is as valuable as it's yours?"

"I won't feel responsible from her reckless behaviours."

"Yes, Samuel you are right," William says, giving us what we want to hear.

I grew up with him, I know his tone when he is hiding his true thoughts, but I won't accept this one. Everyone has blamed me for many things, this won't be one of them.

Brushing my waves back, composing myself and helping Rosita cleaning her wet cheeks, I guide her out of the office, walking to the entrance under the close look of anyone crossing paths with us.

Matteo is at the entrance, "take Rosita to *Little Castle*, I have to attend the gala."

"Are you serious?"

"Stella incident has reach the press by now, the last thing we need is to let it overshadow the event."

"I can take you."

"I will take a taxi," I assure, walking to the assigned place for them, giving the address and reaching the apartment before I can let my mind register all what has happened today.

The moment I exit the taxi, my body turns to autopilot, getting ready, driving to the event, giving the speech Helena has prepared before she decided to don't show up, my mind easily build a lie around the absence of Ruby. And before I get to control myself again, I am on the drive back to *Little Castle*.

Everything is quiet when I enter the house, despite how early it is. I head straight to my office on the lower floor, taking of my tuxedo as I fall over the leather chair.

The door opens, I pull my head up and find Ruby standing there. A copy of her edition of SaStel is on her grip while she slaps the door with her other hand.

I hate when people do that, trying to mark a stupid point, making everyone aware of how angry they are.

She seems frustrated, and pissed off at the same time. *Welcome to the club, angel.*

A few hours ago, it was just us—I was just focused on taking care of her, giving her the world, but now everything is a nightmare.

Her gaze is burning my skin, studying me, I don't move, I just wait for her to throw at me all what I know she held in yesterday.

She doesn't move either, her pulse accelerates as I approach her.

"Did you miss me already?"

"You are a son a bitch. A liar, a manipulator, a narcissist—"

"Careful angel."

"Or what? You will punish me? Or you will fuck me like a dirty whore?"

"What the hell are you talking about?"

"Do I need to explain the pile of lies you have given me the past few weeks? Or the things you have done to manipulate me so I wouldn't have the chance to think clearly?"

"I don't know what you are talking about," I lie.

"You might how cross my path accidentally, but I was a sick plan since that moment. You used me for your interest and benefit. You knew I was moving to the cottage since that weekend, and you forgot to let us know you were about to be our next-door neighbour. You knew about Advik, and you acted surprise of everything you find out—"

"I can't afford the people around me keeping secrets from me."

"But you can keep all the secrets of the world."

"My secrets don't affect your present, neither your future."

"Of course, they don't, because I never want to see you again. If you dare to step close to me or the kids, you will know what I am capable."

"Be aware, he might find you first."

Without another word, throwing the magazine my way, I duck and once again I let her walk away.

Nothing that I do will change the words I have just said or the actions I have taken.

I am a piece of shit.

Walking inside the kitchen, passing by Calvin, Jackson and Logan I walk to the liquor locked cabinet.

"Samuel," Jackson warns me.

"There is no reason to be sober anymore."

Rosita storms inside the kitchen, holding my arm, taking the bottle and tumbler away from me and throw it to the other end of the room.

"Was that necessary?"

"What have you done?" she shouts, "everything was perfect, she accepted you, she was open to support you–"

"I don't need anybody's compassion, as I don't have it for anybody either."

"How dare you?!"

"She is unsatisfied, you are, they are, you can all fuck off!" I exclaim, opening the double door, disorientated as the memories of the past, the ones I never know if they were real or nightmares run through my mind like a movie.

yelling in pain, I run my hands over the cupboard, throwing all the bottles ad tumblers across the room, splashing my body in liquor.

I pull my waves back, burning my throat as I let all the anger, pain, frustration and confusion to leave my system.

Exhausted of holding the world over my shoulder. Of caring for everyone when nobody give a fuck about me.

They never did.

I born to be a type of grandson, son, brother, husband, friend, neighbour, business associate,--

All men I could never transform into.

I wanted to be myself with Ruby, I wanted to be redeem from my sins. I wanted to transform into a better human been, one worth of love, sympathy and kindness from others.

But the shadow of my past is far too large.

The echo of my name bothers me, anxious of feeling all the eyes on me, their pettiness.

The room spins when my back hits the opposite wall, my gaze take a few minutes to focus and find Jackson holding me by the collar of my button-up shirt. Shaking me until I return to the kitchen, to the mess I have just made.

"Listen to me son of a bitch!" he yells on a growl, "Stella is gone!" he grunts, letting go of me and making me hit the floor harshly.

The ground shakes around me, an irritating noise rings far too loud in my ears, my heart stops beating, my lungs close up, and I can't found the way to stand. The wall feels miles away, and the surrounding floor has open, leaving me in the centre surrounded by the fire of hell.

Pulling my body up, Jackson pulls me away from the kitchen, pushing me inside a car that Calvin is driving. I shake my head, watching as Logan and Jackson, each on separate bikes, ride away disappearing in the darkness of the night.

It's takes me a few minutes to control myself, to shell myself up and let the harsh Samuel take the lead. My palms brush my face, and push my waves back.

"What happened?"

"William called, Stella is gone."

"How is that possible?"

"She will have to explain it," he says, speeding up to the city, heading to the hospital where hours ago I left her in what I thought was safe hands.

Hours has passed, the sun is about to rise in the horizon and we have no idea where my sister is.

The night nurse was doing her round where she found the medicine cabinet forced and multiple medication missing. She set the alarm, the hospital was locked, all the patients were inspected and they found an empty room where Stella should have been resting.

Three coffees and many miles driven after, we return to *Little Castle*, coming face to face with the scenario where the three women that matter the most to me stand against each other.

Chapter Seventeen

Ruby

After spending the entire night awake, sharing a deep, dark, and painful conversation with Matteo about Samuel past. Asking him to look after the kids once more, I walk to Samuel's house with a tray filled with sandwiches, quiche, cookies and fresh bread.

It has been a productive night after all, giving me the opportunity to prepare food for the boys, Rosita and Scott, make sure they are all taken care of while they go through the sensitive situation of Scott's mom.

Walking in by the back door as I did earlier, I head to the opposite door from his office–the kitchen.

Rosita is sobbing by the island, I rush to her, pacing the food on the dining table and curling my arms around her.

"What happen?"

"Samuel is mad, I can't do this anymore, poor Scott, I can't take care of him like this–"

"Have he woke up?" I ask, seen how the sun fights in between the houses by the glass garden doors.

Shaking her head, I brush her cheeks clean.

"Do you want me to check on him?" she nods. "I brought some food, do you want to prepare some coffee while I go upstairs?" she nods again.

"Up the stairs, left, door on the right side," she says, indicating to me where I can find Scott.

Kissing her cheek, I rose, and quietly reaching Scott's bedroom door, opening slightly and sliding in.

Gasping at the decoration, I look over my shoulder, shocked at how real this bedroom resembles a jungle, how real the dinosaurs drawn in front look. Mr. Wrinkles sleepy walks to me and I brush him behind the ears.

"I need you to take care of him," I whisper in his ear, "I will get you a special breakfast, deal big boy?" licking my cheek, he agrees with the deal.

Making sure Scott is comfortable, kissing his cheek, I walk back downstairs. Pulling my hair up on a messy bun, brushing my eyes as exhaustion starts to kick in.

I pause at the bottom of the steps as I hear a woman screaming, I rush inside the kitchen, halting as the last person I ever thought to be here stands in front of me.

Her curls aren't shiny and smooth, her skin is dry and without life, a hospital gown cover her small body, she is barefoot, and when I study her face once more, trying to make sure what I am seen is real, I gasp when the same eyes Samuel has, once I haven't connected before, drill a hole in me.

"What are you doing here?!" Stella screams, pointing at me.

What is Stella doing here?

"I asked you a question!" She yells.

"Stella. What–?"

I am not the only one unsure of what is happening. My minds starts connecting dots and the coldness of reality falls over me like a bucket of ice water.

Samuel has this all planned from before, nothing was a coincidence. "Where is he?!" She asks shouting at Rosita and me.

Rosita approaches her, her trembling hands doesn't make it close, when Stella pushes her way, turning to me and facing me too close.

"You are the whore that has kept him so distracted," she mumbles.

This close, I can see there is something not right with her, her gaze is dark, empty, her pupils are so dilated that there is barely any turquoise left to be seen.

The way she anxiously nibbles her bottom lip, leaving red marks that might turn into bruises or worst blood if she doesn't stop.

The way her body shakes, or that she bounces side to side, or her hands play with her curls before she fist them, mumbling something on a whisper.

"I should be his priority!" she yells, "He promised–" she pause, mumbling something else I can't understand.

"Stella, why don't you have a tea with us while you wait?" I ask, stepping away from her, bringing the safe distance I feel I need.

"You aren't more than a street rat. I knew it since I met you. I could see the hunger for money, the ambition for more inside you. But you should know something about me, I can get rid of things easy," she says, snapping her fingers, "to start, you are fired, and second, I want you out of here before I have you removed."

Her voice changes as she tries to intimidate me, some words are clear than other, I don't have to ask, she is Samuel's sister, Scott's mom and the reason why everyone is hanging by the edge of the cliff.

If I wasn't alert, observing her every move I would have miss the moment that something clicks on her head. I jump to the door and block it, but she easily push me aside, and walks away. I hold her forearm and my cheek turns into flames as her stupid fake nails scratch the skin on my face, making me lose the grip for long enough for her to run away.

I rush behind her, reaching the bottom of the staircase faster than she does, "Stella, please understand he is resting," I say, holding my arms across.

Defending Scott as if he was my own, I have done it many times, I have took multiple punishments to save them, and this won't be a battle I will easily give up to.

"You won't get to him," I yell, as she jumps over me and I push her away. Her small body falls on the floor and she cries in pain for a second before she tries to jump on me again.

"What the hell is going on?!" Samuel shouts, walking in.

Rosita is by the door, sobbing and holding her chest, Stella is inches away, ready for another round of punches and pushes. And I hold my position not ready to give up that easily.

From three of us, after all what we have all been through, despite who each of us are in his life. Samuel rushed to me and brushes my bleeding cheek.

"I will take care of this," he whispers, kissing my temple, covering me with his body and turning to Stella.

"Are you for real big brother?!" she chuckles.

"Stella, let me help you," he says, approaching her, embracing her on his arms, where she breaks down, sobbing in pain.

The room grows silent, Jackson, Logan, and Calvin stand by the front door, observing her every more.

"I can't do this any longer," she cries, as he cups his face and rests his forehead on hers.

Samuel is in pain too, he loves to pretend he is the tough guy in the room, the invincible, the heartless.

In this moment as he holds his sister in his arms, I can feel the pain they both have hold over them for years. I don't see two full grown-ups, I see two harmed kids, exhausted physically and emotionally of pretending and I hope letting out their fears, their emotions it will set themselves free.

"I don't want be like this anymore," she says, holding his wrists, pulling back so he will look at her in the eyes. "That old lady and that whore need to get out of our lives."

"In my house we talk to each other with respect," he

says, pushing her hands away, stepping back and breaking the connection they shared instants ago.

"You are blind!" she yells, pulling her curls, walking in circles. "She is after our money, and she–".

"You should shut up! Just talking out of pure ignorance," I shout back, marching to her, stopped by Matteo as he entered the house by the same way that I did.

"I am done with you," Samuel says, pointing at Stella, pulling his mobile out of his pocket and calling someone called William. "She is here, take her in. I have things to work out."

At Samuel's words, Stella chose to rush to the front door, coming face to face with Logan, sharing a silent message through eye contact, his arms open and she hides her face on his chest, hugs him, as he brushes her curls and whispers on her ear.

Pushing aside the curiosity, I look over my shoulder, Matteo stands there, far too close, but at the same time making me less strange in a room where I thought I knew someone or something. But now is clear, I was just a visitor on a stranger house.

"Go home, I will be there soon," he says, pointing at the back door.

Without second thoughts, letting the room come back to live I chose to step away, to leave them behind and make sure who matters, my babies are fine since Matteo walked away.

Making sure all the doors and windows are locked, I head upstairs, where I observe them sleep for a while, before I head to the shower, leaving the door open so they can follow the noise to find me, washing away the past many hours that this day has last, I pick one of my thin floral dresses, comb my hair and let it fall on my back, check on them one more time and head downstairs, collecting the newspapers that has been delivered with some other local mail and head to the kitchen, opening the back door to let the fresh air of the morning clear the house and I start mixing ingredients, mumbling a song I had on a playlist I randomly filled up every time I like a song, and I enjoy a warm coffee to shake away the sleepless night.

Letting the headline of the paper take my full attention for a moment.

<u>Smith's family under attack.</u>

On the century celebration of SaStel's first magazine been launch.
A new scandal over shadow the event of the year from the hand of the princess of the family.
After years since she stepped away from the social city life she was living on, Stella Smith covers the news one more time with a new scandal. The supposed allegations of an attack on herself at the property the family owns in Blue Valley by an employee.
This wouldn't be the first-time inexplicable events happen to the heiress of one of the biggest empires in the world.
Was it an accident? Only time will tell.

Disgusted by the way the press uses a human's life, I throw the paper away, remembering it is something similar to what Samuel did to me and my business.

Did he really thought he was helping?

I don't see it that way, the opposite. He has now associated his name to my company as if I owe him something, when in the contrary, since he stormed inside my life nothing has gone the way was planned.

The focus has turned to him, and even I did fulfill my orders, I need to be honest to myself. Scott birthday stop been my priority many days ago, overshadow not just by us moving to this gorgeous cottage, but by the time I gave to Samuel, the trip to London, and everything that follow those choices.

Now standing here, with no orders to work on, or idea of where the future brings me, by the hand of that hideous article at the posh magazine.

"Knock knock," Matteo calls from the door.

I wave with my hand, inviting him to enter, serving him a coffee and refilling mine.

"Why are you here?"

"They just left, Stella was taken to a private facility. Samuel went to the city and Rosita is resting while Jackson keeps an eye on Scott."

"You don't have to come and report me everything," I assure, "I have no intention on having anything else to do with that family, so I rather step aside and forget it all."

"That's it? You are done with us, like we have no value?"

"I am done with Samuel, he is your boss, your best friend, I don't want him around my children, not knowing all what I do now."

"I thought you had feelings for him," he says.

"I thought he was being honest to us, turns out not everything is what it seems like."

"So, what now?"

"I have the Summer Fair coming in a few days, that should help recover what I now have to refund Stella for the cancelation of the party–"

"You don't have to do that."

"I don't want that money–"

"Doesn't he deserves a party?"

"Of course, he does, he is the sweetest boy, all of this should not be happening to him."

"Then don't cancel anything. No matter what Stella said, or where Samuel is. Do it for who matters that day, Scott."

"The kids will wake up soon," I say.

"*Little Castle* is open for you, the kids could have some time together, you are not alone Ruby, please don't let Samuel take that away from us."

I nod, watching him leave, reconsidering his words. What I believe is the correct thing to do.

After hours of cooking, I message Sarah and Miguel, inviting them to visit us, enjoy the cottage and give myself a touch of who I was weeks ago, talking with them might help me find who I feel keeps slipping from my fingers and is turning into another idiot a man can control.

"Amiga, your life is like the telenovelas that plays in señor Miguel village," Sarah laughs, after I give them a small resume of what has happened.

"I can't say anything."

"Why would you say that?" I ask Miguel, who had been seated in the kitchen table for hours now, silently hearing what I have to say.

"You want to hear the 'I told you so's'?"

"Maybe."

"He blind you with his money, extravagant life, attention, looks, words. Those men are experts in getting what they want, and you fall on the rabbit hole in a matter of hours."

"I will say yes to the things he said and the way he took care of us without asking anything–"

"He asked something in return, your time, your mind, your heart, your body. It wasn't a clear open question, but he took what he wanted giving you the crumbs of what you needed."

"I made a mistake, should I pay–"

"You didn't make a mistake, you lived, innocently and blindly, and thankfully you stepped away of it before he fully transform you in God knows what. But–"

"Knock knock," Rosita calls from the door, "someone here wanted to pay a visit," she says bringing Scott inside the house.

"Good afternoon," he says politely, rushing to my arms, hugging me and whispering in my ear, "thank you for the special breakfast," he says, aware of the little batch of pancakes I left in *Little Castle* secretly while my kids had breakfast.

"Don't tell anyone, is not allowed to snick in people's houses," I whisper back, making him giggle. "Naima and Aidan are playing in the family room," I say, inviting him to go and find them.

Tilting my head at what is happening after just a few minutes distracted with Scott. Rosita has introduced herself, Sarah is serving lemonade, and Miguel is in full on conversation with her. His cheeks are like two cherries, his round belly raises as he laughs, and he nervously fix his hair as she talks.

"What happen to this two?" I ask Sarah by the counter.

Serving Rosita and Miguel their drinks and stepping out with Sarah, taking some fresh air, funny fact as it's one of the hottest days of the month.

"Something like what happen between Samuel and you," she says, answering my question.

"I made a mistake."

"No amiga, you try to move on, there is nothing wrong with that, except that you jumped a thousand step and went to the front of the line without knowing the rules of the game."

"Do you know what I realized these past few days?" I ask, inhaling as I open up for once, "I doubt I have felling for him, I don't miss him, I miss what his attention make me feel, I miss how easily with one kiss, one word, one touch, he could make everything become insignificant. Oh gosh I am horrible."

"You aren't," she assures.

"For starters that is what men does to us all the time,

and its great you acknowledge it, so you stop doing it. I can't blame you, that man is as delicious and addictive as chocolate. Who can look and not have the temptation of try it. He gave you the green light, and you took it all the way in."

"I can't be the woman Samuel needs, I don't like his world, all the extravagant lifestyle, the security following everywhere, the crap the press says about them, the mysterious past–"

"What mystery?"

"I can't put my finger to it yet, but there is something in their family history, something happened, and that make them who they are today, insecure, cruel, heartless, selfish."

"I wouldn't ever use those words to describe him, but I don't know him at all. It's obvious he has an ego as large as his body. But he looked kind and attentive."

"Yes, but like Miguel said, in his own advantage. He being nice invite him to spend the night with me."

"Is he good?" she teases.

"Sarah!" I giggle, "I have nothing to compare it to."

"That doesn't mean you don't know if he is good or not."

"There is something in them–"

"Who?"

"Samuel and the men that work for him."

"They look good too?"

"Bona sera," Matteo says, walking in the garden by the bushes hidden spot, Sarah's jaw hits the floor and I grin, aware she has just experienced what I was about to explain.

"Everything okay?"

"I was left alone," he says, with a sad face, "I thought my incredible neighbor might be lonely too, but I was wrong."

"The cottage has become the new meeting point."

"With that food and coffee, I am the number one uninvited guest you can expect all day."

"I'm Sarah," she says, offering her hand forward, Matteo takes it, giving her one of those smiles they all have just for women and I laugh loudly.

"This is Matteo, right hand and best friend of Samuel."

"I see," she says, nodding, hiding the hand he just hold behind her.

"I was wondering if the kids would like to come and watch a movie, we can order–"

"Do not say take away," I warn him, "I can cook something."

"Is that a yes?" he asks, holding his bottom lips under his teeth, hiding the smile I can see growing in the corner of his mouth before I answer, "he is not coming, I promise, just us."

"I have company–"

"They can come too, after all we own a castle," he jokes, making Sarah giggle, completely absorbed by his charm.

One I am getting used to, but I can't deny is there.

Letting Jackson take care of the pizzas I have placed in the large ovens, I walk out to the cinema room.

This place was stunning before he bought it, now is a place I wouldn't want to walk out of, Miguel gave me the look when we enter the kitchen, and I hide it as best as I could.

This is my dream space, make of beige marble, stunning wood cupboards, all the appliance and tools available in the market, a dining table to accommodate a large group, and a brand-new walk-in fridge or freezer at the back, sadly empty as this people are not used to cook fresh food.

The movie room is a complete cinema, dark velvet couches spread around the room on a way that no matter who seats in the front, everyone can watch.

Matteo has found a good kids friendly dinosaur movie, and the kids are enjoying the time with some popcorns when he invites me to walk outside.

"I need to talk to you," he whispers, "Samuel is an arsehole, we know that by now," he continues, "but before you walk away, Rosita and I believe there is something you have to know first, something we haven't allowed Samuel to know just yet."

"If he can't know it, why can I?"

"Because that is the only way to know who he is, where he comes from, the little boy he keeps hiding away, maybe that way you can learn who he was meant to be, and–"

"And what Matteo?" I ask, holding his arm when his head fall, exhaling loudly, "please, talk to me."

"I don't want you to give him a second chance," he confesses, "if he hurt you again," he pauses, "promise me you will learn all of this impartially."

"You want me to imagine I don't know him?"

"Something like that," he says.

I nod, letting him lead me to Samuel's office, apprehension grows in my chest, the fear of find him inside, but I don't, it's empty, I turn, "thank you Matteo, you should be on his side, but I can see you care for us too," he nods, closing the door behind him and leaving me there on my own.

Taking in the space, a grand, thick, shiny wood desk, with a tall brown leather chair. The wall behind is large bookshelf, randomly filled with books that are laying not standing as they should. Behind the desk, on the corner that face the front of the house, and over a couch by the window are piles and piles of documents.

Some has the shape and look of old document, some are hand written, curiosity wins, and I move around the room exploring what secrets hides under those piles.

It's dark outside by the time I finish arranging the documents in different piles next to the couch. I reconsider the categories, there are far too many things that only Samuel should organized. There are legal documents, bills, contracts of the company, letters, and others that I have no clue what they could be.

After I have separate things by time frames, as some of them go back to the 50s, they must be Samuel's grandfather.

What has me intrigued are the letters, some are inside envelopes that haven't been open, while others are without one and the paper has got damaged with the years.

Randomly picking on, I open it, it's from 1956. A

beautiful female handwriting makes me travel back on time where this was the only way of communication.

Dear Scott,

This will be the last letter I can send as a free woman.

News might have reached you, after all, my engagement has become the gossip in the village. This wasn't on my plans, but we both know an over eighteen years old should not be unmarried, especially on a small town like ours.

Since Mr. Baird passed, my father has struggled with money, and my paints can't cover a full family need.

Father was delighted that a family from a high social level as the Murray are, chose me to be their elder son's wife.

I haven't met him, that won't happen until the day, but the new girls in town, the ones that came all the way from Ireland to witness the wedding, are running around the village talking of how well-mannered and handsome he is.

You know I never seen the physical beauty in people, and I hope he can grow to see my inside as he can appreciate my outside.

And most importantly support and respect my art career. After all, he might be able to help me to put my art out there.

I wish you all the best in the Great city of London, and leading *your father's company to the success I know you will.*

Never forget how much I loved you.

Yours forever,

Catherine Thomas.

Scott must be Samuel's grandfather, and he was in love with a woman that marry other man.

I search for other envelopes with her handwriting, but I can't found any. She mentioned send that last letter.

Wouldn't that mean that there should be more on these piles?

Bringing far too many questions to my mind, I push aside all the close envelopes, and nearly miss one letter. The paper is so fragile that the three pieces way is fold in, is nearly falling apart.

Someone will blame it to be dated back to 1952, but something tells me this letter has been read multiple times, more than the others, and I can't wait to know why.

Dear Catherine,

With great sadness, I write this letter to inform you of the death of my lovely parents on their journey back from London. Their funeral will take place on a week time at our graveyard. I will appreciate your assistance.

These circumstances have turned me into the owner of SaStel, and the head of a family where I am the only member.

I will have to change my residency to the Great City of London. I will finish my economic studies and run the company more efficiently from there. I want to honor the memory of my parents, even when that was not the future I had in mind.

I don't want to go alone, I don't want to have all of this just for me.

Please come to me as soon as you read this letter. Here at the castle or in London if you must.

Let's make our dreams come true on a way, side my side, in freedom.

Forever yours, Scott Smith.

I gasp as I brush my fingers through the letter, closing my eyes and feeling all the emotion he used as he wrote these words, but as well the one coming for a darker place, that couldn't be Catherine.

What woman on her right mind will take this letter on a negative way?

If Scott was something like Samuel, he must have had a line of women waiting at his doorstep. He loved Catherine, I can feel it on the way he begs for her closeness, even just on a friendly way.

But she must have not loved him enough, if she didn't show up, and then agree to married another man.

The office door opens and startles me, I jump to my feet, holding my breath as a tormented, exhausted, broken version of the Samuel I know stands steps away from me.

"I didn't know. Matteo said." I explain nervously.

"I apologies, I didn't know where to go," he says,

rubbing his eyes with the back of his hands, pulling his waves back.

Everyone is on a spiral of sleepless nights, I wouldn't be surprised if I walked into the cinema room and find the grown-ups sleeping and the kids watching, keeping an eye on them and their dreams.

"I will get the kids, it's late–"

"What are those?" he asks pointing at the piles on the floor.

"Documents–"

"You arrange the office?" he asks in disbelief.

"Everything was piled in corners, I just separate it," I explain, nervously playing with the material of the dress.

Aware that perhaps I over step this time, thinking it will be helpful for him, but in reality was my curiosity turning to be more important than his needs.

Wouldn't that make me selfish too?

"You separate it," he repeats, and I nod, "into what?" he ask, stepping more inside the room, but keeping the same distance.

Making me wonder what has changed that now makes him want to put a distance in between us.

"I thought it will help, if things were organized in categories," I explain.

"May I?" he asks pointing at the piles, I step aside and observe as he seats w, resting his back on the couch, facing the piles I have separated, "do you mind guiding me through them?" he asks, pointing at the other side of the documents where I am standing.

Taking a seat, nibbling my bottom lip nervously, rearranging the letters I open, I explain him what each are.

"Legal documents shouldn't be here, that is Nathaniel's responsibility," he points out, I nod and let him talk, "Invoices and bills belong in SaStel. Those are the properties contracts and blueprints," he point out to a large pile, making me wonder how many properties this family owns. "And those–old junk, I guess, it can go–"

"Excuse me?" I ask offended, "that it belong to you grandfather."

"Who died over two decades ago, and by the look of them, they are just old letters."

"That is how much you care for you legacy?"

"My what?"

"They aren't just old letters, that is your grandfather story, the one that brought you where you are today–"

"You read them?" he asks, I look away, standing and fixing my dress, excusing myself and running away, ashamed of been told I have overstep.

"Ruby, wait!" he exclaims, catching up by the foyer.

"I didn't mean to," I explain.

"Is everything alright?" Matteo asks, walking out of the cinema room.

"None of your business," Samuel says, with a darkness his eyes and a ruthless tone of voice.

"Why do you talk to him that way?" I ask, not liking his attitude towards someone he should be friendly and kind.

"Because I am having a conversation with you, and he is unnecessarily interfering once more."

"I let her inside the office–"

"I didn't mean to disrespect you, I was curious," I explain, embarrassed of my behavior.

"What is happening here?" Rosita asks walking out of the kitchen.

I turn in frustration, wanting to run away so people will stop coming out of rooms, and this conversation will be over.

"You were curious about my past," Samuel repeats, brining me back to the previous conversation, ignoring the surrounding people, "have you ever been told that curiosity kill the mice?"

"Samuel!" Matteo and Rosita exclaim.

"I am not scared of you Samuel, I was trying to help you, but it is clear you don't appreciate nothing that is done for you, which is nearly everything, because *Mr. Lord of the Castle* thinks we are just his subjects, and our duty is to do as he please."

His head tilts, his brow raises, his eyes come back to life with a spark I haven't seen before, and his tongue runs through his bottom lip, as the corner tilts up slightly.

"Leave us," he orders, Matteo grunts behind me, "now," he says, and I hear how both do so, my eyes are fixed on his.

Studying this man I lost my mind four days ago, the same one that has shown me multiple personas living inside him, and now is watching me as a predator does to his prey before devouring it.

"Ms. Rao, would you mind if we continue this conversation in the office?" he ask, stepping aside and pointing the way he wants me to follow, "please."

Squaring my posture, I walk slowly, holding my gaze to his, looking over my shoulder, shaking in a mixture of sensations as I observe the way he studies me from head to toe before I walk inside the room.

"Have a seat," he offers, holding one of the chairs facing the desk, he walks to the other side and take his place on the large leather chair.

Time pause, the silence is thick, and my entire body burns under his penetrating eyes study me.

"Is disrespectful to stare at people," I say, breaking the silence.

"May I touch?"

"No, you can't," I chuckle, "what do you want Samuel?"

"What do you want Ms. Rao?" he asks on a low raspy voice.

My head tilts, aware of the game he is playing, considering if I am interested or not in follow it.

"An apology."

"I am sorry," he whispers, resting his body back, pinching his bottom lip, trying to hide a smile.

"Sincerely."

"I am sincerely sorry."

"You are so immature," I chuckle, "I am not doing this," I say, pushing the chair back to stand.

"Ms. Rao, despite of your believes, your assumptions, your little knowledge," he pause, pointing at the documents, "you prove me once more how little you know me."

"I am not interested, anyway."

"That is not what your behaviour reflects," he says, irritating me with this new serious tone in his voice.

"I already apologies."

"There is the point, Ms Rao. If life taught me something, is that *'I am sorry'* is not enough, those three words change nothing, they are enough for some people and under some circumstances. But the reality is, every action has a reaction, and that reaction comes with a consequence."

"I won't seat here while you treat me like a naughty child."

"Have you been naughty?" he asks, "don't answer," he says, as my lips part, "I am sorry if my words make you feel that way."

My brow raises, irritated of this conversation since the moment I accept entering the room.

Wondering what will his point be and why he thinks I want to hear it all.

"And I am sorry for your cheek," he says, pointing at the bruise I hide under my hair.

"You have nothing to do with that."

Actually, he does.

"Actually, I do. Because I didn't tell you who I was, who my sister was–"

"You lied."

"I am sorry."

"That doesn't change what you did."

"That is my point, your apologies for digging in my past, one that I refuse to dig in, and I have to take it gracefully. My apology is not enough to excuse the secrets I kept from you."

"Are you comparing?" I ask, pointing at the documents, myself, him, confused on the point he is trying to make here.

"I miss you," he say, watching my reaction.

"I don't."

"When are you going to put your fucking guard down and accept the truth?"

"When are you going to put your guard down and saw me who you really are?"

"Who I was has nothing to do with who I am."

"And that is where you are wrong, Who you were, what happen in your past, all of that," I say pointing at the documents on the floor, "that has brought you to be the man you are today."

"That man," he points at the piles, "or this man," he points at himself, "neither of them are good enough for you."

"Sam, that is where you are wrong too. I saw who you tried to hide inside yourself. There are moment, when something has happened, I have said a certain thing, an old memory has crossed your mind. At that time, that instant that if I wasn't looking I would have missed is when the real Samuel came to the surface."

His jaw clench, aware of what I am talking about, and perhaps not happy with been exposed in such a vulnerable way.

"I have an idea," I say standing, the deep frown grows in

between his brows. "Do you have something to blindfold you?"

"Are we playing games, angel?"

"No pervert, I want to try something," I giggle and after many days, so much pain and frustration I get to listen to his laugh.

"You will have to go to my bedroom."

"Me?" I ask astonished.

"Your idea," he points out, making me change slightly the plan I had, looking out of the window, it's the middle of the night, and if wasn't for the desk light and corner stand I light up before, we will be in the darkness.

"Where is your bedroom?"

"Stairs, big door on the right," he says, pointing with his finger. I nod and walk my way out.

Taking one step at the time, a heaviness grows on my chest, a mixture of fear and courage.

I am unsure of what will this help with, if something might change in between us. But something I know is, Samuel need to learn how to talk, and let that pain and trauma come out.

My heart miss a few beats when I open the double doors, in the darkness, the park view on display by the large full wall window lights enough the room to let me see what I have around.

The door opens behind me and I step aside, to a corner where the light doesn't touch hiding me, starting the little idea I have in mind.

"Hi, I am Ruby," I say, using a sweet, innocent and

younger tone of voice.

"Hi, I am Sam, nice to meet you," he replies, forcing a boy's voice to hide his raspy normal one. "I like your accent," I grin.

"I like yours too. I am from Texas, from a small village called Shepperton."

"I am from Edinburgh, from a *Little Castle* in the mountains."

"You live in a castle? wow. I live in a farm."

"Do you have many animals?"

"We have chickens, but I don't' like them, they are naughty and loud," I say, smiling as he laughs, brushing my back on the wall and taking a seat when I see him sitting at the center of the room.

In the darkness, with this game and voices, I can see young Samuel, as clear as the sun.

"We have a horse, but papa says I am too young to ride it, maybe when I turn sixteen. And we have cows, Moon and Dalia. They are naughty too, but I think they understand me, and they are just trying to play with me so I won't feel lonely or bored."

"We have horses too. Stella just got one this morning as her Christmas present. She is my sister, she is twelve in a month, so her presents in the holidays are bigger than anyone else's."

"What about yours?" I ask, feeling the pain in his voice as he mentions the attention Stella receives that I think he doesn't.

"I don't have one. Well, I used to, but they took him

away. Father says I stress him out, and he got mad."

"Did you? Stress the horse?"

"If I did, I am not aware of it, he didn't let me ride him, so I used to take him for walks, read him some books, teach him where he came from in the first place."

"Do you believe he understood you? That maybe he just wanted to break his enclosure at your castle and trot freely around the world?"

"I do, but father said that was madness. They didn't tell me, but I think he killed it. That is the easiest way to get rid of things that bother you."

"How old are you Samuel?"

"I will be thirteen soon," my heart breaks.

The idea of this game is to share with the other when did we broke, what happen in our lives that killed who we were and make this new version born.

"Did you said it's Christmas at your castle?"

"It is indeed. The fields are white from the snow, the house is noisy from the grown-ups Christmas Party, kids are not allowed inside." he said, with a touch of resentment in his words. "We are allowed, just to walk around the room while a bunch of strangers shake our hands, squeeze our cheeks, say stupid things to our faces or over praise our beauty, then we have to leave," he explains.

Proving something, I knew it was not a made-up thing, but a reality. Samuel has had everything a boy might have want or need in life. But there were many side things that he has to go through that he might have disagree and somehow needed to be done as a duty.

"Stella is hiding in the library with Nathaniel, and Will, Logan and I are in the family room," he says.

I want to pause him, even ask if what I just heard is correct. Nathaniel is the name he mentioned earlier as the man that should take care of his legal documents. Is Will, William the doctor they mentioned last night when Stella had her breakdown? And hold on, Logan, his employee, his security guard was with him as a child?

Confused, I push my questions aside, listening to the rest of the story.

"William has teased me to break into the liquor cabinet, it's time we find out why is under key, I want to taste it, that will make me feel like a powerful, loved by everyone man like my grandpa or my dad. Should it?"

"I never liked the smell of liquor."

"The idea was to messed up the bottles, give it a little taste, maybe hide them somewhere else and have a laugh later on," he pauses, "Sometimes. there are things that. I don't do it on purpose."

"What you did Samuel?"

"When I go through those trances, everything turns dark, other is a blurry image running in front of me faster than I can focus. I didn't. That wasn't my intention."

"What happened that night Samuel?"

"I can hear their cries for help, the horror on their voices, the cracking of the wood, the glass shuttering around me, everything echoes inside my head, is too loud," he anxiously explains in between sobs.

My chest aches at what seats just steps away from me. A

grown man, reviving this moment, this memory as if it's happening right now.

"I didn't mean to. You believe me right, Ruby?"

"I do believe you Sam. What happen after the incident?"

"They wouldn't let me live there anymore. Neither take me to London. Nobody wanted to be around me."

"It was a mistake," I say, horrified to think a family will reject him for a mistake, no matter how big the aftermath was.

"I was sent to Gordonstoun, a boarding school to high-class boys. That was a prison, a life punishment, a military treatment to break us, and mold us back to the man our parents needed us to be. Heartless, cruel, ready to overpass everything and everyone on the journey to reach the pick of the mountain."

"How long here you there for?"

"Five years. You leave when you are eighteen, straight to college. In my case straight to SaStel."

"You took care of you family business from a young age."

"No, I didn't," he inhales loudly, "I was called back home before graduation, my grandfather was dying. He was a really important man. The sweetest, brightest, kindness, most smart men I ever met in my life. So, I was grant a special permission to say my goodbyes."

"I am really sorry Sam. What happen after that?"

"I followed his words, I knew the destiny standing in front of me. Life in London, working at SaStel, event after event, engaged and married before I hit twenty-three, a bunch of kids before I hit my late twenties, and a life of fakeness, misery and unhappiness."

"How did you avoid it?" I ask, scared to think that could be past he is trying to hide, what will make his previous lies become insignificant.

"I run away. I pack my things. Took money from the safety box and run away from them for good."

"For how long?"

"The first time, three years. I heard a rumor about my parents and thought I should come back and check. I don't want talk about that tonight."

"That is okay Sam, thank you for sharing this with me. You said the first time, can I ask about that?"

"Yes, I came back, I recover. I was trying, but I make a mistake that I," he pause, hiding his face on his palms, sobbing loudly.

I crawl to him, softly moving his hands away and embracing him, brushing his long waves, kissing his temple while he cries on my chest.

"I am so sorry you went through all of that Sam."

"Please, don't go tonight," he begs.

"The kids, I left them in the cinema room."

"They are in their bedroom," he says, I pull him back, frowning, not understanding what he is talking about.

"Their what?"

"The room at the end of the corridor—"

"The one with the arch?"

He nods, I gasp. Remembering our conversation weeks ago in the car, when I shared what I will do with that room, how it will be the children bedroom.

"Can you please stay, I just want you to hold me," his eyes become glassy and filled with tears.

"Sam–"

"I am scared. I don't want to fall again. Please just hold me for tonight."

I nod, gasping as he holds me in his arms, my legs curl in his waist, walking to the mattress and slowly resting me over the soft pillows, lowering himself over me, moving aside after his full body brush mine, resting a leg over mine, an arm across my tummy and his face on my neck.

"Good night angel."

Chapter Eighteen

Samuel

The house is dark and silence when I tiptoe out of bed, collect some joggers and a t-shirt, heading down to grab some water and deciding if I should go back to sleep by Ruby side. Head to the gym and burn my feelings away. Or hide in the office and study those documents with information that nobody has ever talked about.

Jackson and Matteo are in the dining table as I enter, cutting their conversation and staring at me.

"Please don't stop because I am here."

"She is in your bedroom," Matteo points out.

"Yes, *fratello*, she is sleeping in *my* bed."

"You used her again–"

"No, I invite her to stay, since you decide to put the kids in their bedroom."

"What do you want out this?" Jackson asks

"I want her."

"She is not and objective you can possess or use," he

says, standing and facing me with a disapproval look.

"I need her."

"You need the idea of not been alone again," Matteo points out this time.

"Samuel she is not yours," says Jackson, taking some sandwiches out of the fridge.

"She is my past, present and she will be my future," I assure them, after last night everything will be better. "Nobody can tell me what I can or can't have."

"She will have to leave," Matteo exclaims walking to me.

"You don't understand, she was mine before she even knew I existed," I explain, "she saw me in a dream."

"Wake the fuck up *fratello*! That bastard is looking for her, you knew she was in danger and you expose her in a worldwide magazine. Everyone in the full fucking planet knows where she lives. How long until he finds her?"

"That is not. I didn't," his words sink in my head, making clear the huge mistake I made, "we will keep them here, we can protect them, they are just next door."

"You have to let her go, she has survived six months without an incident. You have been in her life for a month and her life is upside down," Matteo says.

"I can't do that, not now."

"You can't keep her while you deal with your problems and feelings."

"She loves me−"

"She doesn't. She is not even sure if she has feelings," Matteo says, "pushing her, will just confuse her. Let her go. If she will meant to be yours, you will find each other."

"How do you know that?"

"She told me. Samuel, get back to the city, take care of Scott, he needs you. Give everyone space and time."

"I don't want to be away from her."

"You are a selfish son of a bitch," he says, stepping closer, "I won't let you break her."

"Stay away from her, I won't say it one more time," I warn him.

"Neither will we," Jackson assures.

"Fuck you!" I exclaim, heading to the gym, ready to burn everything away, taking one by one my thoughts away and transform them into the pain that keeps me alive.

Ruby is not in the bedroom as I walk back, neither are the kids on their bedroom, or in the kitchen where I find a devastated Scott.

"Why did they go?" he asks as I enter, everyone's eyes are on me. Perhaps waiting for my answer to be the correct one.

"There are so many things we can't tell you at the moment, just know that we love you, and we are doing the best that we can to make you feel safe and loved."

"They are my only friends."

"We will see them in few days, for now I think a little break out of this town will help us both a lot."

"What about mom?"

"She is in the best hands possible, we can't see her now, but maybe we could ask when visitations are allowed."

"What about school?"

"You are a week away from summer break, nothing will

change if we leave now."

"Where will we go?"

"Up to you, choose anywhere."

"I want to visit Great Grandpa's castle," a knot block my throat, I clear it, swallowing hard to avoid chocking, "is that okay?" he asks, looking behind me to Logan and Rosita.

"Nobody has been there in years," Rosita reminds.

"How about this? We will use the days away to clean the place, fix what it must, get the place ready for a summer in the mountains."

"Can we uncle Sam?"

"Anything for you," I say, embracing his little body, sending him for a shower and change before we can leave.

I turn to the others as he leave, meeting complete disagreement from them.

"If you don't want to come, be my guest. Scott and I are going."

"Samuel, you haven't been there since—"

"I decided I should face my past, that by making peace with it, I will be able to move forward. I don't expect any of you to be ready to return. But you are more than welcome.

We reach our biggest possession in Edinburgh by sun down, everyone decided to come, and I chuckle when I see Aberdeen by the front door with a basket of fresh fruit.

"Look who we have here!" I exclaim, walking to her and hugging her. I haven't seen her since we were kids, she is the same age as Stella, always running around her, as the only girlfriend my little sister was allowed to have.

"Look at you! You haven't changed a bit," she says, brushing my waves back.

I need a haircut.

"Tell that to my greys," I joke, "let me introduce you to Jackson, the big guy," he raise a hand like if we are at school and I chuckle as Aberdeen cheeks match her ginger hair, "that is Calvin, this is my brother Matteo," I say, curling my arm around him, ready to stop this weird shit going on between us, "you know Rosita," I say on a tired voice, "that ugly one there is Logan," I point out to our childhood friend, "and the last but not least, this little man, the best in the family, the future of the Smith, Scott."

"Is this?" she pause, looking in between Scott and Logan.

"Stella's son," Logan says, I frown and Aberdeen giggles.

"Pleased to meet you Scott."

"The pleasure is mine Aberdeen, thank you for the basket."

"Are you the most adorable thing ever?" she asks, giggling and handing me the keys of the house. "Grandma hold them all these years, she knew you will return one day."

"I am so sorry for her lost," I say, giving a sympathetic smile.

Walking to the front door, I turn the key and push the heavy doors that open my path to the past.

Taking one step at the time, hearing how the other enter by the kitchen door, and are steps away, but on a place like this they feel miles away.

My chest aches at the memories fall over me. The day I

walked in to see Grandpa for the last time, the last look over my shoulder.

And the reminder of the day, I thought I was following a simple national gossip.

Ridding back here to find my little sister as the head of the family, my parents given to us in a jar without notion of what happen to them and without the possibility of retaliation or reconciliation been taken away from me.

My mother, the first woman I ever loved, someone I would have burned the world down for, she was gone, taken forever, I was a bad son, and that day I star paying the consequences of my actions.

The next few days fly by. The boys and I have been busy repairing anything that time has damaged, and exchanging old furniture.

Rosita, Aberdeen and a few other ladies from the village have helped with cleaning, refilling the pantry and purchasing all to turn these ruins into the castle that everyone knew not so long ago.

Now with a new family, a new heir, and a fresh new future ahead of us.

Scott didn't take long until he made friends at the farmer's market on one of Rosita's visits and now has a bunch of kids running around with Mr Wrinkles and him.

Life is hard, but simple. Time never seems enough to do what we want in one go and keep me busy enough.

I remember Ruby and the kids every time I pass by mom and grandpa's flower garden, or every time Scott laughs.

I want to believe she is at peace and happy now that we aren't around to complicate her life more than it already is.

That doesn't make the nights any shorter when I sit in the darkness and train my brain to bring her to the box of my past, where many live and it helps me to don't be haunted and affected by their loss.

"Can't sleep?" Matteo asks, entering the library, I shake my head, "neither do I."

"The ghost that inhabits this castle will never let me."

"Do you feel it?"

"Speak about it sounds insane."

"I swear, there are unexplainable things happening, noises, misplaced things. It sounds fucking insane."

"Grandpa never left this place. I can hear his footsteps that used to wake me up at night, when he was−" I pause, the things that I saw as a child, his words the last time I saw him. I wasn't in my best mindset that time, I could have imagined it all.

What if I didn't?

"Everything good?" Matteo ask, while I walk away, heading to the corridor that ends in the kitchen, Matteo is close by, my hands brush over the left wall from the kitchen, nothings feels different under the wall paper that will have to be replaced soon.

From the kitchen door, I walk close to the other wall, looking for a dent, a bump, something out of place, brushing my hand through the paper feels less old on this side.

"What are we looking for?" Matteo whispers.

As I reach the curve of the corridor, steps away from connecting with the rest of the house, besides a full body painting, next to the thick wood frame I push a piece that seems too reattached to it.

We step back when a loud cracking noise grows around us, the painting moves slightly forward, and with Matteo's help, we move it all the way.

"What the heel is this?" he asks once we have enough room to fit our bodies in.

"My grandpa's secret."

"How do you know?"

"I saw him when I was a kid, and he told me before he died. I thought it was a dream."

"This noise and nobody ever heard it?"

"The place has been unused for over two decades, it's normal that everything sound rusty."

Sliding behind the paint we found ourselves on a dark corridor with light at the end.

"Where is the light coming from?" Matteo asks.

"It's the middle of the night," I say, walking towards it.

Looking above our heads to a ceiling made out of glass, I can see the outside of the castle, we are underground.

How can we miss this place from the outside?

"Who ever made this room, knew what it was doing."

"As I'm aware only grandpa knew of it."

Proving I was wrong when I check boxes and a dresser in the corner, all of his belonging rest there. Hidden, making clear this is how they could take everything away without been seen.

"My father knew of this room, this are my grandfather belongings, they disappeared after he passed, he took them away and wash him out the household as if he never existed."

"It might have been his best way to grief."

"He didn't live here, it was just Stella, Rosita, him and I. He had no rights to do that, and clearly Stella didn't fight back once I left."

"Is that all what is in here?" Matteo asks.

We walk around, using the torch of our mobiles to light the room until I find some candles and matches. the space is bigger than we thought. Perhaps the size of the half of the castle.

"There are boxes of files," Matteo says, holding up one of them.

"We will have to check them, Ruby found some aback in *Little Castle*, here we might find what was missing."

Placing any document, we find by the side of the corridor we walked in to some family antiques, not the things we have on display at the house, this look expensive, unique even.

"There must be a fortune in stuff here," Matteo points out, moving all of them to another corner.

"This can't be," I mutter, aware that there has to be something more than expensive decoration and old paper.

Ruby read things, there was a big story on those letters that I wasn't aware of, but she knows it.

Without thinking at all, I dial her.

"Who the hell are you calling?" Matteo asks.

"Hello?" she was awake, I check the time, it's past 3 a.m.

"What was on those letters?" I ask anxiously.

"Samuel?" she asks surprised.

"You called Ruby?" Matteo asks, grunting and pushing me, "you are out of your fucking mind."

"Ruby, I know is the middle of the night. I need to know what was on those letters."

"I only read two," she explains.

"You must have found something to know they were important."

"There was one, from a lady called Catherine to your grandfather, informing of her weeding with a rich family. I think she was middle class, as she make special emphasis on how good was for her family that the new husband was wealthy."

"What else?"

"The other, was from Scott to Catherine, he informed her of your great-grandparent death, invite her to the funeral, to join him in London, and to spend life together."

"You are telling me he was in love with Catherine and she marry another man?"

"That is what I thought too."

"What about the other letters?"

"I didn't open any other, the handwriting match, but many were fully sealed, like nobody ever open them."

"Who was Catherine?" I ask, on a way to Ruby and Matteo, in other to myself.

"You will have to read them all," Ruby says.

"I am not," I pause, reconsidering telling her I run away

for the best of both of us.

"Do not tell her," Matteo says, reading my mind.

"I will do so, thank you Ruby."

"Sam–uel," she calls.

"Yes?" I ask placing the mobile back on my ear.

"I know you'all move away. I just hope that is helping Scott, let him know the kids miss him terribly," she says on a low voice.

She is crying.

"He miss you too," I assure, "we all do," I confess.

Matteo shakes his head in disproval, but I do not care. I miss her every second that a day has, plotting in my mind any excuse to return and see her again.

"If you changed your mind, I had all of Scott's birthday things ready. Sorry, I shouldn't have say that."

Fuck I forgot, after tomorrow was meant to be Scott's party, with everything we been through that was the last thing in my mind.

"I will love to celebrate his party, we could organised it as a surprise and take him there, I need to plan it."

"I can move everything for Sunday if it's more convenient," she says, giving me full Friday to organise and Saturday to travel.

"I can have someone bringing *Little Castle* keys, and yes Sunday will be better. Thank you Ruby, after everything we put you through you are still thinking of all of us."

"It will be good for Scott, have a special day. I will take care of everything. Thank you Samuel."

"Good night, Ruby," I whisper, before she hangs up.

"What the fuck!" Matteo exclaims.

"What?! She knows things we don't, and she just remind me about the party."

"And you think that take everyone back to Blue Valley, and share a party is the best idea?"

"We are doing it for Scott," I say.

"You are doing it for yourself. Anything we should look for in here?"

"Catherine." Matteo questioning expression makes me laugh, "she was my grandpa lover, before my grandma of course. if he kept the letters, they must mean something."

"Here are only books, fucking collections that must cost a fortune in a good auction house, but nothing–" Matteo steps back, a crack and a dusty cloud forms from behind the bookshelf when he pulled one of the large books.

We pull it fully open holding the mobile torch, stepping inside another room.

"For the love of God!" I exclaim.

There are sculptures and pieces older than history, chests of multiple sizes spread around, paints covered up on the side wall and at the end of the room facing the door, hiding under white transparent fabric is the portrait of a young lady seated on a library.

Charcoal curls fall on the side of her face, while the rest is pulled back on a high up do. Her skin is the colour of chocolate, heart shape face, full cherry lips, wearing a light-yellow dress.

"Samuel, the eyes," he says.

Pulling up the torch I gasp, they are the deepest turquoise

I've ever seen. My head tilts, observing all her features.

"Catherine," I whisper, "it can't be," I say, revealing the painting on the floor, finding a lot more of her portraits, until I come up to a picture.

The quality is hideous, she is covered with a white sheet, her curls are loose, she is smiling and looking straight to the camera.

"*Fratello*, is that Stella?"

"It's Catherine," I mumble, "she was my," I search for more, opening everything I find, looking for more pictures, the paintings won't show me how she looked in real life.

Inside a wood chest, under dresses, jewelry boxes, shoes, a burgundy coat and drawings is a small box, holding it out, I come face to face with what I was looking for.

There are hundreds of pictures of Catherine, my grandpa, them together, them as a couple.

"Holy shit!"

"She was my grandmother," I assay out loud, holding a picture, that anyone will swear for their lives it was Stella.

My sister has spent years hiding away our natural hair colour, and her curls. But I have seen them.

"It's incredible how alike they are."

"We have to take all of this out."

"The house is a mess as it is, where are you going to put all of this?"

"Let's wake up the boys, we can put everything in the library," I say, walking out. Running to the old employees' cottages where they are staying until we finish all the rooms in the house. "Guys!" I shout, banging the door of Logan's old house, heading straight to the others.

"What the hell Samuel?" Jackson protest, walking out, pulling a t-shirt over his head.

"I swear this was not my idea," Matteo says, throwing me under the bus.

"Dressed up, I found something," I say, running back to the house, followed closely by three sleepy heads and a pissed off Matteo.

"What you are about to see is a secret, nobody can know about it until I find more information," I explain, guiding them through the corridor, and into the room that holds *her* portraits.

"Where is all this going?" Jackson asks.

"Library this and that," I point at all the art pieces, "documents to the office."

Everyone is hands on, taking the last bits out when the sun fully enter through the glass ceiling.

"These fake ceilings are another world," Calvin says.

"What?"

"They are fake ceilings, you won't see it from the outside, it's probably covered with some fake grass too, but what it does it, takes any light from the exterior, now is the sun, before was the moo, magnifies the intensity and transform it into a natural light that works all day long."

"You are fucking encyclopaedia with legs," Jackson jokes, holding the other end of the dresser with me.

I hear her gasp of surprise before I see her, turning the corner of the corridor, coming face to face with Rosita.

"Buen día," I greet her.

"What are you doing?"

"Moving things around," I explain, letting Calvin take my

side and walk away.

"Because you can't sleep, you can't just move around like a ghost–"

"Wait a second," I say, interrupting her.

Letting my mind tell me what has been tickling in the back of my head for years and she just confirmed it.

She is complaining that I am moving things around, but she haven't asked where this come from.

She knows where this comes from.

"We didn't finish cleaning the library and you already–"

"Come with me," I request, taking her to the library.

I turn to face her once I am inside, studying the way she looks at Logan, the way she is coming face to face with all of these things and nothing surprises her.

"Did you know," I ask walking in circles.

"No," they say both at unison.

Proving that my suspicions are real, they both knew of the existence of these items. What makes her a liar, as I have asked her for years about our family past and she has always said the rumours where just not truth.

That my grandmother was a regular woman that died at childbirth, that grandpa was curious and loved to build things, but nothing out of the normal.

"You lie," I tell her, "how could you? after all–"

"After all what? I gave my life to this family, they forced me to keep things hidden, I didn't ask for all of this."

"When asked you, everyone was dead, you didn't have to hide anything."

"What I know, will have to stay with me until my last day."

"Rosita that is enough," Logan says.

"And you?"

"Me what? I am just the butler's son did you forget it?"

"Why?"

"Because Stella's life and mental health matter more."

"What does Stella?"

"Uncle Sam?" Scott calls from the door, we all turn to him, Rosita reach him, "is everything okay?"

"You caught me!" I exclaim, "we were having a little secret conversation."

"Mom says, 'keep secrets is not save'."

"Your mom is a wise woman, but this is a little surprise for you. Go and get breakfast,.."

Rosita takes him away and I turn to my childhood friend, the one that now choses to use the 'butler's son' car with me, proving what I suspected it, he is still madly in love with Stella.

"The conversation is not over, think what you can't and can say and better open, before I crack your stupid head open," I warn him.

It's dark outside again by the time we finish cleaning, organising, separating by time frames and topic all the documents, and carefully place away all the antiques.

After many sleepless nights and a hard work of nearly 24h I head bed and wake up with the sun warm up high at the next morning.

Joining the boys, ready to remove the last part of the wood floor at the top level and the wall papers to replace them all. Only Rosita and Scott are home, Aberdeen is back in the city and the ladies won't be needed anymore, so if any more secrets are revealed, I am surrounded by the people I trust the most.

Today should be an easy day, I will wait for a couple of hours before I find an excuse to move to London for the surprise party.

Or so I thought until Rosita rush upstairs where I am fixing the end of the house wood floor with the boys with my mobile in her shaky hands.

"Samuel!" she shouts, I stand, holding the mobile in my ear.

"Sam?" Helena is at the other side, I can hear her nervous breath, shaking as she calls my name.

"What happened?" I ask.

The boys leave what they are doing, standing, guard up ready to anything she says as warriors ready for battle.

"What does, oh Sam I'm really nervous—"

"Where are you?"

"Your office," she says, locking a door in the background.

"What has happened?"

"Do sunflowers mean something to you?" she asks, sobbing.

Memories of that afternoon when I purchase them for Ruby, the way her skin turned pale, the fear on her eyes as she nearly fall, the pain on the cry she let go on my arms.

"Why?" I ask once more.

"Sam, someone came inside your office."

Turning the speaker on, I let the boys listening to what she is saying, "repeat that, the boys are listening."

"Your office is filled with sunflowers," she says on a sob, "someone came inside your office, Sam what the fuck?"

"Was that?" Matteo asks.

"Advik, he is haunting her."

"I'm on it, boss," Calvin says, rushing downstairs, I hope ready to check the office cameras and find out how was that possible.

"Helena, did you brought *Little Castle*'s keys to Ruby?"

"Of course, yesterday at the Summer Fair as you asked."

"Call Natasha, I need her in Blue Valley. Stay in my office, we are on the way."

"But Sam—"

"I need eyes on Ruby while I get the team there, do not leave the building, did you hear me?"

"Yes, I will stay. Be careful Sam."

Without another word, thankful that I got the bikes sent to us, we each jump on ours and hit the highway on a fast speed, skipping every car or truck on our way, determine to reach Blue Valley before I have to do something I haven't done before with my raw hands.

Half way through, refilling the tanks, Matteo approach me with something I didn't remember until he mentioned it.

"*Fratello*, she will be busy with the party, she is fine," he says.

"She should be in *Little Castle* by now, that place is a fucking fortress."

"Where are the children?"

That is when his point hit me like a dagger on my heart, cursing under my breath when I realise I don't have anyone's number, and calling Ruby will just scare her unnecessarily.

"I want you burning the gas down, Ruby is with the party preparations, we don't know where the kids are--"

"I will send someone there, she will be fine *fratello*."

Jumping in the bikes once more we reach the village before midnight, the neighbourhood is quiet, the roar of our bikes echo across the streets warning we are coming.

From the distance, I can see *Little Castle* and the cottage's lights turn on. Not surprised she is full hands-on deck, she was determined to make the best party ever from the day Stella hire her.

What is does it's the mess Ruby's cottage is as we walk in, the front door was ajar, I rush to the kitchen, finding ingredients spread on the floor, tools everywhere, I rush upstairs, clothes are thrown from one side to the other of the corridor, like they have packed as they run away.

"What happened here?" Jackson asks.

"Samuel!" Calvin's shout for help nearly makes me want to jump down the window, but I do down the stairs. Running to my front yard, "the door is locked, bro I can hear her."

Jackson breaks down the door as if it's made of paper.

I can smell her and the food as we enter the foyer, the kitchen, and the cinema lights are on, that is all we have to see something around us.

Walking cautiously around, listening to anything that gives us a clue of what is happening.

Jackson enters the kitchen, shaking his head as he doesn't find her baking as I wish he did.

Calvin enters the cinema room, shaking his head, shocked as what I can see from the distance is a fully decorated room.

Matteo walks inside the office, shaking his head when he doesn't find her reading my family letters, or organising my past.

The silence grows thicker inside us, I reach the stairs, closing my eyes, feeling her presence, guide it by her scent, freezing when a strange scent hits my nostrils.

Is a strong, dirty, disgusting scent, male body odour, mixed with chemical and alcohol.

Something drops steps away from me, I jump the last steps up.

My vision blurs, all my demons unite as one, my blood turns into flames and I can't recognise the beast I guide towards the noise in my room, finding the last thing I ever thought I will have to witness.

Chapter Nineteen

Ruby

The Summer Fair was beyond my expectations, Samuel departure took away my ability to sleep, think, or function properly.

In my benefit that gave me the opportunity of worked longer hours and have far more stock I had planned.

Which was sold out before the fair was finish, guaranteeing that new customers will contact me soon.

That doesn't take away my sadness at the cancelation of the party, Scott deserves it all.

And as much as I hate to agree, I have miss them all every second of every day.

Wondering if they were fine, if they found the happiness, safety and peace we couldn't found together.

I reconsider answering Samuel's call, my chest ache at the sound of his voice, and I bite my lip so hard to hold my word that I tasted blood.

But it was for the best, after all he was calling to make

sure a service that was well paid in advance was taking place at the location and time he chose.

Who was I to ask for anything else?

Sarah, who now has her children living with her, agree on keeping mine until Sunday. Otherwise, it will be impossible to organized things in between stores and houses.

A knock on the door brings me back to the cottage, to the kitchen where I was organizing the party boxes.

A stunning woman stands in the other side. I have never seen before, but her smile tells me she knows me.

"Morning Ruby, I am Helena, Samuel's assistant," she says, extending her hand for me to take it.

"How can I help you?" I ask, she raise her other hand, offering me a set off keys.

"*Little Castle,* Samuel said you are preparing Scott's party?"

"That is correct, you will stay?"

"No way, they are for you. Give them to him on Sunday," she says, waving goodbye and walking away.

The mention of the possibility of seen him in less than 24h, makes me nervous, growing a knot under my chest, unsure how seen him again will be.

How are we supposed to behave after everything ended, after his childhood confession, after he left me in his bed and walked away without a word?

Calling Miguel, I ask him to meet me there, where he will drop all the decoration that he helped to print back in the day when Stella didn't cancel the party yet.

"How does it feel to be here?"

"Inside his house?" Miguel nods, "I can't deny the memories I have around, even I was here for just hours. But, in that spot I pushed Stella, in that spot he chased me and held me closely, up there he opened his soul in a way I think he has never done before."

"No matter how much we love someone, sometimes is better to let them go."

"That doesn't make it hurt any less."

"When two people are meant to be, no matter time and distance, they will find each other again."

"He will be here in a few hours."

"You know what I mean," he laughs, making me smile.

"I thought he could someone take away my past."

"Nothing and nobody will be able to erase that from you, time can will give you a better future, but your past will unfortunately always be there."

"I felt save around him, and so did the kids."

"He had a great team of *machotes*," he says, faking the muscle.

"They were kind and thoughtful with the kids, understanding what they need and how to be around them all the time."

"You will find that sense of security again."

"Not while Advik is looking for me."

"The offer I made months ago, still stands."

"The thought of runaway scares me even more."

"It could be a simple break until they find him, or he

finds something else to distract himself with."

"Don't say that! The thought of another woman falling under his control and abuse breaks my heart. You have cared for us since we moved here, and I will never have chosen a better person to care for my kids in case it was needed."

"The offer wasn't just for them—"

"You are our *protector*."

"As you like to call me."

After hours cooking, decorating, organizing and setting things up. Sending Miguel back home to rest, I call the kids for a quick before bedtime chat.

"How was your day, mama?"

"I've been busy all day, baby."

"We want to be there to help," she complains.

"I will love that very much, but look how late it is and mama is in *Little Castle* cooking, and you will be sleeping in the island while I finish cooking by now, I can't do that."

"We have a bedroom," she says, reminding me that gorgeous room Samuel made for them.

"You will be here in a few hours for the party," I remind her.

"Can Sarah's children come too?"

"I don't see why not? Her son is Scott's age," I say, spreading oil over the dough and storing it in the fridge.

"Babies is bedtime," Sarah reminds them, "Hola amiga," she waves to me.

"Thank you darling, the day has not been enough to

finish."

"Remember to sleep, you have a bed in there too," she says, sending a wink my way.

I laugh at her inappropriate comment. The last time I was inside this house, that room and that bed, was in his presence, in his arms. A lifetime has passed since then.

It hurt when I woke up to an empty bed, a quiet house, and he was gone. Perhaps the reason he opened up the day before was to let me know why he can't be the man I deserve. The one I wanted so badly to be him.

Now is too late, I didn't understand my feelings soon enough to confess them, and I kept silence once he was gone. Giving him the space, he needed, the time to heal by the side of his nephew.

I will lie if I deny that when I saw his name on the mobile something inside me felt warmer. The hope light up, but he just needed me for Scott. To do as I have done, think about the little ones and forget us. We do not matter as long as they are happy. But should I chase my happiness to show my children it's possible to spend every day laughing and smiling, and not worrying about anything.

Saying my goodnights to the children, thanking Sarah for the millionth time, and waving goodbye to everyone, I hung up.

Giving my full attention to the list of appetizers, crossing the warm ones off, they are halfway ready just to be cooked around an hour before the party.

The cold ones are resting on the walk-in fridge, and it's time to work on the final touches of the cake that is cooling down on the metal rack.

I take that time to clear up the counters, organized all the ingredients and work on the cream that will cover the sponge, cooling it down with the rest of the food.

Preparing one more coffee, using a stool for height and comfort, I work on the fondant figures for the cake, cupcakes and cookies.

That is not all what Stella ordered, I have taken the liberty of a couple of changes that I think will be a success with the little ones.

Everyone will take cookies inside their goody bags and I have little cupcakes boxes too, that way they won't eat much sweets here, and they get to taste on full all of my creations.

If the Summer Fair taught me something, is that the decision makers in a household are the little ones. If is good for them, it will be perfect for the entire family.

That helped me to sell out, before expected, thankful for my extra batches I always have handy.

It's late when I finish with everything, cleaning and packing, so I take all my tools and ingredients back to the cottage.

Dropping ingredients and tools everywhere, leaving a mess that might take me hours to clear up, but I rather keep *Little Castle* clean for now.

Samuel didn't confirm what time they will be here.

It doesn't really matter as most of the children's food is cold, and while they eat and play, the grown-ups chat around and have some fresh drinks I will cook and serve the warm food.

I give one last look at the cinema room, I am really proud of myself at the way I transform it into a full dinosaur room.

The walls decorated with movie pictures, every couch has a set of explorer outfit, popcorn boxes with Scott's name and a drawing of him and a T-Rex as his pet, the wall around the screen covered with fake branches, that anyone watching will feel they are in the actual jungle.

"The cups," I remind myself, walking to the kitchen.

Miguel did a fantastic work with the decoration details, we teamed up really well for been a last-minute change of plans. Worked until late on Friday after the Summer Fair and until late this afternoon.

I miss the kids terribly, but all the work that we have done in the past two days, wouldn't be possible if they were around.

I grow used to the sleepless nights that I filled up with work to easy up the thoughts that overcrowd my mind.

"Where are the cups?" I ask myself, checking everywhere around the kitchen, rushing back to the cottage, opening the boxes Miguel brought.

Freezing on the spot when a noise that comes from upstairs stand all my hair on end.

It's an old house.

My mind washes off that uneasy sensation of not feel alone, returning my attention to the box I was searching on in the floor, on my knees, when I hear footsteps.

I stand, coming face to face with my worst nightmare.

On the other side of the kitchen, on dirty clothes, a long beard, and hair, is the last man I ever wanted to see.

"My beautiful wife," he calls, grinning as he walks closer, standing at the other side of the island, "have I been looking for you."

My body can't move, terrified, letting trauma and fear take control. Forcing my head to work on an escape plan while my feet glue stronger to the ground.

"I like the new look," he says, circling his finger in the air around my figure. "Did you miss me?" he asks, licking his bottom lip, making my stomach turn.

I can see his intentions before he finishes considering them, his dark gaze reflects everything playing behind them.

Forcing my feet to move, I slide closer to the back open door, that will be the only way to prevent what I can see is coming my way.

"Do not run, we both know how I feel about it," he warns me, making all the old memories to come to the surface, screaming to my body to get out of here.

I scream the life out of me for help as I exist the cottage, it's quiet and the roads are empty, anyone awake should be able to listen to me, and for the first time since I saw this house, I regret that the closest neighbor is over ten feet away.

Considering my possibilities, I head straight to *Little Castle*, covering my mouth as sobs come out every time I exhale.

I head to the kitchen, searching for my phone, that is

nowhere to be found, my mind tries to remember where I kept it when I hear him, his shoes squeak on the marble shiny floor of the foyer, I head to the back of the kitchen, opening the door that will take me to the exit again.

Blood pumps in my ears taking away the sense, confusing my mind, making me fall on the mouse trap.

The back of my head hits the wall, his hand holds my throat so tight I can't barely breathe.

"I told you not to run," he growls in my face.

His dirty and whisky scented turn my tummy upside down, I need to cough, I am getting sick, but he won't release me.

"Are you okay?" he asks, holding my chest, letting me breath, brushing his dry and dirty hands over my face, "I don't want to hurt you," he continues, brushing my hair away, "I forgot how beautiful you are," he murmurs, close to my face, "did you miss me?" he asks, once more.

I hold my breath, swallowing my disgust down, his hands in brushing down my arm and not around my throat anymore.

My mind considers the possibilities I have, all of them end on the same term, his punishment, I just have to determine if one chose or another will mean something less harmful that the hatred I see in his dark eyes.

"I am sorry," I whisper.

My words catch him off guard, he steps back, his drunken feet nearly trip him backwards, brushing his beard.

"Have you done something wrong?" he asks, I shake my

head, "nothing to be sorry about for then," he says, walking away, tapping his chin, facing me again, "something tells me you are lying."

"Please."

"Have you done something wrong?" I shake my head, and he copies me, "did you know where you sent me?" he asks, bringing up what happened that night over six months ago.

"I didn't–"

"You did it all, you fucked up all, we were happy."

Is he absolutely out of his mind?

"Weren't we? Haven't I given you the world? Why you need to be such an ungrateful bitch?"

In another time, in my past life, I would have let his words make me feel guilty, I will plead for his forgiveness, I will do anything he asked for it, I will degrade myself to save myself.

Today, with many months to disintoxicate myself from his abuse, aware of what is real and not, who I am and what I should not tolerate around me anymore.

Is when I can see how manipulative, evil, and toxic he is.

How he fooled an innocent child with the dream of a life filled with adventures. Telling the words, she needed to hear, mentally and physically abusing her into his benefit. Confusing her mind until she run away with him, stealing her   parents'   life   savings. That took her to the first night in the hospital after he drank his weight in alcohol and she couldn't buy the food he wanted. Because he had ended it all the money.

"Why are you looking at me like that?" he asks, stepping closer, "tell me brave girl, I know you have it in you," he teases, brushing his palm over my neck again.

"You are disgusting, manipulative and a murderer," I shout pushing him back, running to the lock front door, and back to the stairs, heading to search for a phone or a place to hide, when my feet fly back and my forehead hits the steps in front of me.

My head hurts, spinning in circles, disorientating me.

"That is my girl," he teases, turning me around, trapping me under his disgusting body, that even for a slim person is a lot bigger than mine, "what else you have to say, I like it very much," he mutters, pressing his groin to my lower tummy.

Moving my body under him I try to push him away, losing the sense of my whereabouts when his fist hits my cheek, and my temple at the other side lands on the rime of the step.

"Say it!" He yells, slapping me this time, over and over again until I shout.

"You are a monster!"

"I am? but you loved it very much," he presses his body against me once more, I try to kick him, hit him with my knees, anything as I protect my wounded face, "what happened with my little girl who loved and appreciate all what I gave her?"

"You are a lunatic" I exclaim, releasing my arms and coming face to face, receiving one last punch that knocks me out.

I can feel my body dragged up the steps, my back and hips hitting every step until we reach the top floor, through a carpet floor and how he drops me over a soft surface.

"Wake up darling," he calls, softly slapping my cheek to bring me back.

My face turns, I can smell him, the fresh scent of eucalyptus and mint, with a touch of cinnamon in the back.

My eyes open widely to find Advik straddling me, memories of that night months ago come to the surface. I was weak then, I am not anymore.

My fist raises, hitting the side of his head and pushing him out of me, I crawl out of the mattress, rushing to the door and screaming as he traps me, holding my hair on a fist, throwing me at the other side of the room.

My back hits the corner of the wall and I lose the little air on my lungs, he stands in front of me, towering me, as he works on his fly.

"I don't need you awake for this one," he assures, holding my neck and straddling me, "Game over darling, I will enjoy your sweet body once more," I fight but he tightens the hold, "You know what I will do next?" I shake my head, "find your bastards, and do use them on my benefit, I have a lot of males interested in gorgeous little girls."

"Son of a–" his fist hits my cheek on last time, knocking me out for good.

I can feel the strength lifting from me, afraid of any harm that he could do to the kids, aware that he is a man of his words when it comes to destroy humans' life.

My knickers ripped apart, my dress is pulled up, and I bring my mind to a hidden place, one where this life ends.

There is no more pain, fear, or harm.

Finally, understanding that happy endings do not exist, that no knight will come on my rescue me.

Because I am worthless.

Chapter Twenty

Samuel

I am not fast enough. I don't reach her before his fist does. I can't hold her head before it hits the floor.

My body launches over, knocking him off, falling under the window.

I will take care of him, just not now.

I rush back to Ruby, in the darkness, in the same spot I seated days ago, opening my heart and soul to the woman I loved more than I love myself.

Now lays her lifeless body, that bastard has damaged her so badly that I barely recognise her angelic features.

"Ruby," I whisper, taking my shirt off, covering her exposed body, "please angel, do not leave me," I choke on my words.

Desperate to hold her in my arms and bring her back to me, but scared of touching her, of hurting her anymore, or worse, causing any more injuries.

"I need you to come back, I can't lose you," I whisper.

Controlling myself, as my mind replay the way he hold her in a grip, before he launches one last punch in the air to her face and lets her fall, the way her petite body reaches the floor and her head hits the carpet in a loud and dangerous way worries me.

"Ruby!" Matteo calls, falling in his knees next to her.

"Don't!" I exclaim, when his hands reach forward, "we need an ambulance, she—"

"She will be fine, she is strong," Matteo says, reassuring himself too.

I lay on her side, brushing my fingertips on her palm, slowly holding her hand on me, resting my forehead on her shoulder and hiding away, letting the boys take control of something I can't think of.

It might be seconds, minutes, hours since I enter the room, I am not aware of. What I am aware of is how Ruby let go of everything, her heart slows down, her breath becomes a small breeze, and I die with her.

"I'm here angel, please don't leave us," I beg her.

The sirens echo around the neighborhood, the lights bright up the roads, giving a multicolour mix under us.

I don't move when William rushes inside the room, kneeling next to her with a group of paramedics.

"Samuel, don't do this," Will says, "she will be fine," he assures.

"Don't lie to me," I say, rolling around, laying next to her, holding her hand and closing my eyes, "she is leaving."

I feel the light turned on and how everyone holds their breath, I hear the plastic packages open, I can smell the blood mixed with their fear.

This can't be the end, everything can't be just taken away from us like this.

Rage warms my blood like the adrenaline shots I grew used to.

Kissing the back of her hand, I open my eyes.

Her angelical features are a swollen, bloody mess now.

Over my shirt and her ripped dress, they have placed the bed sheets.

The carpet is covered in burgundy pools, a trail that starts from the door, where a group of police officers await.

I turn to find the bastard on the ground, a paramedic is displaying a few items from his bags to take care of him.

Not until I am done.

"He doesn't need you," I say, holding the bastard by the neck, standing him, and dragging him out of the room.

"Samuel!" William exclaims, "it won't fix anything," he warns me.

"Let's see about that," I say.

"Mr Smith," the younger looking officer calls.

I look at him, he is tall but small, there is determination in his face, but he doesn't know the rules of this game. One where I do whatever it takes to protect what is mine, or I take care of the garbage that bothers me.

"We have to—"

"Young man, this is my city, my town, my house. You can take care of her, while I take care of him," I explain, holding the bastard around like a puppet, "they can explain you the rules," I point at the other officers.

They won't stop me, never did and never will.

That is the sickness of my wealth, that as long as the person deserves it, I have total immunity, and tonight, inside my house, for something done to my angel, there is no one able to stop me.

My rage grows as I follow the blood trail, reaching the top of the stairs, the house is lit up, and a burgundy stain mark covers at least three steps at the center of the staircase.

He pinned her there, he bit her there, he abused her there.

My grip tightens around his neck, I hold him in front of me, his feet two inches away from the floor, putting him face to face with me, taking in his current features, studying the man that used my innocent angel, broke her into millions of pieces, and took pleasure out of it.

"Samuel," Jackson calls from the side, he can read my mind, the son of a bitch always did it, he knows what I am thinking, "you will break his neck and it will be over," he reminds me.

I turn to look at him, he is right, throwing this bastard down the stairs will break every bone in his body, kill him, and all will be over.

That won't take what I have inside me away.

"I will take care of it," he says.

"Samuel!" Helena's voice echoes in the foyer, her heels clack in the floor and stairs until she is standing one step under me, I turn to look at her, blood covers my vision, I know is her, but I can't make a clear picture of her, "don't do it," she begs.

Taking a deep breath, I let go of him when I fell the boys holding him, Helena's arms curls around my waist, her face hides on my chest, and her tears wet t-shirt.

"I was so scared," she sobs.

"You are safe now," I whisper on her crown, holding her.

I take her to the kitchen, dial Natasha to come and help with her, just to find out she has been all this time in front of Ruby's old apartment block, keeping an eye on the kids that are staying with Sarah.

"What should we do?"

"She won't easily recover from this one."

"Sam, what about the kids?"

"I will have them, if they take me, they are my world as much as she is."

"Scott?"

"Edinburgh with Rosita"

"I saw Stella," she says, serving coffee to both of us.

"She hates me enough?"

"She has never hated you," I roll my eyes, "she loves you, she cares for you. Even when you have hurt her, betray her, lie to her, use her."

"Not the best time to remind me what a bad brother I am."

"It will never be a convenient time to hear the truth," she says, rushing to the door when Natasha walks in.

I look at them, the way they care for each other, the way they communicate without words.

A full language I never learned, but will give all what I

own to have.

I walk out when I hear everyone heading down.

Ruby's unconscious body rests in a gurney, covered up, slightly cleaner than before, but still unresponsive.

"Are you coming?" William asks.

Riding ahead of them, reaching the entrance of the A&E as they roll her in. Invited to a private room to wait, I pull my skin off for the hours that they take to bring her back to me.

"Samuel," Will calls from the door, I can see it on his face before I can hear it, "Ruby is in a coma," he informs me.

The world turns upside down, blood pumps on my ears, my vision turns dark, and my mind plays off all the times I have lost someone, I received bad news from someone I love.

"What now?"

"Wait, give her time, be patient, positive, she is strong."

"We can't lose her."

"I won't let her go that easily," he assures, "go home, arrange things, she has a few more hours until she is ready for visits."

"The kids?"

"Not the best time and day to see her," I nod, tapping his shoulder and walking away.

Thomas and his team are hands on with *Little Castle* when I walk in.

And Jackson, Logan and Calvin are in the kitchen.

"Where is Matteo?"

"He left in a hurry after William called," I nod at Logan's words.

Like it or not, Matteo cares for Ruby as I do. In a different way, on his way, one that I dislike to admit. But I am not stupid or blind, I heard they've been friendly while I tried to keep space between us, I saw the way he looks at her, and worse the way she looks at him.

Everyone has been affected by Ruby's spell one way or another, she changed us and our lives. I can see it on their faces, they can't lose her either.

We wait for hours until I head to Sarah's. There is not much more information that I can give. But Naima and Aidan deserve to know where Ruby is, and to an extent what happened too.

Sarah's facial features change multiple times in the first few minutes. She welcomes me with her sweet smile, to a soft frown, to worry, and full fear.

"Where is she?" Sarah asks, closing the building door behind her.

"London, in the hospital."

"Is she? What. How. This is too much," she says, covering her face and wiping away her tears.

"He found her, I was just on time, but she is in a coma. My friend is doing anything he can, I would like to take the children with me, if they take me."

"How are we going to tell them?"

"Can I speak with Naima?"

"Are you for real? She is six!"

"Please, I will be careful what I say," I assure.

Sarah walks in, returning with Naima shortly, she runs into my arms, I hold her up and embrace her as she hides her little face in my neck, fisting my shirt.

"Tell me she will be fine," she cries on my neck.

Sarah can't hold it much longer, "I want you and Aidan to come with me, I will take care of you until she gets better."

"You promise?" She asks, pulling her head up, looking at me straight into the eyes, "will you take care of us? For as long as it takes?"

"I will do, forever!" I assure her.

Few minutes later we arrived at *Little Castle*. Logan helps bring their things from the cottage, where until everything is not back to how it was, they can't enter, and I help by accommodating their things in their bedroom.

Jackson has been all morning taking care of the food, Calvin of the decoration that Ruby left prepared.

I was shocked when a few of Scott's school friends arrived, and Naima has been an excellent host. I can't be happier to know that after all of Stella's worries, there are kids interested in sharing this day with Scott.

That all the year of loneliness is paying back with what seems to be a summer break filled with new friends to share time with.

Some of them chose to bring their younger siblings for what Naima and Aidan get to meet some of the kids close to their age in the neighborhood.

With Logan, who went to pick up Rosita and Scott from the airport message, I brought everyone to the garden, where he has been instructed to exit from the garage, so Scott will find us here.

Nervous and excited at once, for the responsibility of a little human happiness I stand under the large banner with a T-rex head and his name inside the mouth. I hold my breath when I hear the car engine turn off, Naima and Aidan walk to me, holding my hands, and the instant the door opens, everyone cheers at once.

I haven't seen such joy in Scott's face in a very long time, or maybe ever. Rosita is crying as usual, and I can see Logan getting emotional too.

That arsehole is missing Stella. I know it, and that is boiling my blood, they have history, and we all know it will never work.

"Naima, Aidan," Scott calls, rushing to them and hugging them at once.

Rosita gives me a questioning gaze, and holding my breath I just shake my head.

"Uncle Sam! What is this?"

"Your surprise birthday party, you thought we forgot?"

"Ruby did this?" He asks, my chest tightens, my eyes fill up with tears, and I appreciate it when Naima calls him away to greet his school friends, who he is surprised to see here too.

The party starts and goes by far better than what we thought.

I managed to avoid Rosita the full time, guiding

everyone through the itinerary Ruby prepared and rushing to my mobile when I sent everyone to the cinema room for a Jurassic Park marathon.

"Hey Will, how is she?" I ask, walking in circles in the garden, pulling my waves with shaky hands.

"We can't let her wake up," he explains.

"What? You said she was in a coma," I say, unsure.

Jackson, Rosita, and Calvin join me and I turn the speaker on.

"Let me explain it simple."

"I'm not stupid," I assure.

"I didn't insinuate either, I just want you to easily understand what I mean. She is in a coma, after the fall you were present on, when she hit her back hard against the carpet. That is a normal, safe self-defense mode the body, especially the brain does, to recover fast and securely."

"That is clear."

"This morning we ran some more tests. There are more damages we didn't know about."

"Santo cielo," Rosita cries.

"How bad is it?"

"Broken ribs, spinal damaged, cranial inflammation, displaced jaw,—"

"It's clear," I cut him, not ready to have Rosita fainting.

"We can't let her be awake until we don't help her heal. Samuel if we wake her up, she will be in so much pain, we can lose her easily. It's your choice, this is just my suggestion."

"If I let you prolong her coma, how long are we talking

about?"

"That is difficult to estimate. The stage where she is now, the natural coma she falls into, will probably last a couple of months, we are talking about front and back cranial damage at once that put her in there. We will have to see how she recovers too, by then the surgeries will be done too, maybe two more months after that."

"Four months, you are telling me, in four months, Ruby will wake up and be the woman we all know?"

"I didn't say that."

"Fuck off Will!"

"Samuel, I will live by her bedside every day of those months if that makes any difference. But as any doctor will tell you, we can't guarantee Ruby will wake, or ever be the woman she was," his words cut my chest in half, keeping my composure, I mumble, letting Jackson take the mobile, walking to her cottage, entering the place by the back door.

I walk around, remembering that night in her kitchen, by the table, the scent of her cookies, her low voice when she sings, the way her breath changed when I walked close to her.

Falling in my knees in the center of the room, I let go of all my pain, shaking my chest, burning my throat and emptying my lungs.

I can't lose Ruby.

There is no world I can live where she is not alive. I could accept it if she didn't want me, but she will be alive.

Chapter Twenty-One

Samuel

Eight Months Later.

It's been the longest months of my life. A journey I would have never imagined possible, but an experience that was filled with concern for Ruby not recovering as we expected, was filled with happiness, kindness, and love.

After the summer was over, Naima, Aidan and I. Together with the boys and Rosita minus Matteo. We moved to Hammersmith, to the house that decades ago belonged to my parents.

Is big enough for everyone, a walking distance from their school, and a short drive from Ruby's hospital and Stella's new home.

It wasn't just me who couldn't stay any longer in *Little Castle* without replaying what happened that night.

My little sister and Scott are working on her full recovery, her struggles and fears, with constant security supervision from Jackson.

And I am working on my duties as a guardian for the kids, a shoulder to cry on after every visit to the hospital, and a playmate at the end of the day or on the weekends.

Today, on her birthday, with the largest bouquet I could find, a homemade card from the kids, and a little gift from Miguel. We are heading to the hospital for the hardest decision I ever was asked to make.

William was concerned when her natural coma was extended to three and a half months, her body was healed from the surgeries, her angelic face was back to the woman I meet nearly a year ago, but her brain wasn't recovering, she was put into an induced coma that was meant to last under three months, but got extended to five.

And I have to explain this to a seven-year-old, so she understands that her mother, the only blood family left they have, will be pulled out of that stage, disconnected, and we will have to wait for a miracle to happen.

One where her blue oceans meet me once more, where her smile warms my heart, and where these children have a lovely mother grow up with them.

I never had that opportunity, my mother was taken away from me, I am guilty on encourage her to choose this, to let them bring her back, I am the selfish arsehole that rather risk losing her out of anybody failure than see her in that bed unconscious one more instant.

William is by the door waiting for us, guiding us to a room we have enter more times that I like to count.

I hold the kids back when we reach the door, Matteo, my *fratello*, my best friend and loyal right hand is standing there.

Like me, these months had made him age, reminding me of what I suspected, witness it, and over thought about for far too long. He loves her.

Doesn't matter which way, but he does.

I knew it when he left, and I can see it on his face.

"I thought I will never see you again," I say, holding my hand forward and taking the hug he pulls me to.

"It took me a long time, but I found what I was looking for," he assures.

I frown, stepping back, the kids wave at him, and I tense when a couple walks out of the waiting room next to Ruby's room.

The man is tall, wide shoulders, large build, a thick moustache, toasted skin from the sun and sad blue eyes. The woman is shorter, long dark waves fall on her side, deep, glassy blue eyes too, heart lips, and a floral dress.

"Samuel, these are—"

"Ruby's parents," I cut Matteo off, and finish his sentence.

"Pleased to meet you, I am Samuel," I say, stepping forward, offering my hand.

"Buddy Brown, this is my wife Maria," Ruby's father says, I nod.

Brown? I thought she was Rao.

Naima startles me, when she steps closer, holding my leg and Aidan closer, I look at them, smiling, inviting them to be polite and greet their grandparents.

"I am aware it is not my place to do this," I say, exhaling

loudly, "Mr and Mrs Brown, these are Naima and Aidan," I say, holding my little man on the arms and the princess hand, brushing my thumb on her shaking palm.

Maria kneels, breaking me into pieces, when I see Ruby's smile, in a version of herself in around twenty years more, holding her palms forward, inviting Naima to hold them.

The moment she does so, the room turns silent, nobody dares to breathe, as the strong little girl, scared of being touched, of strangers, of certain noises, that I met months ago builds the courage to greet her grandmother, that unfortunately in her mind never existed until now.

"Hello," she whispers, Maria bites her lip, holding her tears on edge, "my name is Naima, and I am seven."

"Hello Naima, I am Maria, and I am a lot older," she jokes, making Naima giggle.

"I can see mom in your hair," she says, on the air brushing her wave. Not touching her, neither inviting her to do so, not yet. "On your smile," she says, drawing the shape of her lips. "On your sad eyes," she says, touching her when a tear betrays Maria's control over her emotions, opening the door to a full flow when Naima speaks again, "are you my abuela?" Maria nods, sobbing in her grandchild's arms when Naima steps forward and embraces Maria for the first time.

Everyone shares the same emotion, making me lose it when Aidan asks to be put down, walking to Buddy, asking him to move closer with a simple wave, resting his small hand on each of their cheeks, giggling, and hiding in between them to be cuddled too.

How is it possible that the same kids that before couldn't share a room with others, now are hugging Ruby parents?

That is simple, they feel what we all do. Ruby is the mixed version of them, a portion of the aura they hold, their features resemble their mom, and even we I know nothing about them. I can feel their humble and kind spirit.

"It's time," William says.

We give Ruby's parents to enter first, bringing everyone to tears as they reunite after over fifteen years.

"How did you find them?" I ask Matteo, aware that Calvin tried, now it makes sense, they don't share the same surnames.

"Visiting every single farm in Texas until I found Shepperton. That place doesn't exist on the map."

"This will mean the world to her," I assure, he nods.

Giving me way when they call us in, standing away, letting the nurses follow William's instructions.

As they step away, the kids walk to her, holding her hand as usual, climbing in bed easily, now that there is barely any wire attached to her.

Aidan's face rests over her chest, and Naima on the other side, brushing her waves back, smiles, talking to her.

"Mama, it's me, I am here like always, but I have a birthday surprise," she says, smiling back at us, "Abuela Maria, and grandpa Buddy are here," she says, in a chocking sob.

I step closer, holding her, curling my arms around her and reassuring her that she is fine.

"Happy birthday my angel, I made a fool of myself, bringing the biggest bouquet in the store, to find Matteo with the only gift that matters. Your parents are here. They came to see you angel, please open your eyes, come back to us," I whisper, kissing her temple.

Hours have passed, the sun is lower in the Thames River. Maria's head rests in the bed holding Ruby's hand, her father is distracting the kids with some songs and clapping game, calling Maria attention, she starts singing, crying and laughing at once.

Stopping, gasping and jumping out of the armchair she was seated on.

"Bud do that again!" She exclaims, Buddy looks at her as confused as we all do, "do it!" She orders, with her eyes fixed in Ruby.

I jump out of my own sit, rushing to her side when I think I saw what I've been waiting for far too long.

Buddy starts singing again, Ruby fingers move, and the corner of her lips stands, Maria cries in joy and I kiss her forehead.

She can hear us. She is coming back.

The next few hours are the longest I remember going through, like my live is playing in slow motion. And I am watching from outside, when I am just in the further corner, in an anxious need for speed up, keeping my fear under control, and my nerves hidden.

The children are in a bedroom next door sleeping, supervised by Logan, ready for me to come and give them any news.

I am just observing how with every minute that passes, Ruby muscles wake up, gesticulating, changing the rhythm of her heart, the way she breathes, flapping her lashes until she pushes her lid up slowly, blinking multiple times, staring forward. Everyone holds their breathes.

Stepping out of her sight line as William's suggested earlier, not forcing her mind and body to react to anyone's presence.

"Good evening, Ruby. My name is William. Can you hear me?" He asks, she nods. "That is really good. Ruby, you have been sleeping for a long time, I will need you to follow some instructions," he explains, she nods.

Standing at the foot of the bed, he instructs her to close each fist at the time, wiggle her toes, blink, smile, frown, close her eyes and look each side for neck mobility, and lastly the only thing we have fear the most.

Have those head injuries affected her in any other way?

"Can you tell me your name?"

"Ruby, Ruby—" she pauses, looking around, her heart beat raises.

"Ruby, you are safe her, this is just a simple exercise."

She nods, taking a deep breath, clearing her throat, looking at Will and talking, "Brown, I am Ruby Brown."

"How old are you, Ruby?" He asks.

Ruby searches for something in her mind, an old sign that will give her the answer, but she can't find it, frowning and nibbling her bottom lip.

"That is okay, in what city you are, can you remember

that?" Searching in her mind once more, she shakes her head again.

"Who is your next in kin?" Her heart beat goes off charts, "Ruby, you are safe her, I am not contacting anyone, this are just regular questions," she nods, taking a deep breath.

"I don't have a next in kin, sir," she says, on a thicker Texan accent that I am used to, "please do not call anybody," she begs.

"Ruby, can you tell me your last memory?"

"Do I have to?"

"It might help to determine what the next action will be."

"I'm scared," she says, holding back her tears.

The only thing I want to do is rush to her side, stop hiding away from her, hold her in my arms and remind her she is safe, loved, that nothing and nobody will ever hurt her again.

"I understand that, but I have a little secret," he says, she frowns, on that sweet way she used to, and I smile, grateful of having her back. "This is my hospital, and you're a special patient for me, you are safe. Whatever or where ever is that you find yourself as last memory, is a place you will never return."

"He will find me," she whispers, letting tears roll down her cheeks.

"He won't, never will. He doesn't have access to you anymore."

He doesn't exist.

Maria face hides in Buddy chest, covering her mouth to hold her heavy breath, seen her daughter awake after many years apart, witnessing the pain she has been through.

"I don't know how I end up here," she explains, "my last memories are being imprisoned against my will, by someone that call himself my husband," she continues, "I am scared for my life, I made a mistake, and I want to go home."

"Where is home Ruby?"

"Texas, sir."

"Thank you, Ruby. Now, I need you to remain calm. I have someone I want you to see and tell me who it is, can you do that?" Ruby shakes at the words of Will sink in, "you have nothing to be afraid off," he assures.

William signs for Buddy to step forward, standing next to him, Ruby scared expression changes.

"Ruby, can you tell me who this gentleman is?" William asks.

In between sobs, Ruby talks, "he is my papa, sir," Buddy exhales loudly, looking up the ceiling.

William signs for Maria to step forward, standing next to Buddy, she breaks down when Ruby recognise her, bringing both into tears.

"I have one last person," Will says, signing to me.

Stepping forward, keeping my gaze low, standing next to Maria, who holds my hand and rest her head in my arm, I take a deep breath and look straight at her.

Her bright blue eyes connect with mine, I chew the inside of my cheek, taking in her waves falling around her face, her rosier cheeks, her cherry heart shape lips, holding a smile when she bites her bottom lip to hold her own smile.

She doesn't remember me.

Not as she remembers her parents, there are memories in her mind of them, in a way I am a complete stranger, what should shutter me into a million pieces. But seen the way she looks at me, how she is forcing her memory to bring it forward, that is enough to give me hope that this won't be a full lost cost.

"Sir," she says, talking at me, "I apologize," she continues, the corner of her lips raising, "I think. I can't. This is—"

"Ruby, it's okay," Will says, it's not okay.

"It's not okay, sir."

Thank you, angel.

"I know this gentleman, I am struggling to remember from where," she explains.

"And that is alright, I want to give you some time with your parents, and I will be back shortly," William says, giving them the green light to step forward.

I watch from my position how two parents are giving a new chance in life to have her daughter back.

Meeting William in the corridor, to have a conversation nobody is ready for.

"I am fine," I assure as I exit, standing side by side with Matteo, who has watched it all from the distance. If she doesn't recognise me, she won't recognise him either.

"I am not concern for her not to remember the past year, she has two young kids. She can't remember when was her last memory."

"She might not remember them," Matteo says the words none of us want to express out loud.

"She will," I assure them, receiving two stunned faces, "she recognised me, she couldn't remember the moment or place, but she knew I am not a complete stranger."

"You can't put the children through that," William complains.

"Can I talk to Naima and come to a decision?"

"You are out of your fucking mind," he assures.

Ignoring his words, I head to the room where they are, finding Naima awake, standing by the window, exhausted, but waiting.

She is just seven.

"Sam," she calls and rush to me as I enter, "how is mama?"

"Big girl, we need to talk," I say, taking her with me to a close by couch, holding her hands on mine, lowering my gaze to keep the composure I find the words to say, "mama head injured has taken some memories away from her."

"She doesn't remember?"

"Her memory is working slowly," I explain in easy words, "she recognised me, but forgot exactly from where, does that make sense?" She nods, "we will keep Aidan here, I will take you in her room, but you have to promise something," she nods again, "you will follow William instruction, not rushing to her, let her invite you to step closer."

"I promise."

Holding her hand, I guide her back to the room, where Will has already mentioned to Ruby that someone else will walk in. Maria is seated by her side and Buddy holds her hand from the close by armchair.

"Take your time, do not force your mind—"

"The princess," she whispers, her eyes filled with tears, and I fall forward, exhaling in relief. She remembers the dream, that is why I am not a complete stranger.

"Yes, Ruby. She is the princess, your princess," I remind her, sharing a secret that nobody else understands.

"And you are—"

"I am the beast," I end it for her, when she doubts that dream could be real, "it wasn't just a dream," I say, taking one step at the time, bringing Naima with me, encouraging her to step even closer, until they hold each other.

"I miss you, mama," Naima whispers, bringing tears of joy to everyone's face.

Her eyes are on me, she is studying every inch of me like she did many times before, but there is something different, this time her mind doesn't remember me, but her body does.

I can feel it when I seat close to her, when I took sleepy Naima from her arms so she could rest, when I arranged her bedsheets because her parents went to have a shower and some food.

That is the smallest sign of hope I need to keep me going, to know that it might take time until she recovers her memory.

But is not like I have nothing better to do.

I wait until the sun is out, after they help her having a shower, changing into regular clothes, and having breakfast to bring Aidan in. He is too young to understand what is happening. And Ruby mind can't overshadow her heart.

The way she looked at him, cuddle him, play with him. That is pure and raw love of a mother towards her children.

And for as long as I can help, I will make sure they build up their relationship as if her mind wasn't taking anything away from her.

"I will bring them back in the afternoon," Logan says, taking the kids back home.

"May I ask something?" Ruby asks, once we are left alone, I nod, grinning as she becomes nervous. "Are we?" she asks, pointing in between us.

"What angel?"

Her cheeks blush, warming my chest, remembering how curious her mind can become, ready for anything she might be considering.

"We aren't married," she points out, I shake my head, "but you are the children guardian," she continues, I nod, "how could I trust you so much to let you have my children like that?"

"It wasn't just like that, you didn't came to me and ask me for it, was a common decision in between the people that was safe around the children while you were in a coma."

"The coma," she says, pensive looking away, "that coma save me, didn't it?" I nod, "how long has it been since it happened?"

"Does it matter?"

"It does, because in mind I am back at least seven years ago, what means I last saw my parents six years ago."

"Can you remember the year your mind is stuck in?" she shakes her head, taking a few deep breathes before she looks back at me, her blue oceans talk words she doesn't feel safe to say yet.

"Is it bad to say I don't want those seven years back?"

I shake my head, resting forward, offering my hand that she takes for an instant, pulling it away as I make her feel what we always feel around each other, another easy reminder of how well her body knows me and accepts me.

"That makes me a horrible mother,--"

"It doesn't. because even when you don't remember them, you have been lovely to them, especially to Aidan, he hasn't noticed his mama doesn't remember him, he just thinks his mama needs to sleep more, which is ironic," I say, making us laugh.

"Did I make you happy?"

"No happier man exists in the world," she smiles brightly, making it contagious.

"Was I happy?" she asks, aware that I could lie to her easily.

"You were tough, you were strong, you were secure, you were aware of what you wanted and not."

"That doesn't sound like me," she says, with that sweet frown.

"The Ruby you remember, is not *my* Ruby."

"Will you tell me more about her?" she asks, yawning.

"After you promise me to rest."

"I'm afraid," I frown now, "what about if I don't wake up?"

"I will wake you up."

"Will you?"

"Always, *my angel*."

Chapter Twenty-Two

Samuel
Two years later.

Life changed that night. That night I lost the woman I loved in the hands of a bastard. That night I became the guardian of her children. That night I have to learn how to live without Ruby.

She was taken in an unfair way, forcing us to build a life where all we had was the memories of a past filled with cookie dough and wildflower scent, with a sweet smile, bright blue eyes, and strong spirit.

Giving us three, an opportunity for redemption. A fresh start, a blank page that we could fill up as we wish.

And even when in my pages Ruby was always the main theme, the one thing I couldn't stop thinking of, the motivation to be a better man, one that can be a role model, a safe place and love her children the way she will want me to.

The old said, will encourage any human to hold on to hope, for it to be the last thing we lose. But with every minute that passes, turning into weeks and months, I found it extremely hard to hold on into it.

Just to find that my poor wounded heart was right all alone. Life gave us a second chance. A redemption out of all the injustice we face all our lives.

I witnessed her rebirth, when she took her first breath on her own, opened her eyes, and spoke up.

Anyone else will have run away the moment she didn't recognise me. But I didn't, I could feel it in my heart, I could see it in her eyes. What her mind couldn't remember has nothing to do with what her entire being did remember.

It was hard to leave her at the hospital, watch her learn how to walk, eat on her own, and after two months of rehabilitation head back to a life she couldn't recognise.

Her mother's instinct never faded away, but grew stronger. This new version of Ruby didn't experience half of the horrific circumstances the other did. This was not a broken soul that fought for years to protect her children in fear for her life.

Those were only Naima's memories, ones that this new opportunity with Ruby, help fade away and easily be replaced with happy memories.

For me was the second chance not every human can have in life, and that I possibly will have never had if that night never existed.

I got the possibility of conquer Ruby, day after day, one step after another, giving her the version of Samuel that she deserved all alone.

The man I knew I would have been if my past never broke me.

And even when I was just the neighbour next door for months, the one who couldn't cook and always was in need for something as an excuse to meet her every day as many times as possible.

The man she trusted her children with when she was busy bringing her business back on track. That was enough for me.

Because now, two years later, I am the man who taught her how to love and be loved, the man that holds a smile on her angelic face every day, the man that drives her crazy in far too many ways, the man that she can find comfort, protection, and pleasure on.

There are no safe words, no boundaries, no limits anymore. It's just us, exploring each other to unimaginable limits, aware that there is nothing to fear, that inside our dark desires is a bright world where only Ruby and I exist.

My hands shake as I turn the little black velvet box in between my fingers, my mind rehearses the speech that I had prepared, and I train my heart to slow down and my lungs to breathe.

"Are you ready?" Matteo asks, resting his palm on my shoulder, "she will say yes, so stop worrying too much about it."

"Maybe her birthday is not the correct day to do this?"

"*Fratello*, I would have put that ring on her finger the

day she woke up. You waited two years, you made her fall in love with you all over again, you built a life and a family with her. Any fucking time of the year will be good."

I nod, taking my place inside the party room, the one that has hosted multiple events when I was a little boy, and today will celebrate the first step towards the future I never thought could be mine.

"Do not forget this, today is not just your engagement, or her birthday. Today is your step into continuing the family traditions."

"Today our family grows," Stella assures, stepping closer, brushing my cheek, "not just in members, but in love and strength. You are the New Heir. The head of the Smith Empire. The keeper of the SaStel Legacy."

I nod, grinning when the door opens, and she walks to me, shocked as everyone cheers for her birthday around us, when the only thing I can see is the woman of my dreams standing next to me, looking at me as if nothing else exists around us.

I step back, kneel, and with tears in my eyes, I ask her to be mine *forever.*

The End, for now.

Thank you so much for reading The New Heir.
Book One of The SaStel Legacy Series.
Don't miss the upcoming books with Stella, Scott and Sebastian as Main Characters.

About
the
Author

Nadia Marsoli was
born in Spain and
raised in Madrid.

In 2015, she moved
to London planning to start her dream family and pursuing
growing in her career.

Since she was young, stories will come to her in dreams, or
experiences in life will leave her with the feeling a most
excited end would have been incredible. One day she wrote
to take those thoughts out of her head, and found herself
with an incredible, mysterious romance, creating powerful
characters has become her addiction since then.

Acknowledgments

Thank you so much for reading The New Heir.

Welcome to The SaStel Legacy community.

If you have enjoyed Samuel and Ruby's story, if you want to know more about the story, we invite you to read the next books. And why not share a genuine review on Social Media.

This book was wrote during a time where I lost the believe on real love, on the possibility of finding true love.

But who knows?

I have to dedicate this book to my children, for how much support they have showered me with, for laughing, crying and enjoying every single step of the journey. Without them I wouldn't be able to be where I am today in many ways.

So, for my always and forever love of my life, Ni Luh and José, I love you to the moon and back. ;)

Links To Social Media

Instagram
@nadiamarsoliauthor

Facebook
www.facebook.com/nadiamarsoliauthor

Spotify
Listen to the full playlist while you read
www.open.Spotify.com/playlist/3l1A7xAqcglHHCSOqA0w
EH

Feedback and Suggestions for next books?
Email it to me; team@nadiamarsoli.com

Books and Merchandise
www.nadiamarsoli.com